BAD INTENT

Heath Overton is missing and his wives want him back...

When the Overton clan — one husband, three almost-sister-wives, and their eleven children — arrive in Mallard Bay, summer on the Shore heats up. The Overtons and their television show are ready for prime time until the family patriarch disappears. Lightning Strike Films wants their leading man in front of the cameras in two weeks, and Heath Overton's wives want him home yesterday. Everyone's upset, even before the murders start.

It's been nearly two years since attorney Grace Reagan landed in the touristy little town on Maryland's Eastern Shore, and so far, every one of her plans to leave has backfired. This time it's Grace herself who's holding up progress. She may, or may not, be getting married. Or going to France for her dream vacation. Or starting over somewhere on the far side of The Bridge. She has big decisions to make, but first, the Overtons need her help. As the body count rises, Grace is torn between duty to her clients and the fast-moving changes in her own life. **Can she stop the**

killings before she becomes the next victim?

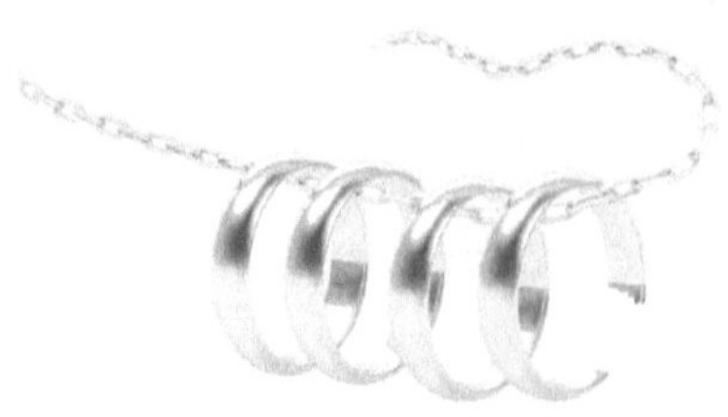

— Come on over to Mallard Bay —

The weather's fine, the water's warm and murder is on the menu!

For ***A Commission on Murder:***

"… A witty thriller and great summer read…"

"… Strongly recommend adding this selection to your summer reading list."

"… A real page turner…"

"… Another great offering in the series…"

Advance praise for ***Bad Intent:***

"… Suspenseful, funny and tragic and filled with more mysteries than Grace wants or needs, *Bad Intent* is Cheril Thomas's best offering yet."

BAD INTENT

CHERIL THOMAS

A truth that's told with bad intent
Beats all the Lies you can invent

WILLIAM BLAKE
Auguries of Innocence

Chapter One

Melanie and Whitney Overton weren't the strangest clients Grace Reagan had handled in her brief tenure with Cyrus Mosley and Associates, Attorneys at Law. Top honors in the strange category went to a murdered billionaire, with honorable mention to a pair of neighbors in a death feud over a six-foot python and three dead chickens. Grace liked to think she'd learned from both cases, and yet here she was listening to another set of clients who needed a magician, not a lawyer.

"You should work with the police," Grace said, keeping her voice even and her words short. The women didn't look like they could handle complicated. The Overton sisters were trouble, plain and simple, and she didn't want to represent them in their search for their missing husband. A runaway polygamist would definitely rate a slot on the Strange Client list.

"We can't," Melanie wailed, tears leaking from her brimming eyes. "They already think Heath's a car thief."

Whitney backed her up with a glum nod.

They favored each other in the way of before and after photographs. Both were on the short side with dark hair and large blue eyes. High cheekbones and oval faces made them pretty, but only Melanie made an effort beyond that. Despite her I'm-on-the-edge persona, she'd taken time with makeup and wore a sundress with wedge sandals. Whitney's messy bun, loose tank top and yoga pants said she'd gotten dressed, and that was all anybody was getting from her.

"We want you to do that for us," Whitney said.

While Whitney had explained the reason for their appointment, Melanie had listened anxiously, wrapping her stick-thin arms around her bent torso and crossing her legs. Now she gave herself an extra twist by tucking one foot behind the chair leg, locking herself into a pretzel shape. "The police think we're crazy, but they'll believe you, Ms. Reagan," she said in a breathy voice.

"Our firm doesn't do this type of work,"

Grace tried again. "If you don't want the police, I can recommend a private detective."

"No. You're the one we need," Whitney said. "We need to find out everything the police know about our husband. You're a friend of the Police Chief's, so you're perfect for the job." She reddened slightly and added, "I'm sorry, that came out wrong. I should have said our neighbor recommended you."

Grace didn't have to ask which neighbor. The keeper of all gossip in Mallard Bay, Maryland, lived next door to the house the Overtons were renting. Avril Oxley had been talking about the large family for weeks.

"I appreciate that," Grace said, trying not to sound sarcastic. "But I'm not sure I can help you."

The silence grew as Grace waited to see if her words were sinking in. Billable minutes ticked by. The screensaver on her computer monitor changed from a vineyard in Bordeaux to a lavender field in Provence, and she wondered if it would be in bloom when she arrived in France in six weeks.

Whitney Overton broke the impasse. "We haven't been in town long, and we don't have any connections here, except our neighbor. You have to help us. When the police came to our house yesterday morning, they said Heath stole a rental car. I was only trying to protect the family, and now I see that was a mistake."

"She lied," Melanie said.

Flicking her sister an irritated glance, Whitney said, "I made a mistake."

Grace rechecked her notes. Between tree pollen and Benadryl her head felt like a hot, soggy sponge. She was still adjusting to the sisters' tale and assumed her slowed reflexes had caused her to miss a vital piece of information. Such as the part of the Overtons' story that would make sense. "What kind of mistake?" she asked.

"As I said, unfortunately, we had to lie — "

"*You* lied," Melanie corrected in a whispery voice.

Whitney briefly squeezed her eyes shut, then started again. "I lied about knowing where my husband — "

"Our husband," Melanie said.

Grace wanted to slap duct tape over the woman's mouth just so her sister could finish a sentence. "What did you lie to the police about?" she asked, looking at both sisters to cover her bases.

Whitney looked exasperated. "I told them we knew where Heath was when we really have no idea because he's *missing*."

"Since last Monday, May 7th. Got it." Grace circled the date on her legal pad.

Whitney's top knot had been sliding loose as she talked. Now she yanked on the elastic holding it together and resumed her story while finger combing the mass of hair that fell past her shoulders.

"Heath flew into Baltimore a week ago Sunday, rented a car, and drove over to see us. He went back to Atlanta on Monday. On Wednesday, the rental car company called me because they had my number as an emergency contact. He hadn't returned the car before he flew back home. The daily charges were still being paid by the credit card, so they'd let it slide for forty-eight hours, but he wasn't answering their calls, and they wanted their car back. I smoothed things over and authorized an extension to the lease."

"That was the first lie she told," Melanie said and dabbed at her eyes. "We have to protect the family, but if they'd called me, I might have handled it differently."

"By crying and handing me the phone?" Whitney snapped, then colored. "Sorry, we're both very upset. Anyway, except for us being worried to death, and not being able to reach Heath, nothing else happened until the police showed up yesterday. Without saying anything to me, the rental company reported the car stolen despite the extended lease."

Both women looked expectantly at Grace.

"Why did you lie about knowing where your husband was?" Grace asked.

The sisters looked at each other in surprise, and Grace hoped they were reconsidering their choice of law firms.

Whitney scraped her hair back up and began twisting it while Melanie nervously fiddled with a perfectly coiled curl of her own. Neither of them answered Grace, who was thinking the Overtons' bathroom drains must be perpetually clogged with all that hair flying around.

Topknot secured once more, Whitney said, "I had to lie because of who we are. The Overton family? *The Plurals Next Door?* I'm sure you've seen the promo ads on the Different Lives channel? We can't risk the press getting wind of Heath's disappearance. It's totally counter to our family's mission statement."

Grace was trying to remember the last time she heard anyone refer to a family mission statement with sincerity when Melanie untwisted herself and stood up.

"We need you to find our husband. Can you do it?"

Grace meant to say no. She even opened her mouth to say no. If the billionaire's murder and the snake case had taught her anything, it was that some clients aren't worth the money. Cyrus Mosley had barely recovered from the newspaper headlines generated by those clients. Two sister wives searching for their husband would probably kill the old coot.

She'd be leaving Mallard Bay in less than six weeks. When — if — she returned, it would only be as a visitor. There was plenty of work to occupy her until she left. Good, steady, boring work.

Whitney said, "We'll pay double your regular hourly rate."

France was expensive.

Grace said, "Where would you like me to start?"

Chapter Two

Whitney produced a business card from a Detective Sergeant Desiree Marbury of the Maryland State Police and one from Mallard Bay's Chief of Police Lee McNamara. As Melanie described their family, Grace made notes and added Marbury's information. She was having lunch with Lee McNamara in an hour and could get his take on Heath Overton then. With any luck, she could avoid the State Police officer. They'd met last year, and Grace wasn't eager to repeat the experience.

Handing the business cards back to Whitney, Grace said, "You must be very worried. I'll try to help you, but I need to understand your situation better." She'd already learned that the sisters, the husband they shared, and their nine children were making a TV series for a Baltimore based independent film company. The show had just been picked up by a large cable syndicate, a deal that would fall apart without Heath.

"You need to use the right terminology when you talk about us," Melanie said. She dabbed at her eyes and the steady trickle of tears that dripped down her face. "We aren't polygamists, and Heath isn't a bigamist. There's only one legal marriage. Be sure to refer to us as a plural family or as committed polyamorists. Do you know what polyamory is?"

"More than one lover," Grace guessed.

"No, but that's one reason we're making this show," Melanie said. "We have a message to share that will help so many people find the families they need. It isn't a new concept, of course, but most people don't understand the value of this lifestyle. Everyone knows about polygamists, but we're different. 'Polyamory' means being in love with more than one person at the same time, and we believe that's how nature intended it to be for the man in the family. We, Whitney and I, are in separate committed, moral relationships with Heath, and soon Felicia will be, too. Did I mention Felicia? She's our fiancée."

Grace wondered if she could live without antihistamines. Somehow, she'd missed a third sister wife.

Melanie seemed to gain energy from telling her story. "The show's about how we'll live as three couples, sharing our love for our children and the responsibilities that come with family life. We aren't sealed in a religious sense, the way the husband and wives are on some of those other families you see on TV."

"In fact, religion doesn't play a part in our decision to have a plural marriage," Whitney added. "We stay away from that topic on the show. No sense alienating any viewers. Especially when we're advocating for a quality of life most traditional marriages lack. Heath says we should share what we've found and show the world how happy we are."

"It's a modern, middle-class, communal way of living," Melanie said. "We're devoted to raising happy, productive families in love and peace."

Grace wondered how the sales pitch would stand up to their husband's apparent defection. And car theft.

Melanie said, "Since the police showed up yesterday saying that the car rental agency had reported the car stolen, we've been frantic with worry. And the children are scared. The three oldest boys are at a camp for child actors, but we have Felicia's two kids in addition to the other six of ours. They're wound up like you wouldn't believe."

"To recap," Grace said, hoping to get the women back to the issue that had brought them to see her. "You haven't heard from your husband in over a week, and a rental agency is accusing him of stealing their car, but you don't want to involve the police. Are you sure? Knowing he is missing could mitigate the theft charge, at least for the time being, and the police have the resources to find him."

"No! We've already lied," Whitney said. "We can't go back and tell them Heath's been gone a week or it'll look like the family's falling apart. Lightning Strike Films is very sensitive to adverse publicity."

"But you're okay with them thinking he stole a rental car?" Grace decided she hadn't missed anything that would make these women sound reasonable.

Whitney looked offended, but Grace thought she saw a corner of Melanie's mouth quiver. It might have been a smile, or she could be getting ready to cry again.

"I paid the lease through Saturday," Whitney said. "The rental company refused to renew again unless Heath contacts them, but if he returns the car, all they can do is charge the penalty rates. So, that's what has to happen."

Something was off. Something basic. "Did Detective Marbury tell you why she was there with Chief McNamara? As you say, your husband is technically only a few days late returning the car, and the rental company thinks you know where he is. I guess I can understand them calling the local police department to check you out, but why are the State Police involved?"

"How would we know why they do anything?" Melanie said. "Please, just get them to leave us alone. We'll keep paying the rental charges, and Heath will show up soon."

"Where do you believe he is?" Grace asked.

Melanie wailed, 'I don't know' at the same time Whitney said, 'with Felicia' and handed her sister more tissues.

"Felicia says she hasn't heard from him since he left Atlanta, but I think she's lying," Whitney said.

"We can't risk violating the terms of our contract with Lightning Strike Films," Melanie said as she dabbed her face. "It took over a year to set everything up with them and we'll be broke if we can't meet our obligations." She paused and gave her sister a dead-eye stare. "Felicia is fine and onboard, and so are we. Right, Whitney?"

Grace made a mental note to double her standard retainer in case the double billing rate only resulted in higher unpaid invoices.

"Here," Whitney said, holding out a thick envelope. "This is a copy of our contract for the show. We have six episodes finished and ready to go, but filming starts again on June 4. We have to get Heath and Felicia here as soon as possible. I've included basic information on Heath that you'll need, and I added copies of the credit check and background report we ran on Felicia. That should speed things up for you."

Grace looked at the envelope but didn't take it. "Did you get permission from Ms. Jones to acquire that information?"

"You think we'd invite someone into our family without doing due diligence?" Whitney said. "The only thing we knew about her was that she worked with Heath at the car dealership. Of course, we checked her out thoroughly. But, yes, we had her permission. I also gave you a copy of her release and authorization for the reports."

"If you think he's with her, Whitney, why don't you fly down to Atlanta and see for yourself?" Grace asked.

"She couldn't just leave us," Melanie said. "We're both needed here with the children. Plus, it would look like we didn't trust Heath when it's Felicia we have our doubts about."

"Got it," Grace said, thinking Paris and

Provence had better be worth it. "Well, I can start with a call to Felicia."

Both women said 'No' just as Whitney's cell phone buzzed. Grace didn't have time to register the *We Are Family* ringtone before the intercom on her own desk phone began to blink. She excused herself and found her secretary, Lily Travers, waiting for her outside the office door.

"I'm sorry, but Chief McNamara just called. There's a fire at the house next to Avril's. It's contained, but someone is hurt. One of the children told the Chief that her mother and aunt were with you."

Before Grace could respond, Whitney Overton appeared in the doorway. Melanie stood behind her, clutching her sister's arm.

"There's been an accident," Whitney said. "Something awful at our house, we have to leave."

Grace thought she'd never seen two people less fit to drive than the quivering sisters. "Lily and I are going with you," she said.

Chapter Three

Aidan Banks didn't know how it happened. One minute he was responding to a call about a fire in the historic district, the next, he was holding a sobbing child. Then two children. Then he lost control and ended up on a sofa with a toddler in his lap, a small girl under one arm, and another child of indeterminate sex clinging to his leg.

He remembered long unused words of comfort, which he whispered to the children, mostly so no one else would hear him. Not that he had a reputation to uphold — not a good one, anyway — but he was a police officer. If he couldn't be front and center of the scene in the backyard, he should do something besides babysitting. Baby whispering.

A pretty girl ran into the room, saw him, and made a beeline for the sofa. She picked up the child attached to Banks' leg, but instead of taking over, she settled beside him.

"I'm Hallie Overton. The oldest girl," she said, as if that explained something. "Sawyer will be fine, thank goodness."

"I know," Banks said. Did she think he'd be sitting inside with the children if there had been a real emergency to handle? He decided not to pursue that train of thought since it would only lead to reminders of his shortcomings. "Where are the parents?" he asked, nodding at the toddler on his lap.

"I called Aunt Whitney," Hallie said. "They're on their way."

Banks wondered if she was old enough to take over responsibility for the children. Her eyes were red-rimmed, and she was very pale. She seemed calm enough, but he didn't have confidence in his ability to read women. She might blow at any time, and he wouldn't be surprised.

"Do you know what happened? What caused the fire, I mean?" Hallie asked. "It's scary how fast it spread."

"Well, it's under control now," Banks assured her. "The firefighters I talked to said it could be a mulch fire. People don't realize how flammable that stuff is."

The girl looked even more frightened, but the child he was holding started to whine distracting both of them. Banks resumed whispering and bouncing his knee, just a little. More children joined them, stair-step sizes, boys and girls. All had somber faces, some with tears that eased, then stopped once they joined the sofa group. He and Hallie were soon covered with small, slightly smelly, and very wiggly bodies. Older children, too big for laps but needing comfort, settled on the floor near the sofa.

Banks kept up a running monologue. *It's all right. You're okay. Everything's okay. Your parents will be here soon.* When the standard child-minding protocol wore off, he switched to the only bedtime story he could remember, a version of Hansel and Gretel with Snow White and Cinderella all involved in a benevolent tale with no danger or evil adults. What his mother had lacked in imagination, she'd more than made up for in common sense.

The scrambled fairytale worked longer than Banks would have thought possible. Still, when two frantic women burst through the front door, followed by Grace, Lily, and Mallard Bay's Chief of Police, bedlam resumed.

"I see we've uncovered your true talent," Chief McNamara said, raising his voice to make

himself heard over the wails of the smaller children and Melanie Overton.

Banks stood and surrendered the last child
he held into the outstretched arms of a woman
he hoped was its mother. The smell of urine hit
his nose, and he saw the big damp spot on
his leg.

McNamara followed Banks' gaze, but only
said, "Good job, Corporal."

Banks thought the Chief sounded sincere
and decided to leave on a positive note. He almost made it to the door before being grabbed
again by a small boy. One look at the little up-
turned face and Banks was lost. Or found, he
wasn't sure which.

And as it turned out, Brayden Overton had
quite a lot to say.

By the time Banks got outside to the scene of the
fire, the temperature had dropped a bit, and a
light rain was helping the Mallard Bay Volunteer
Fire Department. The far end of the garage was
a smoldering ruin. The Fire Marshall's office
would ultimately get involved, but Banks knew
he and Chief McNamara would handle the initial investigation. McNamara was inside interviewing the home's occupants as best he could in

the chaos. So far, Banks' sole contribution was to get peed on.

He considered asking if anyone had called the other parents. The house must be in use as a daycare center, although he couldn't imagine such a thing happening in this location. An elderly woman came around the corner of the house and headed his way as if he had summoned her for an answer.

"Anyone hurt?" Avril Oxley demanded. "I just got home, or I'd have been here sooner."

Banks had no doubt on that score. As the locally acknowledged village historian and busybody, Avril knew everything and everyone. Disasters, natural and otherwise, were magnets for her, and this time, she lived right next door to the action. She carried a huge black umbrella instead of a broomstick, but the witch resemblance was still there.

"Well, what's happened?" Avril started to walk around Banks but stopped when he shook his head.

"An accident," he said. "Some guy visiting the family living here got hurt. Looks like he was caught in the garage when a fire started."

They both looked toward the group gathered near the smoldering garage.

"Then where is he?" Avril asked. "Everyone's just standing around."

Banks could feel the righteous energy rising from her tiny frame and knew he only had a short time to diffuse it. "There's nothing to do, really…" he hesitated, trying to decide how much to say. The Chief didn't like it when Banks over shared.

"Is he dead?" Avril asked.

Banks wondered why he bothered trying to keep anything from her. Even the Chief had trouble with the nosy old woman.

"Well? Is he?" she demanded.

"No, he'll be fine," Banks said, then stopped abruptly when the Chief came out of the house.

Banks remained where he was with Avril and decided to throw her under the bus if details of the fire got out while they were still on the scene. After all, anyone could have told her the injured man was a guest of the residents and that his injury wasn't bad. Banks didn't know anyone who could keep secrets from Avril Oxley, and he was only a lowly village cop with baby pee on his uniform.

"Are the mothers inside?" Avril asked. "How about the girl, Hallie? I'd better go help."

Banks described how the children were being cared for while easing her back to her house with a promise to call if anything changed. He knew she was only pretending to be cooperative, which was fine by him because he was only pretending he'd call her. Besides, her side porch offered a clear view of the Overton property, including the ruined garage. Avril could be back in a flash if she saw something interesting.

He hoped he was long gone by then.

Chapter Four

Lightning Strike Films sent a crew to care for the Overtons and film their newest drama. Melanie insisted that she and the children couldn't breathe the acrid smoke-scented air, and within an hour, the family was packed up and on their way to the Egret Inn. Grace and Lily saw them off and returned to an unusually quiet office. Cyrus Mosley was rarely around in the afternoons, and Marjorie Battsley, Mosley's long-suffering, and perpetually unhappy office manager, had taken the day off.

"Kind of nice, isn't it?" Grace said when they'd finished comparing notes on the Overtons. "Having the place to ourselves, I mean. We could try to finish with the Simpkins file while

Marjorie isn't here to tell us what we're doing wrong."

Lily looked uncomfortable. "I guess Mr. Mosley didn't mention it, but I'm leaving early. In about ten minutes, actually."

"No, he didn't." And neither did you, Grace thought. When she'd turned down Mosley's offer of a permanent place in the firm, Lily's disappointment had flattered her. But as Grace's departure date grew closer, Lily's unhappiness increased. Now, her once indispensable secretary was behaving as if Grace had already left the practice.

She was tempted to put an out-of-office message on the phones and take the rest of the afternoon off, too, but the stack of files on her desk was a reminder of the work she had to finish in the next few weeks. There'd be time to relax in July.

The quiet office was peaceful after the hectic morning until Grace's cell shimmied and buzzed with calls from her fiancé, David Farquar. She sent them to voice mail. The smiling David in the photo on her contact list was not who she'd hear if she answered. They were having a long-running argument, and at the moment, Grace thought the best thing about their relationship was that he was on the other side of the Chesapeake Bay.

Too wired with fading adrenaline, she couldn't concentrate and flitted from one task to another, accomplishing nothing. When Lee Mc-Namara arrived, she wanted to hug him.

"How did you know I needed to see you?" she said. She'd have to be careful in asking about Heath Overton, but she needed all the help she could get. Plus, she was just happy to see Mac. Their friendship was one of the best things to come out of the time she'd spent in Mallard Bay.

"I have that kind of radar," he said as he followed her through the empty reception area to the kitchen and the coffeepot. "Where is everyone?"

"They all, even your sister-in-law, have better things to do this afternoon than work."

"The day's looking up," he said with a grin.

They both knew that if Marjorie had been in the office, she'd be standing between them. She made no secret of her disapproval of their friendship.

"We missed lunch," he said.

"We did, indeed. It's been a stressful day." Grace poured a cup of coffee for McNamara and grabbed a bottle of water for herself. Lately, afternoon coffee had been leading to evening indigestion. It was one of several new and annoying signs of aging she couldn't fight. It wasn't fair that McNamara, in his mid-fifties and nearly twenty years older than Grace, still drank the stuff around the clock.

"Now, about that lunch?" he asked. "Are you hungry?"

She looked at him, leaning up against the counter, smiling at her as if he hadn't just spent several hours with two upset mothers and a houseful of very active kids. She wanted that — the calm vibe he had. "Not very," she said, "but I could be tempted."

He raised an eyebrow, making her laugh. Setting the coffee cup down, he said, "I'm sure you think this is coffee, but I hope it tasted better this morning. Let's go. We should be able to get a porch table at Morsels, and you can regale me with the latest details of your trip. You still leaving the first of July?"

And with those words, her happy mood vanished.

For weeks, he'd made it clear he didn't want her to go, and when she didn't change her plans, he acted as if it wasn't happening. This fake enthusiasm was new. If it was fake. He might be ready for her to leave. After all, he'd started dating again, something that had both surprised and dismayed her. She'd been so shocked by her visceral reaction to the news that she'd redoubled her efforts to wrap up her temporary job with Cyrus Mosley's law firm. The good times, like the lunch he'd just ruined, seemed to happen less and less as the gossip mill breathlessly reported on the Police Chief's growing social life.

She had no right to begrudge him happiness wherever he found it, but it was hard not to with the increasingly mixed signals he sent. Her calm, kind, rock of a friend was turning into someone she needed to tiptoe around, and her life was already full of people like that.

"Nothing new to report," she said. "Tell me about the fire. How did it start?"

McNamara took the change of subject in stride. "It appears a pile of mulch somehow ignited and spread to the walls of the garage. It must have gone up fast. I don't know why people are always surprised to learn that shredded wood can be a fire hazard. Anyway, Hallie Overton, the oldest child at the house and the one left in charge of the others, said she smelled smoke and called 911. The young man who was hurt, Sawyer Renne, got there around the same time she made the call, and he ran into the garage. He said he wanted to save what he could, but was overcome by the smoke. He was too choked up to talk, but rebounded pretty quickly once help arrived."

"Sawyer's the Overtons' associate producer," Grace said, remembering the introductions Melanie had made. She'd said 'associate producer' with a tone of pride. "Sounds like the fire moved fast. It was brave of him to go into a burning building."

"Or stupid," McNamara said, shaking his head. "In fact, what he did made no sense. It's an old garage at a rental house. Melanie Overton said there was nothing in it of theirs, yet he entered and stayed much longer than it would have taken him to see that the place was empty. I had questions, but the paramedics whisked him off to the hospital."

McNamara stopped to look at his buzzing phone, turning the screen slightly away from Grace's line of sight, but not before she saw Ashley Greenburgh's name flash across the screen. Rumor had it that the new veterinarian in town had done what no other woman had managed in the decade since the Chief's wife had died. Lee McNamara was dating again.

Grace could feel the shift in his attention and demeanor. She took his cup to the sink and washed it to give him privacy, and herself a chance to do some deep breathing.

"Nothing that can't wait, so let's go," he said as she heard the swoosh of his answering text being sent. "I'm starved, and you look like you need food and sunshine. You're a little pale these days."

This time it was her phone that interrupted

them. It lay on the counter between them, David's face visible on the screen.

"You going to answer that?" McNamara asked.

The irony of it all was too much. She should take the call and look straight at Mac while she did it, but she pushed the button to silence it instead.

"Would it be very wrong of me to smile right now?" He was already smiling.

"You go ahead," she said, letting her irritation get the better of her. The kitchen alcove suddenly felt crowded, and she moved around him into the hallway. "I need to finish a few things here. Why don't you call Ashley? Maybe she's up for Morsels."

She walked the short distance to her office, not waiting for his answer. They had never discussed his new social life or the woman at the center of it. It seemed to Grace that Ashley had moved to town, set up her business, and attached herself to Mac all in one smooth move.

"What does that mean?" he asked, following her. "We can't have lunch because I made a joke about your fiancé?"

Lately, Grace had noticed that when anyone referred to David that way, she had to stop herself from wincing.

"No," she said, drawing the word out to

make sure he understood how much patience she was expending. "It means you have a girlfriend to go out with, and I have work to do."

Laughter was the last thing she expected from him. She couldn't believe she'd found him charming just a few minutes before.

"Well, okay," he said. "I'm going, but not to see Ashley, who, since we aren't in high school, isn't my girlfriend. You can stay here and not take calls from David, who actually *is* your fiancé, something that didn't seem to matter when you asked me to have lunch today."

"Are you gone, yet?" she said without turning around.

A chuckle was his only answer.

Just as the front door close behind him, she remembered she'd wanted to ask him about Heath Overton. It was all she could do not to scream.

Chapter Five

"You have to keep the police away from us." Whitney Overton's voice was low, but anger punctuated each word. "We can't afford this kind of publicity."

Grace had welcomed her newest clients' call when it stopped her brooding over the embarrassing conversation with McNamara. Now, in the cramped sitting room of Melanie's suite at the Egret Inn, she was having second thoughts. The three youngest children were watching *Daniel Tiger* in an adjoining bedroom. The music and singing cartoon characters made an unsettling backdrop to their discussion of the fire and the Overton family's missing patriarch.

"Another crisis!" Melanie said. "I just can't

handle it, especially since Heath isn't here. I have such a hard time without him." She sat on the edge of her chair, hands tucked under her legs and shoulders hunched up to her ears. "First, he disappears, then the police say he stole a car, and now a fire in the garage. We're all about showing the world how our version of family life can be peaceful and harmonious, but we keep having one disaster after another. We should project the happiness we had in the early days when we had our babies, and Heath was doing the work he loved. That's the picture we're selling."

Whitney groaned and said, "Not *selling*, Mel. For God's sake, watch what you're saying."

"I'm not in public," Melanie said. "Grace needs to know what we're doing if she's going to help us."

"She knows, already, don't you?" The look Whitney gave Grace said if she didn't know, she'd better fake it or they'd be there all day.

Grace said, "You're demonstrating a polyamoric family life in a positive light by making a television show, and you hope to have a lot of viewers and advertisers and make money. Is that about right?"

The sisters nodded, and Melanie said, "We want it to reflect how happy we were in the years when Heath was a minister. That's really all he's ever wanted to be. Besides a doctor, I mean. Pediatrics was his first love, but all that schooling takes so long — "

"Mel," Whitney tapped her watch. "We're paying by the minute, here. She can read his bio online."

Grace's face hurt from trying to maintain a neutral expression. "We'll roll this time into the initial consultation fee," she assured Whitney. "No additional charge for today." She couldn't see how any of it was relevant to her finding the missing man, but she wanted to hear more. "Why did he leave the ministry?"

"There!" Melanie said to her sister. "I told you someone would ask that." To Grace, she added, "We grew out of the church, in a manner of speaking. We changed as a family, and it wasn't something the congregation understood. When you have a calling, you should answer it, don't you agree?"

Whitney said, "Get on with it, Mel," and made a rolling motion with her hands.

Melanie leaned away from her sister with an injured air and gave her attention to Grace. "When we left the church and moved to Atlanta, Heath found a job selling cars. We initially had our doubts, but he turned out to be just as good at that as everything else he did. We got back on our feet, financially, and refocused on our family's calling. Heath met Felicia at work, and they became friends. When we started talking about another wife, it was natural to consider her as a candidate."

Whitney's expression said not everyone had been on board with the calling or the selection of a third wife.

Melanie carried on, clearly enthralled with her own story. "We're not part of a religious or social group promoting plural marriage, so we didn't have support or guidance. It was a real problem figuring out how to add Felicia to our family and make it legal."

"How did you solve it?" Grace asked, hoping they already had an answer.

"Actually, it was simple. I agreed to divorce Heath so he could marry Felicia and adopt her children."

"But then neither of you will be married to him."

"That's right." Whitney smiled and patted her sister's arm. "It's a huge sacrifice for Mel. But since we're birth sisters and sister wives, our children are first cousins and also half-siblings. Heath will always be their father, regardless of who he's legally married to. Mel and I maintain separate relationships with Heath, and nothing will ever change that. Once he marries Felicia and adopts her children, they'll be half-siblings of our children. Three emotional relationships for the adults, one family with all the children. Understand?"

Not in a million years, Grace thought, but she said, "Well if it works for you."

"It does," Melanie assured her.

"My inclination is to call Ms. Jones," Grace said. "But you didn't seem in favor of that. May I ask why?"

Whitney's worried expression returned. "She's a bit excitable,. and we can't risk her thinking our agreement isn't rock solid. We need to appear absolutely confident that the plan is still on track, which is why we can't ask the authorities to look for Heath or do anything to upset Felicia. Our deal with Lightning Strike only works if they are both here on time for filming. We have a tight schedule to get them married on script."

Melanie jumped in, saying, "You see why we're so worried, don't you? Everything is riding on this show. And the show's only marketable when we add Felicia and her children to the storyline. But to do that, Heath and I have to divorce, even though we're still very much in love."

"That's it, Mel. You don't talk about this on

camera," Whitney said. "You make it sound mercenary."

"We ha*ve to* be mercenary." Melanie turned on her sister, eyes flashing. "We have to keep that contract foremost in our minds because for sure and certain no one else is."

Grace sat back, shocked, and watched as Melanie gathered speed. Whitney sat motionless, and Grace saw that she had misjudged their personalities. Melanie was the weak sister and Whitney the strong one, but only as long as Melanie allowed it.

"Lightning Strike is already asking questions about Heath." Melanie spit out the words. "We can't turn up short a new wife, and we can't start over with a new woman. We're going on as if nothing is wrong. Got it? Because I'm tired of arguing about it."

Whitney turned to Grace, her resigned expression giving nothing more away. "I think my sister has told you enough to get started. Despite how it sounds, we love our husband, and he loves us. We've all sacrificed a lot for this television series, and we need Heath here soon, or we'll lose everything. We want you to find him, discreetly, while keeping the police away from us and Lightning Strike."

"Okay," Melanie nodded. "That's better, sister. Now, Grace, how are you going to do that?"

~

Sawyer Renne's arrival with a large fruit basket saved Grace from explaining a plan she didn't have. A chorus of squeals from the children announced him, and by the time he came through the sitting room door, the sisters were on their feet. Whitney accepted the basket and began distributing the contents to the children who followed in Renne's wake, while Melanie launched herself at him for a hug.

"Where have you been?" she cried. "I thought they weren't going to keep you at the hospital?"

Renne glanced at Grace before answering.

"She's our attorney, Sawyer," Whitney said.

Melanie told Grace she could leave.

"No." Whitney dropped the basket on the coffee table and sent the children back to their cartoons. "We need to talk, all of us, while Hallie has the other kids at the park. I want to make sure we're all on the same page on handling the publicity about the fire."

"But the fire doesn't affect us," Melanie said. "Sawyer will get us another house, a better one, won't you?"

Renne was slender with carefully tousled light brown hair and eyes so pale they were his most arresting feature. Only slightly taller than

Melanie, he looked like one of the children as he floundered about for an answer to her demand. Grace wondered what kind of film company sent someone this young and inexperienced to handle a group like the Overtons.

"Uh, no," he finally said. "The house is habitable. The fire marshal released it, and the rent's paid in advance. You can stay here tonight, though." Renne still smelled of smoke, and Grace thought the whole house probably did. He would have a problem getting ultra-sensitive Melanie back in there.

Whitney said, "What have you been doing? You said you were fine, and we needed you."

"I said I was okay, not fine. I was a light-headed from the smoke, and my chest hurt, so the paramedics wanted the ER docs to check me out."

This brought maternalistic tsking from Whitney, but Melanie still looked put out.

"Also," Sawyer added, "I needed to call the office and fill them in. I didn't think talking with the police around was a good idea, and things seemed under control. I'm sorry, I guess it rattled me. When I left the hospital, I went by the police station to give them my statement. I talked with the younger cop. He asked a lot of questions, and it took forever."

"I don't understand. Why?" Whitney asked.

Again, Renne looked at Grace. "I'm not sure why you need a lawyer, but I'm not comfortable talking with her. She doesn't represent Lightning Strike, so I have no protection."

"From what?" Grace asked.

"The cop said the fire wasn't an accident."

Chapter Six

For the first time in weeks, Grace quit work at six. It had been a long day, and she was ready for it to end. After making his upsetting announcement, Sawyer Renne had insisted she leave. Whitney had agreed with Melanie that Grace should focus on her original assignment. She'd left the sisters huddled with the producer and decided to end her arrangement with them as quickly as possible. The Overtons weren't being completely honest with her, and she didn't need a complicated case when she was so close to leaving Mallard Bay.

On the short walk home, she let the beauty of the little village soothe her. Her favorite street was a narrow lane lined with tiny eighteenth-and nineteenth-century watermen's cottages. Their simple architecture, neat gardens, and air of history always made her smile. At the corner, Georgian and Victorian structures claimed the landscape, and the houses grew larger. When she turned onto Barclay Street and saw Delaney House, her steps slowed. It was getting harder and harder to come home these days.

The mansion and its grounds covered the largest residential tract in Mallard Bay. Grace's work to restore her mother's family estate had occupied most of the last two years. Acclimating to life on the Eastern Shore while renovating the historic building had been both wearing and exhilarating. Accomplishing her goal was thrilling, but after the initial rush of happiness had come a sharp let down and the inevitable question — what next?

She was getting married — maybe. David's insistence on setting the date and her reluctance to do so was the source of their never-ending argument. Before she did anything else, she was going to France for an extended vacation, and she was going alone. David didn't want to go and didn't want her to go. Neither of them was budging.

She was selling Delaney House — sort of. Eventually. If everything worked out. It made her head ache to think about the long-range plan she'd let her cousin, Niki Malvern, talk her into.

If all went according to her new business partner's proposal, the risk was moderate, but complications were already arising. The latest one caught up to her as soon as she stepped through the front doorway.

High-pitched laughter floated down from somewhere on the upper floors. The open hallway with its domed ceiling three stories above provided excellent acoustics for the women who were discussing the merits of a Rococo style bed. Grace preferred clean lines, but her main concern was the decorating budget. She was the one funding it, and she'd specifically instructed Niki to purchase sturdy, hotel quality furniture for the guest rooms. She'd also refused to give into Niki's request for a professional designer.

She found her cousin on the second floor, laying large swatches of upholstery material across a worn velvet fainting couch and talking over someone on her cell. Niki saw Grace in the doorway and ended the call, but not before Grace recognized Niki's mother's voice running on as her daughter hung up on her.

"What are you doing here?" Niki asked.

"Last time I paid the bills, it seemed like I still lived here." Grace looked around at the collection of battered furniture she hadn't seen before.

Since agreeing to let Niki open an inn in Delaney House, the cousins' relationship had grown rocky. Even though Grace had never planned to live permanently in Mallard Bay, she was reluctant to turn the restored mansion over to Niki. The property had been listed for sale for a year with no serious offers, but Grace was still confident the right buyer would walk in the door. Eventually.

Niki's plan, while emotionally tricky to execute, could work. She owned a successful bed-and-breakfast operation, the Victory Manor Inn, but the four rooms she rented didn't bring in enough income. Adding a sister inn with six more bedrooms and large reception areas would change that. In the business plan, the additional revenue from room rentals and events would repay Grace's startup investment and give Niki a modest salary. Then, in two or three years, Grace could sell her property as a profitable business or a single-family home. Niki would have time to find another property to replace the lost income or, more likely, sell the Victory Manor Inn and go on to a new career choice, debt-free. Grace had decided her cousin's proposal was better than letting the newly renovated house sit empty, waiting for a buyer with deep pockets.

The ink wasn't dry on their agreement before Niki started trying to take over Grace's life.

Ignoring the dig, Niki said, "Well, I'm glad you're here. I've had a fabulous idea."

"No. Not if it involves recovering antiques with," Grace looked at the information tag on the nearest fabric swatch. "Two hundred dollars a yard? Are you crazy?" She was beginning to think she should have agreed to hire a decorator. Having a consistent third person in the mix would have given Niki someone to bounce ideas off of besides her interfering mother. Connie Delaney was always happy to suggest ways to enhance her daughter's business enterprise using Grace's money.

"Hush. That's retail, not my price." Niki gathered up the swatches and changed the subject. "Do you know what happened on Jefferson Street? There were a lot of sirens earlier. Avril stopped by here on her way back from Baltimore, but left as soon as I told her. She hasn't called, and I can't get Aidan on the phone. When I see him, I'll kill him for worrying me."

Niki and Aidan Banks had been a couple for so long, their tumultuous relationship seemed normal. Niki was always irritated with Aidan about something, but they talked to each other several times a day, if only to continue an argument. It hadn't occurred to Grace that Niki might not know about the fire. Telling one half of the duo anything usually meant both heard the news.

"I'll bet it had something to do with the TV show," Niki ran on. "I started to cut through the woods to see if there was a film crew there. Then Mom called, and I couldn't get away from her. Was that it? Were they filming? I'll die if I missed my chance to be in a scene."

"No, you didn't." Grace explained about the fire and left her cousin on the phone, contributing to the spread of the news.

After changing into shorts and sneakers, she went for a run. She'd hoped to clear her mind, but thoughts of Niki using Delaney House as an inn circled in loops with the day's events. Both work and home provoked anxiety and pushed her to run faster. When she returned to Barclay Street, it was getting dark. Niki's car was gone, and she'd left every light on downstairs. The house glowed like a jewel, but Grace only saw dollar signs. And then she noticed David's black Porsche parked across the street.

She climbed the front steps slowly, trying to muster some enthusiasm for her fiancé's unexpected visit.

Her former boss and lover had come back into her life last winter. She hadn't said 'no' when he got down on one knee and presented the iconic blue box. She hadn't said 'yes', either, but details rarely got in the way of what David wanted. The box and its sparkly contents remained in her jewelry drawer unless he was in town. Her only significant acknowledgment of her engagement had been to increase the amount of her homeowner's insurance. She wasn't wearing the ring now, a detail guaranteed to set him off.

An hour later, she wished they only had the ring to argue about.

Chapter Seven

Grace insisted on cleaning up before getting into the reason for his unusual mid-week visit. She was careful to put the ring on before rejoining him in the sitting room of her apartment on the third floor.

"I walked around downstairs while you were in the shower," he said as he uncorked the wine he'd brought. "Looking good."

Her nerves went into overdrive as she took in the telltale signs. David wore khaki pants and a polo shirt. He'd taken time to change out of his suit after work. That meant there was no emergency, just no notice to her of his plans. The duffel bag by the door said he meant to stay over. The compliment on the house he disliked and the expensive wine meant he was trying to soften her up. But for what?

He left their glasses of wine on the breakfast bar and reached for her. "I have a surprise," he whispered in her ear and kissed her gently.

"Must be something to get you here on a Tuesday night," she said, smiling in spite of herself. He was so handsome, and when she was in his arms, it was easy to remember how much she'd once loved him.

He stroked her back and switched to her other ear, still whispering and dropping soft kisses to distract her. "I know you're worried about what comes next. The wedding, where we'll live, all the details. It's a lot, and I completely understand that you have your hands full with things here."

"What have you done?" she whispered back, mainly because the words stuck in her throat. This had all the hallmarks of being so, so bad.

"I told you I'd handle everything." Another kiss, a real one that trailed down her neck, then lower.

She pushed him away, grabbed her wine glass, and took a fortifying swallow of the merlot. "What have you done?" she repeated.

"Way to kill a moment." He forced a laugh and moved to the loveseat in front of the fire-place. Patting the space beside him, he said,

"Come on. I'll leave you alone until you fling yourself in my arms. It's that good, Grace."

She joined him and tried to tamp down her rising panic. David tossed out good news like candy. He only worked this hard if he knew her immediate reaction would be 'no.'

He pulled a folded brochure from his back pocket and handed it to her. Smoothing it open, she saw it was a realtor's ad for a waterfront home near Queenstown. Under a headline boasting 'All New Construction,' the single-story stucco and glass structure spread out over six thousand square feet and overlooked a massive pool. A long, T-shaped dock stretched from the property's edge out into the Wye River, where a large speedboat was tied off.

"What have you done?" She knew she sounded like a parrot, right down to the squeak in her voice.

"We'll have a real home, Grace. Not a condo in DC, but a home." Despite his promise, he moved to close the gap between them. "Sell this museum, don't sell it, I don't care. Stay here with Mosley and his law practice, or come back to DC and work with me; it's your call. But this," he tapped the brochure, "will be our home. Yours and mine. And here's the best part: you get to finish the inside. It's brand new, and you can design the kitchen and pick out all the finishings for the interior. It'll be finished soon. If you want to live there full time, I'll commute. If you'll give in and live in DC, this will be our fabulous weekend home."

The house was everything she hated in architecture. The 'surprise' was everything she hated about their relationship. His expression was Little Boy at Christmas, and once again, he'd set her up to be the Grinch.

"Why?" she demanded. She couldn't believe they were going over the same old argument again. "I've told you I'm not ready to get married."

"You will be when you see this place, babe. I was there today with my agent, and I'll take you out there in the morning."

He pulled her into a gentle embrace, and she let him hold her. It was easier to talk into his shoulder. "I don't want to do this, David. Buying a house is a huge commitment."

His arms stiffened around her. She rushed on, her words landing on the soft cotton of his shirt. "I want you to be happy. I gave up being me for years, to make sure you got what you wanted." The speech that had been building up for weeks was falling out of her mouth faster than she could put her thoughts together. "I did it for a long time. I made you happy, and I made Mom happy, and I told myself it was enough. It wasn't enough, David, and I won't do it any-more. Everything needs to change."

"Everything such as, what?" He pushed her to arm's length, forcing her to look at him.

"Everything. All of it. Our relationship. I need a break."

"Stop. Just stop talking," David let go of her and turned away. "I shouldn't have sprung it on you."

"No, you shouldn't, but I'd feel the same no matter how you told me."

He stopped at the door to pick up the duffle bag and said, "I'm sorry. I seem to have picked a bad time for good news, but don't go overboard."

In an un-David-like move, he left without drama, telling her to slow down and think things through. Her initial relief vanished when she remembered that he never gave up. Not in a court-room, and certainly not with her. He'd only retreated to regroup.

The ring on her hand felt like a ticking bomb, and she couldn't get it off fast enough.

Chapter Eight

MELANIE

She pulled on a peacock blue sundress, adjusted the fabric, looked at herself in the mirror, and stripped again. The pile of discarded clothing was growing, and the two remaining outfits she had to try on didn't look promising. She'd spent the first ten years of her adult life either pregnant or lactating. She had to work on herself every minute, or she'd never look right again.

"We need to talk, Mom."

Melanie ignored her daughter and picked up a cotton sweater and skinny capri pants. She'd managed to lose another five pounds, but the sweater would add bulk.

"Here, try this." Hallie held up a sleeveless sheath with lace three-quarter sleeves, a sweetheart neck and a retro kick-pleat. "They sent it to me, but I'm going with a more casual look."

The dress was beautiful, and the deep rose color would complement her dark hair, but Melanie shook her head. "If it fits you, I'll never get into it. Besides, it's too young for me."

"Put it on," Hallie ordered. "You're looking at yourself with crazy eyes again."

The family joke made Melanie smile. "It's not crazy eyes, sweetie, it's real," she said as she looked at the dress. "But, I'll try to squeeze into it."

The dress floated over her body, softening the sharp angles and covering the few signs that she had ever given life. "I still look huge, but I guess it will have to do," she said.

"Maybe Aunt Whitney can take it in through the hips." Hallie's voice was tense with concern. "This is a size two, and it's big on you, Mom. You should eat more."

Melanie always ignored such negative comments. She twisted and turned in front of the mirror and pictured herself standing between Whitney and Felicia while the cameras rolled. She'd be tiny and delicate with her sister wives towering over her. No one would ever believe she was the oldest wife and the mother of seven.

"Your silver sandals will go with this, don't you think?" Melanie stretched up on her tiptoes and examined the curve of her calves with a critical eye.

"I was going to wear them, but you can have them. Now can we talk about Dad?"

Ignoring the question, Melanie said, "Pick anything you like from those things on the bed and pack the rest up for Sawyer to return to the studio. That nasty woman from Wardrobe said one outfit each, then we have to use our own clothes. Good thing I went shopping for us last week, huh?"

"Anything?" Hallie eyed the clothes her mother had rejected.

"Nothing's too good for my big girl." Melanie brushed her daughter's cheek with a kiss. "But not the dresses. You have to look the part, honey. Happy Active Teenager, that's your role, remember? Try those cute jeans and the striped boat neck top."

"I will. But before everyone comes back, we have to talk about Dad. He's just out there somewhere. The police said the rental car people couldn't reach him and we can't, either. Where is he, Mom? What's going on? He doesn't even know about the fire yesterday. I really need him."

"Oh, sweetie, we all do." Melanie finished buttoning her blouse and slipped on her old Birkenstocks. She looked like Hallie's mom again as she gathered the girl into her arms. "I know this is hard for you, and I'm sorry. The last few days have been awful, but it'll be over soon." She patted Hallie's back, making a mental note to tell Sawyer they needed a personal trainer. Hallie was getting too soft. "Your father will be here soon, and everything will be fine."

"Are you sure? I mean, what if — "

"I *said* it will be fine. Your father's working on a special project for the show, that's all."

"What kind of project?"

"I told you, developing some sites for a couple of the shows we're filming near the end of the year. Sawyer's handling everything while Dad's gone, so don't worry."

"Yeah. Mom, about Sawyer. There's something else."

Melanie's tone turned harsh. "You'd better not be starting up with him again. I fixed that once, but I can't complain about him now."

Hallie pulled away and sat on a corner of the bed. "He's only a few years older than me. I've already told you I came on to him; he didn't do anything. I was the one who broke the rules, and I did it again yesterday." She squeezed her eyes shut. The rest of her words came out in a rush.

"The littles were happy watching TV, and I went out behind the garage to smoke. Then, one of them yelled, and I think I threw the cigarette down without putting it out when I ran back inside. I'm sure I started the fire."

"Smoking!" Melanie grabbed her daughter, pulling her off the bed and shaking her. "You promised you'd stop. What if someone saw you? How does it look for us if we're preaching moral values and raising children in a strong family unit when you're out there smoking? How could you?"

"Did you hear me?" Hallie yelled. "I started the fire, and Sawyer got hurt."

"Oh, I heard you, and now you listen to me, young lady. You don't smoke, so put the whole thing out of your mind. And as for Sawyer, why did he go into the garage, anyway? Nothing of ours was in there."

Hallie's mutinous look said the confession was over.

"Start talking," Melanie demanded. "Or I'm calling Fred Renne right this minute."

The mention of Lightning Strike's CEO ended the argument. Sawyer had his job due to his uncle's generosity, but the Overtons owed the elder Renne much more than an entry level paycheck.

"I called him," Hallie said. "I wanted to see

Sawyer, and I called him. But when he got here, the garage was on fire, and he ran inside, and everything went crazy after that."

"What was in the garage that was so important?"

Hallie began to cry. Melanie's mind raced as she held her daughter. When the sobs eased, she wiped her daughter's face and said, "Tell me everything, from the beginning. I can fix it all, but you have to tell me."

Knowing better, but wanting to believe her mother, Hallie talked.

Chapter Nine

Grace faced Wednesday morning grateful the long night was over. She'd only slept briefly and woke at three. Unwilling to try to sleep again, she'd walked through Delaney House, letting its emptiness echo in her heart. By six, she was desperate to get out of her own head. She ran her usual two miles, showered, dressed, and went to the office all on autopilot. The brochure on her kitchen counter never left her thoughts.

The opening screen on her computer monitor was a bird's-eye view of the Latin Quarter in Paris. She looked at a small corner cafe and imagined herself at the single empty table on the sidewalk. Her plane ticket was non-refundable. She'd either make the flight in July or lose her money. When she'd bought the ticket, she'd already missed two self-imposed deadlines for leaving Mallard Bay and was desperate for any trick to keep her plans on track. This time she would be successful, but first, she had to do something about David.

She made herself concentrate on finishing the work she'd agreed to do for the Overtons. The sooner she could wrap up that project, the better. She wanted to have a clear idea of their legal situation before meeting with them again, but lack of sleep and impotent fury kept distracting her. Between yawning and mentally cursing David, she didn't get much done. Curiosity nagged at her to go see the house he'd picked out, but it felt like giving in, and pigheaded stubbornness wouldn't let her do it.

Remembering that Whitney had emailed her the promotional video for the Overtons' show, she opened the file, curious to see Heath Overton.

Melanie and Whitney hadn't exaggerated. *The Plurals Next Door* was ready to roll. The production was polished and professional, complete with sitcom theme music and soundbites from Heath, Melanie, and Whitney and, after a dramatic *Tada* chord, their fiancée, Felicia Jones.

Melanie and Whitney looked both younger and more sophisticated than the women Grace had met. Care had been taken to emphasize the sisters' similarities in appearance and wardrobe. Someone had gotten Melanie to open up, literally. She sat untwisted on a couch, laughing and flicking her long hair out of her face as several giggling children played around her. A beaming Whitney, who carried a toddler and led a small boy by the hand, soon joined them.

The currently missing husband appeared next. The shot widened to show a dark-haired man of medium height and medium build. Everything else about Heath Overton was extraordinary. He had a bone structure and natural grace that the camera loved. His smile looked sincere, and charisma fairly leaped from the screen. Whitney handed him her little girl as he joined his wives on the sofa. The child clapped her chubby hands and laughed in delight as he held her in the air before setting her on his lap. The older kids, dark-haired, handsome stair-step miniatures of their parents, filed in and lined up behind them.

Felicia Jones and her children, blonde counterpoints to the Overtons, entered, and the cameras zoomed out to capture everyone. Only one thing kept the group from projecting bland perfection: while the adults welcomed the new arrivals, the teenagers' expressions said trouble was about to break out. Grace wanted to see what happened next with this family. Maybe the Overtons were on to something — if they still had a father and a contract.

Googling 'Overton' and 'plural family' produced links to the websites for Lightning Strike Films and the Overton family. Neither told her anything she didn't already know, but she spent a few minutes studying the family's promotional photos. They all looked relaxed, happy, and attractive. Grace wondered how the women she'd met yesterday had been transformed for filming. Just getting Melanie untwisted and dry-eyed would have taken some work.

Although Melanie and Whitney hadn't asked her to, she read the marriage laws in Georgia and Maryland's 'crimes against marriage' statutes. When she finished, she decided that there weren't any serious issues with their plural family arrangement.

Whitney had changed her last name to Overton, wore a wedding ring, and called herself Heath's wife. The name change was legal; she had the right of free speech and the right to wear any kind of jewelry she wished. As long as she and Heath didn't commit fraud by claiming to be married, they should be in the clear. The only thing Grace found for the State of Maryland to throw at the threesome was adultery between Heath and Whitney, a charge which carried a ten-dollar penalty. Not exactly a deterrent, and who'd file a complaint?

Even bringing Felicia and her children into the mix didn't break any laws Grace could find. If Heath and Melanie divorced and Heath married Felicia and adopted her children, all three women would have the Overton name, as would all the children. In the new family unit, only Felicia would be Heath's wife, although the Overtons claimed not to recognize a distinction between a legal union and their moral commitments to each other.

A review of the contract Heath, Melanie, Whitney, and Felicia had signed with Lightning Strike Films revealed a straightforward agreement. The failure of any of them to perform under the specified terms meant the contract was void for all of them.

She turned her attention to the personal information Whitney had given her on Heath and Felicia. For her husband, Whitney had only provided a copy of his driver's license, social security card, and the phone number of the car rental agency. The two reports on Felicia provided much more information, but little of it was useful.

Starting with the basics, Grace called all the work and home numbers for Heath. The home landline and cell phones went to voicemail, where she left messages. The sales manager at the dealership where Heath and Felicia had met confirmed that neither was still employed, then unloaded snarky opinions of his former employees. By the time Grace got him off the phone, she felt reasonably sure the couple hadn't been in touch with him recently.

Next, she checked public records in Maryland, Delaware, and Virginia. No arrest or citations showed up in either name. They were equally clean in Georgia, where she only found Felicia's divorce from a Robert Lee Jones. Grace hoped she wouldn't have to find the ex-husband in the sea of men carrying versions of that name.

A call to Ernie's Royal Rides in Baltimore got her nowhere. Once she identified herself as the Overtons' attorney, the leasing manager said, 'no comment' and hung up. She briefly considered driving over for an in-person conversation, but knew she was only avoiding the most obvious next step.

She needed to know what the police were thinking. The easiest way to find out was to call McNamara, but there was the uncomfortable matter of yesterday's argument. Her argument. Mac had enjoyed a good laugh at her expense, and calling him now would be beyond embarrassing.

Over the past six months, he'd made his interest in her clear, but in a lighthearted, no-pressure way. She hadn't reciprocated, but she hadn't discouraged him, either. Now here they were — she was still engaged to David, and Mac was seeing someone else. More than 'seeing.' She'd run into the couple last week at the bakery, eating breakfast and looking happy.

Everyone said Ashley Greenburgh was the perfect match for the widowed Chief of Police. A widow herself, Ashley was an attractive, late forty-something with a wide smile and easy laugh. While she wasn't the first woman to set her mind on ending McNamara's single status, this time, he was cooperating.

Another good reason to leave, Grace had thought. If Mac was waking up to women after a ten-year hibernation, she didn't need to be in his first round of options.

So why had she asked him to lunch yesterday?

If she was honest — and she was too tired of her relentless introspection to be anything else — she had to admit it was because she enjoyed being with him. She wanted their friendship to stay that way, friendly. Mac made her happy, or he had until he'd changed from Grace's friend into A Man. The last thing she needed was another one of those.

Chapter Ten

The good news was, McNamara wasn't mad. At least she thought it was good. Grace didn't have much experience with men who didn't hold grudges.

When they'd covered the weather, and she'd assured him she was fine, she asked about the investigation into Heath Overton's disappearance.

"Are you still the family's attorney?" he asked.

She hesitated. Melanie and Whitney Overton had signed the new client paperwork and given her a retainer, but she expected the officious Sawyer Renne to ask them to drop her.

"No one's said otherwise, so I'm still on duty," she said.

"You have a low threshold for positive client relationships."

"Uh-huh." She wasn't going to be drawn into an easy banter that could lead to revisiting their conversation from the day before. "After reflecting on the information they shared with you and Detective Sergeant Marbury, and considering the concerns you both expressed for their husband, my clients asked me to speak to you on their behalf."

"The concern we expressed was that neither of your clients was being truthful as to the whereabouts of Mr. Overton." The humor was gone from McNamara's voice.

Careful not to allow her surprise to show, she said, "Did you and the Detective Sergeant visit the Overtons together?"

"We weren't invited to a party, Grace. Heath Overton rented a Land Rover with a six-figure replacement value, and he didn't return it. I accompanied Desi Marbury to question Mrs. Overton and her family as part of a multi-jurisdiction investigation with the State Police."

She'd envisioned the father of nine renting a van or some other vehicle impervious to spilled food and drinks and sticky fingers. "Investigation of what? The lease was renewed, and the car isn't due back until today."

"That's true," he said. "But on Saturday, the

rental agency received a traffic citation from the city of Anderson, S.C. The Land Rover had blown through a red light in a school zone three states south of the permitted travel range in the rental agreement. The car agency's owner tried to connect to the vehicle's GPS system, only to find it had been deactivated, which is never a good sign in a missing car. That's when he reported it stolen."

"Did you tell my clients all of that?"

"Yes." His tone was genial again. "It sounds like they omitted some important details when they talked to you."

"Mac, if you've spent any time with them, you know the personalities I'm dealing with — just tell me what you think. Where is Mr. Overton?"

"Hang on." She heard him ask for a file; then, paper rustled at his end. "On Sunday, May 6, he passed through the west-bound toll booths at the Bay Bridge around nine forty-five, p.m. and hasn't been seen since he left Mallard Bay. Whitney Overton told us he's called daily and is fine and will be back in town today."

"Mrs. Overton believed that her husband would return in a timely fashion, but she may have exaggerated the extent of his communication with the family. They mistakenly thought a confidentiality requirement in the contract for their television show prevented them from talking to the police. I've advised them they should communicate with you, fully and honestly, and cooperate with your investigation."

"And they made you call for them so they could deny anything you told me."

She made herself count to ten before saying, "So? Where do you think their husband is?"

"No idea, but I intend to find out."

"Those citations generated from traffic cameras usually come with photos. I don't suppose you could tell if there were two people in the car? Another person connected to the family might have been with him. Felicia Jones."

"The fiancée?"

"Yes."

"Are the wives worried about her, too?"

"Don't be judgmental," she said.

"There's only one person visible in the car. Could be male or female, but only one."

She asked for an update on the garage fire. "Sawyer Renne said Aidan told him it wasn't an accident."

"Did he, now? I don't have any concrete answers yet, but you can tell the Overtons I'm looking into it."

An awkward silence fell between them.

A series of beeps from an incoming call gave him a quick way to end the non-conversation, but that only made her feel worse. Their easy friendship was gone, and she didn't know how to get it back.

~

Since she didn't have a single thing on her work list that wasn't unpleasant, she started with the easiest. If Mosley fired her for taking on the Overtons, she could live with it. On her way to his office, she stopped at Lily's desk and asked her to draft a letter to Ernie's Royal Rides asking for a copy of the lease Heath Overton had signed.

"You're keeping that family as clients?" Lily asked, her disapproval clear. "We don't do missing persons."

"For the time being. I'm off to see the big boss about it now."

"Yeah? Good luck with that."

Grace let the moment go. Whatever was bothering Lily would just have to play itself out.

She found Mosley muttering at a golf ball that had become lodged under a glass front bookcase. At some point since her last visit, half of Mosley's large and elegant office had been turned into a putting green.

"You've redecorated," she said as she threaded her way around the conference table and chairs which had been shoved up against his desk. She would have said a lot more, but office decor wasn't her problem anymore.

"Well, I had to do something," he said peevishly. "If I don't keep up with my putting, I may as well quit playing golf."

She knew he was winding up to the argument about how she was ruining his social life by leaving the firm.

"We don't take missing persons cases," he said when she tried to introduce the Overton case as an exciting addition of new clients.

"So I've been told."

"Have Marjorie pass them along to Harry Bork in Cambridge with my compliments. That bottom feeder will know every low life hideout where a man with three wives might go."

"Heath Overton only has two wives, and legally, he only has one. The third woman is a fiancée."

"Ever so much better," he murmured as he abandoned the lost ball and lined up a putt. "These people don't sound like my cup of tea. However, I've asked Lily to give you a few files to follow up on. Simple meet and greets and a few phone calls at most, m'dear," he'd said. "You'll breeze through them in no time. I'm taking the afternoon off. Once you're gone, I won't get many chances to do that."

Only a few months earlier, she'd worried he would never be able to pick up clubs again. As heartwarming as it was to watch the old Mosley return to life, the flip side was she had to work with the manipulative old crank the way he used to be. At least now, she usually knew when she was being played.

She gave in, rearranged her task calendar for the afternoon, and saw she was already running too far behind to accomplish everything on it. David, Mac, and the office personnel problems all had to take a back seat to work, but as the day wore on, her thoughts kept drifting.

She couldn't do anything about Mosley and the staff's disapproval of her decision to leave, and she was afraid talking to Mac would only make matters between them worse. But there was still David to deal with, and she wanted to do it as soon as possible.

Chapter Eleven

One convenient thing about the Overtons' rental being next door to Avril Oxley was that Grace could combine three tasks into a single trip. Once she'd handled Cyrus' assignments and the top layer of work on her own desk, she drove home, parked, and then walked through a dense stretch of trees between her house and Avril's. Ordinarily, she avoided the woods, but Avril liked the shortcut, so Grace had cleared a wide path between their properties. Today, it saved her from parking next to her clients' driveway. With a little luck, she could look around the scene of the fire without drawing attention.

The garage was a small structure built when cars needed a hand crank to start. Grace was surprised to see how close the fire had come to the tree line at the wood's edge. She resolved to send a donation to Mallard Bay's all-volunteer fire department. Without their fast action, Delaney House might not be standing today.

"Will you come on over here?" Avril's call was punctuated by a long barrage of yapping and a single deep *woof.* "These creatures want you for some reason, and they're making me crazy."

Grace was met at the front door by a German Shepherd named Louise, and Leo, a white ball on sticks masquerading as a dog. Grace's dog. The ball launched himself at her, and she stooped to catch him in mid-air. "How's my good boy?" She whispered into his pointy ears.

"Redefining 'good boy' is how he is," said Avril, whose hearing was as sharp as the rest of her. She closed the door behind Grace and called the shepherd to her side. "You have the same taste in dogs as you do in men," she said. "Louise, pay no attention to them."

The shepherd was small for her breed, but standing next to Avril, she looked like a pony. The old woman laid her left hand on Louise's head, as if in benediction. "These dogs are very close. You know that, right?"

"Hello. I'm fine, thank you. And you? Are you well?"

"Oh, for… yes, missy, I am *well*. Please join me in the conservatory for tea and let us converse."

The conservatory was a cluttered sun porch that overlooked her side garden. Tea was store-brand diet soda and a package of Oreos.

"Aren't you supposed to be on a new healthy eating plan?" Grace asked as she accepted the drink and debated the calorie worthiness of the cookies.

"Keep up, girl. That was last month." Avril took two cookies for her own plate and gave the dogs warning glares. "No chocolate. You know you get your cookies at night."

"You give them cookies?" Grace picked Leo up and patted his tummy. "That's the last thing this guy needs."

"Everyone needs cookies, otherwise what's the point? You're born, you die. In between, you eat cookies to make it worth the bother."

"Words to live by."

Avril's face darkened, and she motioned for Louise to lie down. "Yes, well, eating dessert first seems like a good diet plan after yesterday. That fire could've spread, and the dogs were here alone."

"I should have checked in with you last night.

I meant to come and get Leo, but with everything that's going on — "

"You forgot him," Avril finished for her.

"Not exactly."

On top of her miserable day, she was being called out for being a bad dog mother. Grace helped herself to an Oreo. The fat and sugar rush would be temporary, but worth the calories.

"It's fine," Avril said. "I'd have called if I needed you. Besides, you had company. What was Mr. Wonderful doing here in the middle of the week?"

The Oreo was working its magic, and Avril's nosiness made her laugh. "It's a story better told with a bottle of wine, I'm afraid. But not yet. I'm still processing his latest antic."

Despite Avril's protests, Grace changed the conversation back to the dogs. "Thanks for keeping both of them; I know it's a lot to ask. Before all the excitement yesterday, I intended to talk to you about Louise. I ran into Doris Bosworth over the weekend. She said Safe Harbor had to take two dozen dogs from a puppy mill down in Wicomico. They're trying to leave all the foster dogs where they are for now while they use the shelter space for the new arrivals."

Safe Harbor Animal Rescue was a grassroots organization that supported local animal shelters and provided fostering services to relieve over-crowding. Kingston County's shelter would soon celebrate its first full year as a kill-free operation due to Safe Harbor's work.

"The dogs aren't a problem for me."

"You're not getting attached, are you? Remember, I only adopted Leo, I'm fostering Louise."

"And you're doing such a good job with both of them." Avril's smile took the sting out of her words. "But Louise doesn't need to be fostered; she has a home."

Grace looked up from her inspection of what might be the beginnings of a rash on Leo's pink potbelly. The dog had more allergies than she did. "What's happened? Did the woman who adopted her originally decide she could keep her?"

"No. Her apartment really wasn't big enough." Avril snapped her fingers to pull Grace's attention from Leo. "Love doesn't conquer everything, you know."

"You've mentioned that once or twice, and I'm still not going to discuss David."

"We'll see about that. Anyway, this girl needed a home and I'm happy to provide one, so it's settled. I worked it all out with the SHAR folks."

Grace pushed away the immediate worry of

how Avril would manage a large dog long term, even a docile one. The happy grin on her friend's face was contagious. "You're keeping her? That's wonderful."

Avril waved the congratulations aside. "Since you're leaving and these two are so close, I'd like you to give Leo to me permanently. They kind of balance each other in a Laurel and Hardy sort of way."

"You want my dog, too? Are you kidding?"

"One of us has to be practical. You're moving on. Someone will have to pick up the slack around here."

The words hung between them in a rare silence. Grace felt wounded, which she knew was unreasonable.

Avril broke the tension by asking about the Overtons.

"We're not finished with the subject of you stealing my dog."

"Whatever. About those kids. It's the oldest girl I worry about the most."

"Hallie? Why?" Grace asked. "Her mother and aunt said she's a big help with the smaller children."

"I'll bet they think so. The child runs her skinny legs off taking care that brood. It's not right."

"She's old enough to be helping."

"What do you know about children? Hallie always has a bunch of kids in tow, and I never see her doing normal teenage things. She only gets a break when that infantile Sawyer person shows up. He's sillier than the kids. I doubt he's part of any professional production team."

Grace had to agree Sawyer Renne didn't seem experienced, but she didn't want to get Avril off-topic. "What do you think is going on with them? The Overtons, I mean. You obviously have strong feelings."

"I'm invested in them, in a manner of speaking. I own the house they're renting."

Every time Grace thought she knew Avril well, she was reminded their friendship was still young. It impressed her to learn Avril was collecting a handsome rent from Lightning Strike Films for a three-month lease. "An Eastern Shore retirement plan is what my daddy called it," Avril said. "Buy up properties as you can and lease them out. I sold most of the ones he collected, but I like selecting my next-door neighbors."

"Are you saying you thought a family with eleven children would be fun?"

Avril shrugged. "The house has been empty a while, and the agent offered triple the rent for a short lease. I like kids, and I wanted to see how those shows are made."

"Those cheesy quasi-reality shows? You don't even have a television."

"Don't be a snob. Some of them are very entertaining. And for your information, I stream shows to my computer. When you have time, I'll show you how to do it so you can catch up with the modern world."

Why had she ever assumed her friend wouldn't be up to date on electronics as well as everything else?

"I haven't missed an episode of *Survivor* since 2002," Avril said. "But we can talk about reality family drama versus situational competitions another time. I want to know what's up with those *Looney Tunes* sisters and their children. Something's off with them, and someone needs to watch out for Hallie."

It took a while to appease Avril without breaching client confidentiality, but eventually, the dogs had to go out, and Grace made her escape. She wanted to take Leo with her, but gave in to Avril's insistence that he'd be happier staying with Louise.

She walked back through the woods alone, glad for the silence that let her thoughts settle. That peace only lasted until she got home.

"What do you mean you've moved in?"

The day before, the smallest bedroom on the second floor had only held a double bed and a dresser. Now it looked like the aftermath of a rummage sale.

"I'd have told you if you hadn't run off yesterday afternoon," Niki said.

"You would have *told* me?" Grace couldn't believe her cousin had the nerve to sound insulted. Well, she could believe it, but it was irritating. "*Asking* me didn't occur to you?"

"I'm renting the first two floors from you for the inn. What I do with them, I do for the best interest of *our* business, which *I* run. By living here, I have more rooms to rent at the Victory Manor. Groups can rent the whole house, which will bring in more income. You'll be making money before we even get this place open." Niki beamed as she described her new plan.

Grace knew what Niki was saying made financial sense. Still, the idea of living with her perpetually busy cousin gave her a headache, which added to the gnawing sensation in her stomach. For the second day in a row, she'd forgotten to eat lunch.

"Don't worry," Niki said. "It won't be for long. When you're gone, I'll move into your apartment and add this room to the rental inventory."

When Grace was gone.

She agreed with Niki so she could end the conversation and escape to her nest on the third floor. At least for now, she could still claim it for her own, but who knew where she'd be by fall? The unfettered freedom she'd planned for didn't feel right, only lonely.

Chapter Twelve

To Banks' surprise, McNamara took him along to the Overton house on Thursday morning to interview the family. There'd been no mention of what had happened with the children on the day of the fire, but Banks had rehearsed several variations of 'somebody had to do something,' just in case. He'd also taken pains with his shift reports and was trying to be as quiet as possible. He didn't want to be taken off the first interesting investigation they'd had in months. His resolve held out until they pulled up at the Overtons' house.

"Are we here to question the family about their father's disappearance, or do you also think there's something suspicious about the fire?" Ordinarily, he wouldn't ask a question that might have been answered in a report he was supposed to have read, but he wanted to know what the Chief thought.

"Both," the Chief said, to Bank's relief. "The disappearance is odd, and the wife — wives — denying he's missing, then sending Grace to ask questions, is odd. An accidental fire is too coincidental on top of all that oddity. Especially when it all happens to an unconventional family like the Overtons."

Banks nodded. "Plus, that Sawyer guy, the producer, looks and acts like a squirrel."

"Is that why you told him we thought the fire wasn't an accident?" McNamara asked.

"That's not what happened." Banks was incensed and made no effort to hide it. "He came by the office after he got out of the hospital, which was bogus. You should have heard him describing his labored breathing as if he was ninety with emphysema."

"When he came to give his statement, which I asked him to do, you'll recall — what did you say?"

"He asked if we knew what started the fire. I said no."

The Chief's look was steady and far from agreeable. "That's all you said?"

"Dude had a tone. Like we were basic hicks

who weren't doing anything. I said we were still running tests."

"*Dude* told the Overtons we thought it was arson," McNamara snapped.

"Well, we do, don't we?"

The lecture that might have been was interrupted when a white Tahoe pulled up behind them, and a tall woman with shoulder-length red hair got out.

"What's she doing here?" Banks asked. The arrival of Desiree Marbury was an unexpected and unpleasant turn of events. He and the Maryland State Police detective didn't get along. To be more precise, Marbury viewed him with disdain, and he tried to pretend she didn't exist.

"Wasn't sure she could make it," the Chief said. "But it will save time in the investigation since the State Fire Marshall's office is ultimately in charge."

"And they sent the State Police out here for a garage fire?"

"You know Desi and I worked together for a while in the State Police. She's in the area today, and I wanted her take on the Overtons."

Banks was offended and confused, but mostly offended. It wasn't enough that the Chief treated him like a trainee instead of a corporal, but Mc-Namara knew that Marbury was one of Banks' least favorite people. To add to the insult, McNamara hadn't just worked with Marbury, he'd been her supervisor and mentor. And now he wanted to work with her on the Overton case, which despite their relationship, made no sense at all.

"Are you coming, or waiting in the car?"

Banks realized McNamara was speaking to him from the sidewalk where he stood next to Marbury.

"Do we need to bring junior up to speed, sir?" Marbury asked McNamara as Banks joined them.

Banks ignored the comment. "Sorry to keep you waiting, Chief," he said, then added, "Detective Sergeant Marbury, always a pleasure." He'd be damned if he'd stoop to her level. She'd been two years behind him in school and was now light years ahead of him professionally, and she never let him forget it.

"If we could talk about the Overtons?" McNamara said.

Banks marveled at the instant change in Marbury's demeanor. Suddenly polite, she nodded to him, then turned to address McNamara directly.

"A minute's about all I have, sir. There's a development in, uhm, the case I'm handling." She hesitated and glanced at Banks, who felt himself turn red when he realized she didn't want to give details in front of him. Deserved or not, how many times was he going to be insulted before he got down to any actual work today?

"We can handle this if you need to leave, Sergeant," McNamara said.

"Sir. I do have to get on the road, but I wanted to touch base with you." Again, Banks got a sideways glance. "And to get the lay of the land for myself. I'll call you later, and we can catch things up."

"Sounds good," McNamara said. "These women might not know much about what happened on Tuesday, or the daughter may have told them more than she told us. If she can state for sure that she or Sawyer Renne started the fire, it would tie up some loose ends. If not, we'll have to come up with another way to get the information."

Banks felt stupid. What was he missing? Avril had said the garage had only had a few gardening tools in it. What was the big deal?

"I also want to talk to the two mothers and the oldest daughter about the father," McNamara said, drawing them back to the situation at hand. "So far, Mrs. Overton has refused to let us question the children. Now the fire gives me a reason to interview Hallie."

"Don't we need a court order and a social worker if a parent won't give us permission?"

Banks asked, emphasizing 'we,' and hoping he'd gotten that bit of protocol right.

McNamara smiled. "If your magnetic personality doesn't convince the biological mother, yes. But we'll try the easy way first."

Marbury said, "The father's situation could still be innocent at this point — the GPS could be defective, or he might not have read the fine print on the lease. In either scenario, he could show up with the car, and then it's a matter of money wrestling between him and the rental agency. Interesting situation with this polygamist angle. Wish I had time today, but I'll keep in touch."

Banks wanted to say the Overtons were polyamorists, not polygamists, but Marbury was moving away. He noticed that McNamara didn't tell her either.

"What do you want me to do?" he asked McNamara as they walked to the house. "Be quiet and take notes, right?"

"Do what you do best," McNamara said as the front door opened, and four giggling children spilled out.

Banks was amazed the Chief thought he had a 'best' but didn't have time to wonder what it was before he was surrounded.

∽

"My husband will return any day now, I assure you. And when he does, he can answer your questions." Melanie Overton's words were firm and might have been convincing if she hadn't been clutching a large wad of tissues. The interview was just starting, and her face was already damp.

Once the women had learned McNamara and Banks had no news about their husband, they'd been reluctant to cooperate. Banks' good-natured banter with the children had gotten them in the house, and McNamara's offer to take the sisters' statements in their home instead of the police station had sealed the deal.

McNamara said, "I hope Mr. Overton returns soon, but we aren't here today to talk about your husband. There was a fire here that caused quite a bit of damage, and we need to discuss it."

The women looked at each other, then Whitney said, "All right. But we told you everything on Tuesday. The owner of this house understands we had nothing to do with what happened. I'm sure there was something flammable in the garage that ignited somehow."

"Such as?"

"Corporal Banks told my daughter it was a mulch fire," Melanie said.

McNamara looked at Banks, who shrugged. There was no point in denying it.

"We Googled it," Melanie continued, "and sure enough, it's possible for mulch to spontaneously combust if it's piled too deep and the weather is hot and dry. So, there. Like I said, it wasn't our fault."

Banks waited for McNamara to call her out on the unlikely possibility of spontaneous combustion on a rainy day, but all he said was, "You've had a rough time lately; I can appreciate that."

"Well, that's a nice change. Thank you." Whitney rewarded them with a brief smile.

"Just a few questions, and we'll be on our way," McNamara continued. "Why did Sawyer Renne have a key to the padlock on the garage door?"

"What padlock?" Whitney asked. Her sister looked equally confused.

"One of your children, Brayden, told Corporal Banks that he saw Renne unlock the padlock before entering the garage."

Banks felt uneasy. The women didn't look happy, and he worried that he'd just gotten a five-year-old in trouble.

"We know nothing about that," Whitney said. "But Sawyer works for Lightning Strike, and they rented this place, so if he had something stored in the garage, it makes sense that he'd put a lock on the door. Have you asked him?"

"I will," McNamara said. "Who was caring for your children on Tuesday?"

Melanie looked incensed, but it was Whitney who answered. "Our daughter Hallie is sixteen and perfectly able to handle the other seven who were home at the time. She also had her sisters to help her. The twins are eight and are very good with the toddlers."

"None of the children besides Brayden saw anything unusual or out of place?" the Chief asked.

"You can't question the children!" Melanie sat upright. "They didn't see anything, and we don't permit interviews with them. Besides, they're upstairs with their tutor."

"I hadn't thought of that. Interviewing them, I mean," McNamara lied. His tone made it clear he was thinking about it now.

"No," Whitney protested. "You'll have to speak to our lawyer. Maybe we should call her."

McNamara changed tack and steered the conversation away from Grace. "What about Mr. Renne? Was he here when the fire broke out?"

The question seemed to set both women back, but Melanie spoke up. "Hallie was taking care of the children. Sawyer showed up after the fire started. I believe you already know that."

"I have his statement, yes." McNamara waited for the implication to sink in.

"Talk to the landlord," Whitney said. "She's lives next door."

"Miss Oxley was away most of the day," McNamara said.

"Then we can't help you," Whitney said. "When our husband gets home, you can talk to him."

"But he wasn't here, either," Banks said. He'd been getting bored, and since no one objected, he kept talking. "Do you believe your husband and Ms. Jones are together? I was going through the reports, and I noticed that neither of you ever said."

Melanie said, 'no' just as her sister said, 'I hope so.'

McNamara said, "Mrs. Overton, Whitney, would you speak privately with me?"

Banks, uncertain if he'd been dismissed or promoted, stood and said to Melanie, "I'm pretty handy in the kitchen. Would you let me make coffee? I didn't get my usual six cups today, and I could really use some."

It wasn't much of a joke, but it was enough to get the nervous woman on her feet and moving. Banks was rewarded with a nod from the Chief. He was congratulating himself on his success in motivating a witness without brute force when Melanie said they only had herbal tea or instant decaf.

Banks suppressed a shudder and tried to think of the questions he should ask while he had the weaker sister without her watchdog.

Chapter Thirteen

The large, sunny kitchen was an open concept design, which meant children's toys, shoes, and clothes spilled from the family room area at one end and into the kitchen at the other. Running footsteps and the occasional shriek from overhead confirmed Whitney's earlier statement that the children were upstairs.

"I know what you're doing," Melanie said. She opened a cabinet filled with boxes of tea and snacks and waved toward a kettle on the large gas range. "Knock yourself out. You can make tea if you want some, but I'm not answering your questions."

"I don't blame you," Banks said as he filled the kettle. "You can't be too careful, I understand. But the only reason the Chief sent me in here was so he could talk to your sister without interruptions."

Melanie looked indignant at this, so he rushed on. "It's me, you see." He decided the truth might work. "I'm trying to move up, get promoted, but there's nowhere to go in a two-person department. Anyway, the Chief still lets me come along for meetings like these to improve my interviewing technique."

She got up and started for the kitchen door.

"No, please don't do that." He tried to sound desperate, which wasn't all that hard. "This is what I'm talking about. I'll be fired if you go out there."

He couldn't believe it worked.

She turned around and gave him a look that he was sure worked wonders on her kids. "What's going on?"

"It's like this, you've told us all you can and it's clear you're in charge here. Your sister seems very dependent on you and the Chief wants to give her every opportunity to tell her story without, uhm…" he ran out of bullshit just as she was starting to smile.

He turned and grabbed the first box of tea he saw. Raspberry. It figured. He hated herbal tea *and* raspberries. He took another look in the cabinet and found a box of Zebra Cakes.

"Help yourself," Melanie said, but she came

back to the kitchen table. "One of the kids sneaked them into a grocery cart last week and they'll only rot up there. Whitney doesn't allow sugary snacks."

"I guessed as much. Poor little guys." Banks was relieved to see her smile grow. "Well, I mean, dried apricots and granola?"

"I do a lot of baking," Melanie said. "I make sure everyone has wholesome snacks and desserts. Whitney doesn't eat sweets, so I can spoil the kids from time to time."

She didn't look as if she ate anything at all, and he wondered if her idea of spoiling children was to put carob chips in their sugarless cookies. He poured boiling water over the tea bags and tried not to recoil from the aroma.

"Your sister calls the shots on food choices, huh?"

"Whitney likes to think she and Heath run everything, but we're a team. All of us. The big kids help and they have a say in how we do things. We're a democracy."

"Interesting," Banks said. It was also crazy. His mother would have thumped him a good one if he'd suggested such a thing, but Melanie was talking without crying. He took two cups from hooks along the underside of a cabinet and filled them with the red tea. Passing a cup to her, he said, "Is it all worked out with this new woman, Felicia Jones? The kids and you and your sister are all happy about sharing your husband and expanding the family?" He wasn't even sure she still had a husband to share.

She frowned. "Well, we don't involve the children in a decision like that. I mean, choosing a spouse is personal, isn't it?"

"I've always thought so. Are you saying you look at it as if you're marrying this woman, too?" He was losing her; he could see it. Her eyes were watering again. "I'm just curious. For myself, I mean. I've never met a family like yours."

He added the last part quickly and wondered if he'd crossed into forbidden territory. But she was still listening and wasn't crying yet, so he kept on. "My mom always preached at me to be sure I found the right woman before I got married. She says men aren't able to love two women at the same time."

"There are many kinds of love." She took a sip of her tea. "Although your mother was probably right about your father. You were thinking about your father, weren't you? Did he leave you?"

Banks tasted the noxious tea and tried to look too emotional to respond.

"If he loved your mother and the other woman, he could've made it work without leaving his family. Good men don't do that."

"It's not that easy," he said, thinking of Niki. He also felt defensive about his imaginary father's imaginary betrayal. Then he wondered if Melanie was talking about her own husband.

"But it is," she said. "Humans are hard-wired to love multiple people. That's what ensures the success of the species. It's science; a pack mentality. Our family's arrangement developed naturally. Organically, really. We needed help, and Whitney was there. She was wonderful and I understood Heath loving her for it. Of course, I've always loved her — she's my sister. The kids adore her, too."

He couldn't imagine discussing any type of plural relationship with Niki, although he could easily imagine her killing him if he did. "But what about, you know, what about…"

"Sex?" Her cheeks pinked up a bit. "Don't be embarrassed to say it. We discuss it on television, so I'm getting used to the questions and the fact that nobody believes or even listens to our answers. They just enjoy the mental images."

Banks was so flustered, he forgot himself and drank some tea.

Melanie laughed. "Goodness, if you think it's that bad, dump it and get some water."

He noticed that she wasn't drinking her tea, either, but she was smiling. He emptied his cup into the sink. "I'll listen," he took a stool at the island counter. "Tell me about it."

Hallie Overton may have been Melanie's daughter, but McNamara thought she was a junior Whitney. Wide blue eyes glared at him from under a blanket of tousled black hair. She wore cut-off jeans, Daisy Duke style, and a halter top that countered any misconception that the Overtons' plural family might embrace a conservative religious lifestyle. Her appearance in the living room interrupted a line of questions that were getting McNamara nowhere with her aunt. He asked Hallie to join them.

"No." Whitney got to her feet. "No questioning of the children."

"What*ever*." Hallie plopped down on the sofa. "But I can sit wherever I want. You know, I'm nearly eighteen."

Her aunt didn't budge. "You won't be seventeen until next month, young lady, and you will not talk to the police."

Hallie narrowed her eyes and stayed put, but she didn't argue.

"I've heard nice things about you, Hallie," McNamara said. "It sounds as if you did a good job yesterday, keeping the younger children calm and inside the house."

"Go upstairs, Hallie." Whitney had one hand at her niece's arm and her eyes on McNamara.

"It won't take long to get a court order, Ms. Overton," McNamara said. "Or I can ask her some questions now at home with you as a witness."

"You don't need to do either," Whitney insisted. "She doesn't know anything we haven't already told you."

Hallie had lost the 'whatever' expression but made no move to leave.

"I'd need to ask her what she was doing when the fire started," McNamara said.

"Nothing, really. I—"

"No," Whitney interrupted. "She isn't going to answer you."

"Okay," McNamara said agreeably. "Can she tell me what was in the garage?"

Whitney still looked worried but shook her head.

"How about whether or not Sawyer Renne stopped by?"

"She doesn't know." Whitney turned back to her niece and ordered her upstairs.

"No!" Hallie shouted. "Don't treat me like a child."

"It's okay," McNamara stood up. To Whitney, he added, "Please have her available at two this afternoon. I'll return with a court order."

"No, please," Whitney said as Melanie hurried into the room, followed by Banks.

"She's right," Melanie said. "No court orders. It could get into the press. Hallie will tell you what you want to know."

Chapter Fourteen

WHITNEY

Whitney thought her sister only had two basic settings — contented and Category Five. Anything in between was only a wave she rode to Happy Land or Armageddon. The waves themselves were tricky because you never knew which way they were headed. When hurricane speed arrived, it was best to hunker down and let it blow. She and Hallie sat at the kitchen table and waited while Melanie spent her fury.

"You're not to speak to the police without my permission. Disobey me again and there will be repercussions, young lady. You're not an adult, and you don't make the decisions around here."

Finished for the moment with her daughter, Melanie rounded on Whitney. "And you! You're unbelievable. We agreed, sitting right here last night. We had a game plan, and you blew it. What were you thinking?"

"I did the best I could under the circumstances." Whitney stayed calm, at least on the outside. Matching Melanie decibel for decibel never worked. After a lifetime of experience, she still couldn't believe so much anger could boil out of such a tiny person. Her sister needed to diffuse to a place where she could be reasonable.

"You know what happens when we don't stick to the plan. Heath is counting on us to hold up our end." The comment was addressed to both Whitney and Hallie, but Melanie was glaring at her daughter. "*I'm* in charge here until he gets back."

Whitney used her napkin to mop up the chamomile tea that slopped out of Melanie's mug. "Eat a bite, Mel," she said and pushed a plate of cinnamon granola bars toward her sister. "Just a bite. You haven't eaten anything."

"I don't have any appetite, and who could blame me?" Melanie sank into a chair and put her head in her hands. The Big Unwind, as Whitney thought of it, had begun.

Aunt and niece exchanged brief glances, then Hallie said, "Mom, it's my fault, all of it. I should have left when Aunt Whitney first told me to. I didn't think it through, and I'm really sorry."

The last part of the apology was meant for Whitney, who gave a slight nod in acknowledgment. She'd been up half the night before with Hallie and knew how the events of the past few days had affected her. Today's visit from the police was too much. The girl hadn't gotten many traits from her mother, but as she entered adulthood, Whitney was beginning to see emotional highs and lows emerge. She prayed it was hormones regulating themselves, but it was another worry for her list.

"Thank you. You're not entirely to blame." Melanie gave her sister one more look, then turned her full attention to Hallie. "Now, I've decided that it's time we treated you like an adult since we're asking you to behave like one."

Whitney wasn't sure what was about to happen, she only knew it wasn't something they'd discussed.

"Catch."

Hallie didn't move fast enough, and the keyring Melanie tossed to her landed on the floor.

"You're almost seventeen and have a lot of responsibility. You should have a car, too."

Hallie picked up the keys and inspected them. "But these are to the vans. Oh, you mean I get my own set of *keys*."

Melanie broke off a bit of granola and put it on her napkin. "Check with me, first, though. Now, what do I get in return?"

After a few seconds of her mother's withering glare, Hallie pulled a crumpled pack of cigarettes out of her pocket and threw it on the table.

Whitney relaxed a bit. Mel was just grandstanding, and Hallie knew how to play the game. This silly act was only a way for Mel to save face and assert her authority. Things would be back to normal soon.

Jealousy was an unavoidable part of the life they'd chosen, and they each had their coping mechanisms. She always tried to let Mel have these 'first wife and mother' scenes without interfering, but it was growing more difficult as the years passed.

The lecture over, Hallie gave her mother a half-hearted hug and made a temporary escape. Whitney moved to the far side of the kitchen, stabbed at Heath's number on her phone, and listened to the ringtone roll over and over until the voice she wanted to hear told her to leave a message.

"I'm over it," Melanie said, coming to stand next to Whitney. "I'm sorry about how all that sounded, but somebody had to make her see how dangerously she's behaving. She could ruin everything."

"We could lose her," Whitney snapped, finally out of patience.

"We will *not* lose *anything.*"

Melanie's voice cracked on the last word. The tears came next, and Whitney rocked her sister in her arms, just as she'd held Hallie the night before. Why did it have to be so hard? Pieces of her family were falling away too fast for Whitney to catch them.

"Still love me, NeeNee?"

Whitney groaned at Melanie's use of the hated childhood nickname. Her sister pulled away and laughed as she wiped her face. They had reached the end of this particular storm.

"You're lucky to have me, and don't you forget it," Whitney said, then began to unload the dishwasher.

"I never would," Melanie agreed in a sing-song voice. "Before you unload that, can you make lunch for the kids? Nothing for me. I'll go finish the laundry and get something later."

Whitney knew Hallie would end up doing the laundry, and Melanie wouldn't eat.

She heated kosher hotdogs and made a fruit salad, distracting herself with a quick version of her favorite daydream. In this one, Heath showed up, tossed Felicia to the wind, and they all went home to Atlanta. She'd been happy in the old, ramshackle house south of the city. In those years, everyone had their place, and Whitney's role was mom, sister, head cook, and wife to an undemanding, charming, and funny man. Then Heath had come up with the idea of a television show, and everything changed.

She ignored a twinge of bitterness. She couldn't start doubting him now, he was trusting her to hold things together until he could come home and take over. But the troublesome questions wouldn't go away.

His visit had been a wonderful surprise. They'd taken the children to the beach in Delaware, then out to dinner for steamed crabs. Whitney had him all to herself for a long walk while Hallie put the little children to bed. It wasn't until he and Melanie had gone upstairs, and the arguing started that Whitney realized Heath hadn't brought any luggage. He left without telling her goodbye.

Eleven days later, she still had no more from Melanie than 'wait until Heath comes back.'

It was there, at the kitchen counter, halfway through toasting hotdog buns, that Whitney quit making excuses for her sister and their husband. Heath and Mel were hiding something big, and for the first time in their joint marriage, they'd cut her out.

Chapter Fifteen

"Well, that was lame," Banks said. "After all that 'you can't interview the children' crap, they were only hiding Hallie's cigarette habit. At least now we know how the fire started, and it wasn't spontaneous combustion."

McNamara didn't respond, which made Banks wonder what the hell he'd missed this time.

Their first stop after leaving the Overtons was Three Pigs Deli. Banks declared he needed a double pork sandwich and Old Bay fries to erase the taste of the raspberry tea. They got lunch to go, drove to Memorial Park, and ate in the car. Even with the windows down and a breeze off the water, it was too warm in the car, but the view of the harbor was the perfect antidote to their chaotic morning. Also, they were less likely to be interrupted than if they tried to discuss the Overtons in the tiny police station with villagers and tourists wandering in. The time it took for an overheard word to grow into gossip was short in Mallard Bay. The Chief was already getting calls from concerned citizens who wanted news about the polygamists. Polyamorists.

"Why didn't you tell Marbury she was using the wrong word?" Banks crumpled his sandwich wrapper with a satisfied burp.

"You could have corrected her if it bothered you," McNamara said.

"Why? She makes fun of anything I say, anyway."

"You sound like you're twelve."

Banks wanted to point out he'd gotten Melanie to talk while McNamara had gotten them thrown out of the house, but he wanted to keep the Chief talking. And he wanted to stay employed.

"Melanie made their life sound so simple," he said, returning to his report of the kitchen conversation. "But I don't know any women who'd go for it, do you?"

"You never know," McNamara laughed. "Are you thinking about it?"

"Like I'd want more than one woman. I can't afford Nik as it is. But back to the Overtons —

everyone calls them bigamists, but they aren't. They're not really polyamorists or polygamists, either. I'm not sure what they are, but it seems to me they took the parts they liked from both groups and made up their own rules. Polygamy is the closest to what they do, but only the guy gets multiple partners. Melanie tried to explain it." He glanced at his boss to make sure McNamara realized the significance of his accomplishment. "But what she described was actually polygyny, which is what most people mean when they talk about polygamy."

"You've taken quite an interest."

"Well, you have to get past the surface to understand what's going on, don't you? Polygyny is one man with multiple wives. Sororal polygyny is one man with multiple wives who are biological sisters, like Melanie and Whitney."

McNamara set his turkey sandwich down and stared at Banks. "Let's have the rest of it. What else have you learned?"

"That there are all kinds of multiple partner relationships. Bigamy and polygamy are just the two best known in this country. Bigamy is illegal, of course. Polygamy, where the partners don't have more than one legal marriage between them, is a gray area. Same for polygyny and polyamory. And then there's religious versus secular arrangements. The sisters mentioned Heath being a minister back in the day, but they don't seem to affiliate with any particular religion."

"Think their ideas will catch on once they're on TV?"

"Why not? Look at the bleachers at your typical soccer game. There are parents, step-parents, half-siblings, significant others, in-laws, outlaws, you name it. Kids with two moms, no dads, and vice versa. The only difference with the Overtons is they all live together."

"And sleep together?" McNamara asked.

"Not according to Melanie. Besides, how many divorced couples around here do you think hook up?"

"I'd have to ask Avril," McNamara said.

Banks was so intent he ignored the joke. "Heath and the sisters apparently make it up as they go along, deciding what works for them and what doesn't. Melanie isn't that bad, really, when you get her to calm down. She was pretty funny a couple of times. She and Nik seem kind of alike to me. They can look happy, but it's sorta desperate. More of a wanna be happy look."

McNamara didn't interrupt but stored the comment away.

"Melanie said she wants a happy childhood for her kids," Banks went on after finishing the last fry. "She talks about how much better things are now than when it was only her and her husband, poor as dirt and turning out babies every year until she had a breakdown. Seven kids in nine years could do that, I guess."

"What kind of breakdown?"

"No details. Claims she doesn't remember much, except that Whitney and God saved her."

"Not her husband?"

Banks thought for a moment, then said, "Whitney, God, and the kids. In that order, pretty much. Husband seemed to fall into the food and shelter category. A necessity."

McNamara gathered up the paper wrappers. On the way to the station, he described Whitney refusing to let Hallie answer questions about Renne.

"What is it with that guy?" Banks asked. "Why are they protecting him?"

"Another way to look at it is to ask what he might be holding over them." McNamara pulled into the lot behind the police station side of the municipal building and turned off the ignition. "Melanie threatened to sue the department if I talked to Renne and caused them to lose their contract for their TV show."

Banks started to say that Sawyer was the nephew of the film company's owner, and might have the influence he claimed to, but the Chief had moved on.

"There's a lot we don't know about these

people, and it's hard not to be sidetracked by their controversial lifestyle."

Banks reluctantly agreed. "Melanie and Whitney may end up being two sisters with nine kids to raise all on their own. Think they can sell a show about that?"

"Doubt it." But McNamara thought it could be an excellent reason for the women to develop a sideline income that didn't depend on a husband.

Back in his office, he shot off an email to Desiree Marbury.

Chapter Sixteen

Grace's morning was full of irritations and interruptions. She'd had a queasy stomach since last night, and her defenses were low. Naturally, Marjorie zeroed in on her like a mosquito.

"Didn't you hear me ringing you?" the secretary demanded from the doorway of Grace's office.

Grace bit back her first response and said, "I thought Lily picked up the call."

"That would have been helpful, but she's out, again, so, of course it all falls on me. I was trying to tell you a strange woman is asking to see you. I'm sure Mr. Mosley won't approve of her."

"Strange is in the eye of the beholder," Grace said. "Do you mean we don't know her?"

"I certainly don't. She doesn't have an appointment, either, so I told her you weren't available. She's very rude and won't go away."

"What's her name?" Grace asked.

"That's just it. I think she made it up. It's one of those frou-frou first names, and the last name is, get this, *Jones*. And she's wearing sunglasses indoors like some movie star. She's most insistent that you're her family's attorney."

Felicia Jones was a perfect cast member for the Overton family soap opera. She was younger than the sisters by a decade, a tall, blonde, in-your-face opposite of Heath Overton's wives. The three women sat at the conference table in Grace's office, Felicia at one end with Melanie and Whitney on either side of her. All of them looked unhappy.

"Why did you have to call them?" Felicia asked. "You could have just given me the address."

"I don't give out my clients' addresses," Grace said.

"Why did you come to our lawyer's office, anyway?" Whitney said, asking the question that had been driving Grace crazy.

Felicia said, "What choice did I have? I don't

have your address; I've never been here, remember? You all decided you should make the move up here without me. 'One last trip for *your* family.' Wasn't that what you said, Mel?"

"And you've never stopped whining about it," Whitney said, cutting her sister off.

Melanie sat in her pretzel pose, an oversized cotton sweater adding an extra layer to her thin form. She watched the exchange but said nothing.

"I called Melanie this morning when I landed in Baltimore," Felicia said. "Hallie answered her phone and was incredibly rude. She said if I wanted to see any of you, I had to call the family attorney. Which, by the way, I resent. How dare you hire a lawyer and not tell me?"

"I'm really sorry about Hallie. I'll speak to her," Melanie said. "I apologize for how we've handled all of this with you. I hope you'll forgive me."

Whitney didn't bother to hide her surprise or her disgust until Melanie gave her a long look.

"Let's get you home, okay?" Melanie said, turning back to Felicia. "Becca and Sean will be so excited to see you, and we don't need to take up any more of Ms. Reagan's time."

Felicia looked back and forth between the sisters and then at Grace. "What's wrong?" she demanded, then pointed at Melanie. "This one has never been considerate of my feelings or anyone else's. And that one," Whitney got an air poke, "can't stand me, as you can tell. Now that I'm in their lawyer's office, everything's fine? They're hiding something."

"Being apart has really helped us understand our mistakes. Heath said a break was what we all needed, and as usual, he was right." Melanie nodded and smiled her way through her non-explanation.

With a lift of her shoulders and a little smile, Felicia replied, "Yes, he is. That's why when he said I should let him handle you, I did."

"*Handle* us?" Whitney's outburst made Felicia jump. "What are you saying? Do you know where he is?"

"Yes. Right where he said he'd be."

Whitney reached for her sister's hand. The gesture seemed to please Felicia, who opened her clutch purse, took out a wide gold band and slipped it on her left ring finger. Wiggling the shiny ring to catch the light, she said, "I'll forgive you for not congratulating me right away, but isn't it exciting? We're a real family now."

Whitney froze, but Melanie jumped up so fast, none of them had a chance to react. The slap of her hand on Felicia's cheek sounded like a gunshot. "Where is he," she yelled. "*My* husband. Where is he?"

"I, I'm not sure." A stunned Felicia gingerly touched the reddened side of her face. She started to rise, then Melanie leaned over her again.

"Stop it," Grace was on her feet, but it was Marjorie who charged in and restored order.

"Ms. Regan," she hissed, glaring at Grace over the top of her glasses. "Please lower the noise level in here. We have clients in the other offices who can hear these ladies."

To Grace's amazement, the Overton wives straightened up, and Melanie even managed a weak apology. The threat of bad publicity appeared to trump outrage, at least until the door closed behind Marjorie.

"Spit it out, Felicia," Whitney demanded. She stood next to her sister, on guard. "What're you saying?"

"You know we're married," Felicia said in a shaky voice. "Heath told you."

Whitney looked at Melanie, who shook her head.

"We eloped two weeks ago in Las Vegas." She sounded stronger in the face of the sisters' shock.

Whitney sat down abruptly.

'Two weeks?" Melanie asked.

Felicia scrambled out of her chair and moved around behind Grace's desk. With a more substantial barrier between herself and the other women, she said, "Well, you divorced him, Mel. Heath told me you got the finalized papers."

"You're already divorced?" Grace said, struggling to keep up.

"A technicality. It doesn't mean anything," Melanie said, not taking her eyes off Felicia. "I don't believe Heath did this to me."

"To *us*," Whitney corrected. "Felicia, you knew the wedding ceremony was supposed to be a moral union for all of us, not just a legal one for you and Heath. You weren't scheduled to be married until we filmed the Christmas episode. Now you've ruined everything."

Grace decided the producers had missed a great storyline. She'd watch this drama even if she wasn't getting paid. Hopefully getting paid.

"Don't be silly," Felicia said from the safety of the far side of the room. "Heath said Fred Renne was fine with it as long as we kept it quiet."

"The owner of Lightning Strike knows?" Grace asked.

"Well, now I'm not sure," Felicia said. "I thought he told them, too." She waved a hand at the sisters. "Good thing I didn't mention it to Fred when I saw him. I stopped by the Baltimore office on my way here. He seemed a bit nervous, but I assured him everything would be fine and we'd be ready to shoot on schedule."

"You had no right to do that," Whitney said.

Melanie appeared to gather herself and got to her feet. "What else did you say to him, you stupid little girl? Because Fred told Sawyer — our producer, remember him? Fred told Sawyer if Heath isn't here on time ready to film *with no changes to the script,* the contract is void. How do you like that? Keep on bragging about being married and guess what? All that nice money I'm sure you've already spent will evaporate. Get the picture?"

"I've always had the picture," Felicia fired back.

Grace interrupted before the free-for-all could start again. "Wait a minute, please. Felicia, when did Heath say he'd told Melanie and Whitney about your marriage?"

"Right after he did it. He called me after he saw them." She paused. "That was Sunday, the sixth. He said everything was fine, but he was going back to Las Vegas for a few days. He said he wanted to rest before the filming started. That's where I thought he was, Las Vegas. But then Whitney and Melanie started calling me, looking for him. I couldn't reach him, and I got worried. Last night I decided something had to be wrong, and I took the first flight I could book this morning. "

Whitney snorted and said, "Your new husband wanted to be alone to rest? That doesn't say much for you, does it?"

Felicia's smug look slipped a little, but she said, "I understand him. Heath needed a breather after seeing you two."

Grace broke in before the latest insult could sink in. "What I'm hearing is that none of you have talked to him in the past ten days, and you don't know where he is. I think it's time to call either the police or hire a private detective."

"No," Whitney said. She stood, pulling Melanie up with her. "Come on, let's go home. Grace, check everywhere and do everything you can think of to find him without filing an official missing person report. He'll be so disappointed in us if we ruin the deal with Lightning Strike. Felicia, if you're part of this family, then get with the program. This is what we do, we make a decision and stick with it. You can see what happens when we don't. Grace will find Heath and, in the meantime, the three of us will see to the children and work out a way to spin this into an even better storyline."

Grace couldn't believe Whitney wanted Felicia to come home with them and was amazed when the other two women fell in line without protest. The relief she felt when they were gone was quickly replaced by worry over how to find the missing man. She also had to tell Mosley that not only hadn't she withdrawn from the Overton case, it had gotten even more convoluted.

Lilac fields and the glittering streets of Paris had never seemed so far away.

Chapter Seventeen

Thursday night dinner parties at Delaney House had become a thing at some point over the past six months. It had started in the winter when Grace was still recovering from a series of events that had ended with her being injured and engaged — a combination that still struck her as ominous. When David returned to Washington, Avril and Niki set up a weekly party schedule to, as Avril put it, 'make sure Grace stays fed and socialized.'

While Grace recovered physically, her naturally introverted nature kicked into overdrive and left to her own devices, she'd have buried herself in work. At first, she went along with the dinners to please Niki and Avril, but as the weeks passed, she slowly began to enjoy herself. The potluck affairs were often so crowded, guests spilled out of the big kitchen and set up folding tables and chairs in the empty dining room and the twin parlors. Aidan Banks said it was a BYOFFB — Bring Your Own Food, Furniture, and Beer. Sometimes she didn't know half of the people who showed up on her doorstep, but everyone was a friend, or at least friendly, by the time the evening was over. Her total immersion into the social life in Mallard Bay was a crash course that she enjoyed much more than she'd thought possible.

David called it a circus and usually delayed his weekend arrival until Saturday morning. His unexpected appearance thirty-six hours early did not bode well, especially given the way they'd left things on Tuesday. Her surprise at seeing him started the evening off badly. She'd been looking forward to having fun, and instead, she'd be on edge trying to keep him happy and non-confrontational.

Her concerns were realized as soon as he walked into the kitchen. His 'hey, babe' segued directly into 'how soon until we're alone?'

"I wasn't expecting you," she said and moved around him to greet a new neighbor.

They went through the motions from that point on. Grace tried to throw herself into the dinner conversation, but it was clear the Overtons were all anyone was interested in. Besides worrying about David, she had to steer clear of talk about her clients. What low-budget publicity had been slow to achieve, a missing husband and three angry wives had accomplished. The news of Felicia and Heath's elopement was out and traveling fast, and the guests at Delaney House devoured food and gossip with equal enthusiasm.

"What would you call them?" David asked. He refilled his wine glass and passed on food. He'd already talked at length about his seventy-hour work week and the long drive from DC. It was clearly a chore for him to be polite, not that he ever made much of an effort with Grace's friends. His rudeness hadn't hurried the dinner along, so he tried a different tack. "Your clients, honey," he prompted when she didn't answer. "What are they?"

"Besides adults minding their own business?" Avril asked.

David and Avril had an actively antagonistic relationship, and he refused to acknowledge her as he said, "I mean their *ménage a' quatre*, Grace."

"They have a familial relationship," she said, giving him a warning look, which he ignored.

"And they aren't polygamists because, why again?" He took a handful of potato chips from an open bag, bypassing a platter of shrimp stuffed rockfish filets and a basket of warm corn muffins. He was enjoying putting Grace on the spot and was helped along by the other dinner guests who were waiting for her answer.

"You'll have to watch the show for the details," she said.

A chorus of protests made him laugh until her napkin landed on his head.

"Come on, you have to admit they're advertising themselves that way. *The Plurals Next Door* pretty much says it all, don't you think?" David tossed the napkin back to her. "And a good headline would be 'Scandal Rocks Mallard Bay — Again.'"

Up and down the old pine farm table, heads swiveled to Grace, who was fuming. How dare he behave as if her clients didn't deserve the same level of professional confidentiality he gave his own?

But David ignored all the warning signs. "I mean, come on. How can one lawyer in a small town end up with back-to-back Jerry Springer casts for clients? Last winter's disaster was bad enough, but you may have outdone yourself with this bunch. You sure bring a lot of attention to this little backwater place, babe."

The hilarity level dropped, and Grace blushed.

Mac broke the awkward moment, to Grace's relief and David's irritation. "Actually, this part of the mid-shore is quite a fashionable place to be. Has been for years." He settled back in his chair as if moving into a fireside chat. "We attract all sorts of wealthy and famous people. Such as yourself, Counselor." He paused to smile at David. "I seem to recall your first appearance here last year was to represent one of those Jerry Springer types."

The looks the men exchanged had nothing to do with David's disparagement of Grace's clients and everything to do with Grace. Mac was sitting next to Ashley Greenburgh, his arm resting on the back of her chair. The veterinarian looked embarrassed, but neither man seemed to notice.

Aidan changed the subject in his usual abrupt way. "Why'd you come down early this weekend?" he asked David.

"If I need a reason other than this entertaining dinner, let's say I missed my girl."

"Huh," Aidan said. "You mean the embezzlement case I've been reading about in the *Washington Post* doesn't keep you tied to your office around the clock?"

"I'm never too busy for Grace." David snagged another handful of chips and sent an insincere smile toward her side of the table.

"C'mon," Aidan said. "Give us some details.

What's Senator Sloane like? And is his wife as hot as she looks on TV?"

"Hey!" Niki gave him an elbow in the side. "Are you checking out other women?"

"I'm not blind, so, yeah," he said with such earnestness that everyone but Niki laughed. "So, Davey, fill us in on the good stuff."

With exaggerated movements, David brushed chip crumbs off his hands. "You're a police officer, aren't you? You should know I can't discuss my clients."

"Corporal, actually," Banks said. "But you know how we are over on this side of the bridge. News is slow to reach us out here in the *backwater*, and we're not as uptight as all you DC folks. You were making fun of Grace's clients, so I assumed it was okay to get the gossip on yours, too." The smiles he got from around the table were nice, but the glare from David was even better.

The general conversation drifted off to the local theater group's production of *Ten Little Indians* and the YMCA's yard sale fundraiser.

"That'll be a great opportunity for me to finish cleaning out Mom and Dad's house," Niki said. "And who knows what we might find for the inns, Grace."

David gave her his best smirk and said, "Can't wait to see this place decorated from a yard sale." The conversation took off into urban legends of junk sales with unsigned Picassos, long lost Vermeers, and priceless Faberge eggs used as Easter decorations. Unhappy to have been dismissed so easily, he pulled out the brochure for the house on the Wye River and passed it around, accepting compliments on his good taste.

Grace noticed Mac looked at the photos longer than the others before passing it down the table without comment.

Ordinarily, Avril stayed until the dishes were done, and the kitchen was sorted. During dessert, David announced that he was doing all the cleaning up, but if he thought that would rush people through the caramel cake and peach cobbler, he was once again mistaken. The desserts were delicious, and the party kept going.

When the evening finally wore down, and she closed the door behind the last departing guest, he exploded. An hour later, he was halfway to DC, leaving Grace with a kitchen full of dirty dishes and an ultimatum. Come back to DC and marry him or else. He didn't define 'else,' but she took it, anyway.

Chapter Eighteen

On the walk to Niki's house, Aidan said that for a dinner where he had to sit between David and Avril, it was a pretty good night. Niki said she was glad he'd had fun and proceeded to ruin the rest of his evening. When he couldn't convince her he wasn't interested in Senator Sloane's wife, he cut the ridiculous argument short and left her at her door.

Since their first date in the sixth grade, Aidan and Niki had been mismatched soul mates, miserable apart and never really happy together. Lately, he'd been thinking about one of his mother's sayings. Her stock response to his arguments with Niki was always, 'It's better to be alone than to wish you were.'

It was after ten when he pulled in the driveway of his childhood home, but there was a light on in the den. He decided to find out what his mother had been trying to say for the past twenty years.

❧

McNamara dressed in the dark and might have slipped out of Ashley's house without any un-comfortable explanations if her fifteen-year-old Siamese cat hadn't been incontinent. When his foot hit the cold puddle of pee, his gasp startled the cat, whose screech woke Ashley, who turned on the lights and caught him, shoes in hand, at her bedroom door.

"Going so soon?" she asked, rubbing sleep from her eyes.

He had zero experience with such situations and froze, speechless, and without a single useful thought coming to mind.

"Maggie's a watch cat," Ashley said. "I should have warned you."

"She's also made a little mess, but I think most of it's soaked into my socks now." He could have kissed the cat for providing the diversion that allowed him to make almost normal sounding conversation until he got to the front door.

His hand was on the doorknob when she

said, "It's okay, you know. You're more transparent than you think. I knew how you felt when I agreed to this."

He wanted to believe her, to keep going. To go home where he could pretend he hadn't hurt her. Instead, he turned around to apologize, only to see the door shut behind her.

Outside, the predawn air was cool against his hot face. What a fool he was.

After a fitful night spent fuming over Aidan's behavior, Niki went to the only person who hadn't, at some point, urged her to dump her boyfriend. Grace didn't answer her text, but a ride past Delaney House told her David was gone. Forty-five minutes later, she surprised her still sleepy cousin with lattes and lemon poppyseed muffins from the Dunkin' Donuts on Route 50. The coffee and the muffins were both considerably cooler than when she'd bought them, but the twenty-minute ride to Easton was better than risking a run-in with Aidan in the bakery section of Three Pigs.

"Last night was it, Grace. You see it, don't you?" Niki asked as she set the food out on the table.

Grace stood in the kitchen doorway, longing

to go back to bed. Instead, she crossed the room to the rocking chair by the fireplace. "Coffee first," she held out a hand for a latte. "I'm not up to this."

Niki briefly considered leaving, but she had to talk to somebody. She handed Grace a muffin. "I hate to bring up problems so early, but I've wrestled this all night, and I need to talk it out. The way he behaved at dinner just reinforced everything I've been worried about. His behavior is awful."

"I know," Grace agreed. "Everyone noticed, and it was embarrassing. He's ridiculous, and it's exhausting trying to keep up with his moods."

Niki knew she shouldn't be surprised that Grace was so emphatic, but it was rare to have someone else as mad at Aidan as she was. An awful thought struck her. Did everyone else really feel the same way? Were they all wondering why Niki put up with a man who was so clearly inadequate? Fresh anger flared, and all of Aidan's shortcomings rushed to the surface. "He's thoughtless and selfish. And let's not forget ignorant. Sometimes he's so dumb, I can't believe he's made it as far as he has."

"Dumb?" Grace stopped picking at the muffin she wasn't eating. "Thoughtless and self-ish, yes. I'll even agree he's ignorant sometimes, but you really think David's dumb?"

"Who's talking about David?"

It took a minute to untangle the conversation. At first, it was funny. Then it wasn't. The cousins sat and let their coffees go cold in the kitchen that had seen generations of the Delaney family's troubles.

Niki broke the silence. "He says I'm mean." There was a quiver in her voice, and she waited to be contradicted. "I wasn't mean enough," Grace answered.

"I'll dump mine if you dump yours," Nicki offered. It was a last-ditch effort for a laugh, but Grace just looked sadder.

"This isn't helping either of us." Niki decided if Grace wasn't up for relationship analysis, she could switch to their new business venture. Anything beat watching Grace stare out the window and shred a muffin. "If David's gone, is it okay if I come home today?"

"What?"

"Home? Here. I live here, remember? Yes, it was nice of me to sleep at my inn to give you some privacy, but since you don't need it now, I'll come back. I have to redo my room at the Victory Manor, anyway. Freshen it up to the level of the other rooms. I have the whole place rented starting next Saturday."

"Really? With everything that's happened lately, I forgot. I'm sorry."

"Well, snap to, girl. Our business is about to take off." The overly hearty words fell flat between them. "It will be great, I swear."

The worried note in her cousin's voice got Grace's attention. She forced herself to focus on the conversation. "How much of the decorating budget have you spent?" she asked.

"Oh, I'll have plenty left. And the new bedroom suites are being delivered this afternoon. Wait until you see them. Hotel quality, just like you said. Elegant, but sturdy."

Niki's smile was a bit too wide for Grace's liking. Taking out her own phone, she pulled up the calendar they'd set up for Delaney House. "I don't see any reservations here."

"Check July."

Grace flicked the screen forward and stared at the bright red entries. "These are reservations? You've rooms rented almost every night."

Niki beamed. "Isn't it wonderful? Even allowing for cancelations, we should have a sixty percent occupancy — which is incredible for a new bed-and-breakfast. It's the ads I ran. You said they were too expensive, but they paid off."

Paid off. Grace closed the calendar and opened her banking app. A moment later she looked up at Niki in disbelief. "You've spent — "

"I know, I know. It looks like a lot, but wait until the rentals roll in. You'll get your money back by the end of the year. And everything after that is profit for you. I'm taking the biggest risk, remember."

"That's not true." She wasn't in the mood to let Niki do one of her reimaginings of reality. "You'll have operating expenses."

"Which I will cover. We have to spend money to make money. And we're going to make a lot of money."

Grace tried not to let her own lack of sleep and an increasingly upset stomach fuel her words. Her problems weren't Niki's fault; she'd allowed herself to be roped into this harebrained scheme.

"No," she said. "The point is to earn a reasonable return on your investment. Risking lots of money on a small profit margin isn't just dangerous, it's wasting time."

As usual, Niki ignored the lecture and chatted on, telling Grace to concentrate on finishing up with Mosley's law practice and getting herself to France. "When you come back in the fall, you'll be amazed at what I've accomplished. You're free now. Do whatever you want, I've got things handled here."

Grace took another look at the numbers in her bank account. An uncomfortable clammy feeling seized her, and she felt the acid from the latte at the back of her throat.

"Hey," Niki yelped as Grace jumped to her feet and ran out of the room.

She barely made it down the hall to the bathroom in time. When she returned to the kitchen, every trace of the food and coffee had been cleared, and a chastened looking Niki was waiting for her.

"I'm so sorry. I should have left as soon as I saw how bad you looked."

"Gee, thanks."

"Well, you look sick, and you obviously are. Can I get you anything?"

"No." Grace went to the rocker but was careful to sit still. Motion wasn't a good idea. Whatever she had wasn't finished with her.

Niki hovered close by. "I've checked my emails and texts. Doesn't look like anyone else who was here for dinner got sick, so that's a relief."

It was also a surprise to Grace. She'd thought for sure Niki's artichoke casserole had been off.

"It isn't nerves because I spent so much, is it?" Niki asked in a small voice. "I promise you'll get it all back and a good profit, too."

The spending spree didn't make Grace happy, but she knew her underlying misery had a different cause.

Chapter Nineteen

Grace wanted to go back to bed once Niki left, but that wasn't an option. Niki would return soon to resettle into her second-floor room, and Grace was in no mood to continue their conversation. Irritated at the world in general, she dressed and went to work.

Arguing voices greeted her as soon as she opened the front door. The file room looked as if a small tornado had passed through. After a quick check to make sure her own office was still intact, Grace followed the noise into the big corner office where Cyrus Mosley and Marjorie were squared off.

"I said Daniels, not Dumfries," Mosley said.

"I brought both because they're suing each other." Marjorie didn't back down, just waited, holding an armful of files and glaring at her employer of four-plus decades. "Do you want to work on the deposition questions or the motion to dismiss first?"

"Motion," Mosley said. "With any luck, we won't need depositions."

Marjorie nodded in approval, then noticed Grace in the doorway. "Well, look who decided to join us."

"Don't be rude," Mosley said and then waved Grace in, giving her a wide, denture-filled smile. "Lovely to see you, m'dear. Come, fill me in on the Overtons. That lot's gone south fast, haven't they? Do we still have them as clients?"

Grace navigated around the putting green and sank into an upholstered armchair that had been shoved into a corner next to Mosley's desk. This wasn't the solitude she'd hoped for, but at least it was a change of scenery.

"As far as I know," she said. "Not much to do for them at the moment except, continue to look for the husband. For now, everyone's hanging in to see how things turn out when he turns up — or the contract deadlines pass." She didn't add that the film company was undoubtedly busy preparing for a cancellation, while the wives refused to consider that their beloved man might be gone for good.

"I thought we agreed to pass them along to a

firm better suited to help them," Mosley said. "I don't think they'll be interested in my representation, and I'm not sure I can keep a straight face with them."

It seemed to be the old Mosley who was at work today, and, in Grace's opinion, the change was not entirely positive.

She said, "Our clients are three scared mothers and eleven children. I assure you; they aren't funny in the least."

He didn't even pretend to be ashamed. "By all means, until you hand them off to someone else, go to them for your meetings. I can't have children in this office."

Grace ignored the edict and said, "May I assume you're playing golf today?" Mosley's bright green window-pane patterned slacks and a yellow short-sleeve shirt said the golf course was on his agenda.

"In an hour or so. Just setting up work for the next week. It'll be busy."

Grace mentally ran through the following week's calendar. Mosley only had a handful of active clients, but one of them had a motion hearing on Thursday in a zoning appeal for a local restaurant. It was a simple case, but he hadn't been in court for more than a year. He didn't seem nervous, but the client, a golfing buddy, was getting a lot of work for a small fee.

She reminded herself that it wouldn't be her concern for much longer.

"What happened in the file room?" she asked.

Mosley looked up from the paper in his hands. "File room?"

"It looks like a bomb went off in there."

"I'm rearranging a couple of the drawers," Marjorie said. "The way Lily has it set up is inefficient, and since she's leaving soon, I decided to rearrange it."

Before Grace could react, Mosley erupted. "What did I just say about being rude? We've talked about this. I'll not have it. You'll be polite, and there'll be no gossip. Understood?"

Marjorie shrugged and said, "Well, if you don't need anything else, I'll finish up in the other room." Then she was gone, leaving Grace and Mosley staring at each other.

"Lily's just talking to some people," he said.

"About a job."

"Yes. She told me yesterday when she asked for today off."

"Another day off, you mean. And she asked you, not me." Grace tried not to look as hurt as she felt. Lily hadn't even mentioned she would be out of the office.

"She's only exploring her options." he crossed the room and closed the door. Out from behind his desk, he looked years younger. He was stronger than he'd been even a month ago, Grace realized. Lily and Mosley were both moving away from her, and she'd soon be leaving them.

"We've talked. Lily feels she'll have a brighter future elsewhere," Mosley said as he came back to his desk. He removed a file from his middle drawer and handed it to her. "Look at this. I'm hiring a new associate. I rather enjoy limiting my work to morning appointments, and I believe I have enough business to keep this young man happy."

Grace looked at the resume he handed her. "Jacob Briard? Where have I heard that name before?" She scanned the thin document. "Oh, Jake, from the town council office. What can he do for you? Is he an attorney?"

"No, and he never will be at the rate he's going," Mosley said. "Since his wife up and left him and their children, he's had to work two jobs to support his family. He goes to UBC for night classes when he can, but he's not getting anywhere that way. I'm talking to him about clerking here part time and taking a full course load. I've known Jake all his life. He's a good boy."

Grace felt a headache start. Or maybe it was a heartache. Jake Briard was another hard-luck story; exactly what Mosley didn't need.

She said, "Look, let's talk about this. If you want to keep the practice going, but you don't want to work a full schedule, you need an attorney. Jake, nice as he is, will only be a part time clerk. How does that help you? All you're doing is adding another salary to the payroll with no corresponding income."

"I have a plan. Things will work out fine."

"Cyrus, how? Jake's a single father with two kids and two jobs already. Just because he knows the local zoning laws — "

He cut her off, saying, "And he knows local government and local people. He was born and raised here, and everyone trusts him. It may be an investment now, but I'll be repaid tenfold when he passes the bar. I'll have someone to run the firm, and I can move on to full time golf."

"I see," Grace said. Suddenly, she did. Mosley had tried so hard to keep her in Mallard Bay; it hadn't occurred to her he wouldn't wait until she left to erase her option to take over the firm.

"I have to make plans, too, m'dear," he said as if reading her mind. "You aren't the only one who's changing. We all have to get on with our lives. I'd planned to have this conversation with you at some point next week, but we're into it now. We should talk."

There was more? She felt like a delinquent in the principal's office.

"I've taken too much of your time, and I appreciate your patience," he said, then fell silent, seeming to find something of great interest to look at just over her head.

Grace forced herself to wait for whatever was coming. The halting, impatient man who'd suffered a heart attack and a stroke and recovered at the improbable age of older than God, was fading away as the real Mosley returned. Only a newly bald, spotted scalp distinguished this man from the one she'd met when she first came to Mallard Bay. He hadn't needed her then, and it was sounded like he didn't need her now. When he finally spoke, she wished he hadn't.

"I couldn't have asked for a better colleague or friend than you." His tone low and kind. If Marjorie was in her usual spot glued to the other side of the door, she'd have a hard time eavesdropping. "You're ready to go, and I know you believe that's what's best for you. It might be best for me, too."

Grace leaned forward; sure she hadn't heard him correctly. Her stomach was doing flips again. Cyrus thought it was best for *him* if she left? What had she done to make him say that?

Her inner critic immediately began whispering answers to that question, but she waited for him to tell her. Maybe his version would be better than her ever-ready guilt monster's.

"Don't think I'm not grateful," he said. "Life has handed me a lot of entertainment in the past couple of years, and you're responsible for most of it. I've been glad to be a part of it all — wouldn't change a minute, except for the down-time. But I want to get back to a regular routine. And wherever you are, m'dear, there's a hulla-baloo coming, happening or fading."

A hullabaloo? She'd gotten his wardrobe up-dated by several decades, but he was still firmly rooted in the last century. And not the end of it, either. She supposed he'd accuse her of having groovy shindigs next.

He wasn't finished.

"Your idea of a client base and mine are dif-ferent. I thought your changes would be good for the practice, but the truth is, I'm out of my depth with the high profile types you seem to at-tract. The fellows at the club are most impressed with me, of course. The firm's had a noticeable uptake in reviews of wills and estate planning tasks. It seems everyone wants to reassert their client status with the attorneys who get the head-lines. That part is very nice, but unnecessary. And it casts me in the wrong light. I won't be able to keep this pace up when you're gone. My heyday is long past, and it involved politicians, not television stars, not that there's much difference these days."

Grace wanted to tell him he was exaggerating the notoriety of both the case she'd handled last winter and the Overtons, but the tabloids covered both stories, so she didn't bother to argue. In fact, she couldn't think of anything to say.

"Jake's a friend," Mosley said. "He's a young man, but we understand each other. When his wife left, I like to think I was some help to him. We spent a good bit of time together handling the custody details, and I've been a mentor of sorts for him. And now he and Lily are close, did you know that?"

Grace knew Lily's boyfriend's name was Jake, but she'd never put two and two together. Jake was at least ten years older than Lily, but any man who could handle two jobs, children and law school might be a match for her high-energy secretary. Mosley's high-energy secretary.

"Do you think Lily will stay if Jake accepts your offer?" she asked.

"It would be best if she didn't. I meant what I said; she'll be better off in another job. There's nowhere for her to go if she stays here. She's talked about law school, too, but I don't believe she's done anything about it."

She and Lily were both out. Mosley was

bringing in a mini-him, and Marjorie would return to her former status as the Queen of Everything.

Grace promised to wrap up the Overtons and her other active cases, and ready her files for Mosley — or Jake. She gave Mosley a hug and kissed his cheek. The strength of his return squeeze was heartening. He really was back to his old self, and she tried very hard to be glad.

Chapter Twenty

McNamara's early morning routine involved a large mug of coffee and a walk around the yard to check his bird feeders and the status of his latest squirrel baffle. He was enjoying moderate success with the new contraption, a silicone-coated feeder with rounded top and bottom sections which were deeper than the crafty rodents were long. The advertisement showed squirrels sliding off the slippery surface and happy birds eating in peace. McNamara figured it would last until he let down his guard. The squirrels always won in the end.

After ensuring all was well in the garden, he walked down to the beach that marked the eastern edge of his property. The Wye River was glassy this warm May morning, and the Adirondack chair at the end of his dock called to him. But Fridays were peak workdays during tourist season, and even if he'd had time to enjoy the beauty of the river, he didn't want to let his mind wander. He didn't like where his thoughts kept ending up. He had a decision to make.

~

Mallard Bay's police station and municipal operations shared a rambling 1950-style brick building with an off-shoot of the Kingston County Library. The two-room department opened onto a small gravel parking lot that ran up to the side of the Three Pigs Deli. Since the grand opening of the deli's new bakery section two weeks before, McNamara and Banks had fought against the distracting aromas that permeated the station. When the always fickle air-conditioning went out, they were forced to open the windows and front door, the battle was lost.

McNamara brushed pastry crumbs from a report the corporal had given him and winced at the oily stain the buttered croissant left behind. Not that Banks would notice, or care. He was busy working his way through a cinnamon bun the size of a dinner plate.

McNamara tapped the report. "This is good work, Aidan."

"Can't take credit for all of it," Banks said. "Grace called here early this morning and asked me to let you know the gossip at dinner last night was mostly true. Felicia Jones is in town and claims she and Overton are married. Also, the family is confident he'll be returning any time now, but if we get a lead on him, she'd appreciate a heads up. All I had to do was make a few calls and troll the internet and databases for a while."

It was a lot of detail for a case that still might be a late return of a rental car, but Banks had done a good job. McNamara had to admit a missing man with three wives and a State Police all-points bulletin chasing him warranted the extra work. "She say anything else?" McNamara asked, not looking up from the report.

"Who?"

McNamara refused to say Grace's name just to amuse the juvenile corporal. His expression was enough to move the conversation along.

"Only that she expected *quid pro quo.*"

"What?" Startled at Banks' use of the Latin phrase, McNamara forgot he was trying to look disinterested.

"It means she wants a favor in return for the information," Banks said, slowly, enjoying himself. "The wives want Grace to find Overton, and she figures the quickest way is to get us to do the work for her."

"She did not say that."

"No, she said *quid pro quo*."

Banks went back to his pastry, and McNamara reread the report.

Overton sounded like a man with imagination and drive, willing to buck social norms. McNamara wondered if the missing man always looked for the fastest route to what he wanted. Would he quit if he didn't find it?

"Guy's a nutter, right?" Banks said when the Chief set the report down again.

"You sure seem interested in him."

"I have more gossip from last night. Do you want it?"

"If it's about an open case of ours, yes."

Banks reluctantly skipped his observations on the chilly behavior between Grace and David Farquar. "Nik told me that Avril told her the first two Overton wives got into a catfight with the new one while they were all in Grace's office yesterday. A real fight with screaming and hitting. The Bat had to break it up."

Marjorie Battsley's nickname and the mental image it conjured got a bark of laughter from McNamara.

"Despite all that, the Jones woman is staying with the family. Can you believe it?" Banks pushed the last chunk of cinnamon roll into his mouth and groaned in satisfaction. "That bakery woman is older than my mom, but I may have to marry her. God, that was good."

The 'bakery woman' at Three Pigs was all of forty. Maybe. "Niki does a nice pastry," he said and watched the younger man's smile shut down. "You two doing okay?" When Banks didn't answer, he prompted, "That bad?"

"Nothing new. I'm just losing a taste for it, you know? Everything's a fight. Everything. I watched Nik with Grace the other day, and I didn't recognize her. She looked like a different person, and that's when it hit me — she was *happy.* Not the 'wanna be happy' crap, either. They were laughing, and they were both happy. I don't make her laugh like that."

"Does she make you — "

"No."

There wasn't much to say to that. Aidan and Niki were a pair of magnets, alternately attracting and repelling each other. For years, McNamara had counseled, mentored, and tried to drag Banks out of adolescence and into adulthood. Now that he seemed to be making the transition, it wasn't how McNamara had expected.

He crumpled his empty bakery bag and cleared off the table. "Well, let's give Grace her quid pro quo. Check in with the State guys and see if any new information on Overton or the missing car, then finish up the daily report. I'm going back to visit with the wives. Somebody knows something."

Banks looked surprised. "Why? I realize I went overboard on the report, and we have more background on these people than we need. It's not actually a real stolen car issue, yet, even if there is an APB." He stopped and studied McNamara. "There's more, isn't there?"

McNamara broke an uncomfortable silence saying, "Remember Cappy Ulner?"

Banks nodded, thinking he was seriously sick of the reminders of his shortcomings.

"You should be a sergeant climbing the ladder in MSP right now," McNamara said. "And then there was the time you — "

"Got it," Banks stood and reached for his hat. "For the hundredth time, I didn't know Cappy was running that bush league burglary ring out of his parent's upholstery shop. I was a twenty-five-year-old trooper, drunk at a party and running my mouth about having to do surveillance on the midnight shift. I think I've paid for it a few times over."

"You still tell Niki everything?" McNamara asked.

"No." The regret in Banks' voice said it was

the truth, but he'd passed that test before only to fall flat later.

"Talking about the stakeout at Cappy's ended your career with the State Police. Talking about department business limits your usefulness to me." It was a subject they'd covered before.

"Maybe it's time for me to move on."

McNamara nodded. "Maybe it is. Let's both think on it. Meantime, let me get your take on the drugs we found in the Overtons' garage."

"So that's why Desi Marbury showed up yesterday," Banks said. "I thought she might be angling for my job."

"She's not looking for a demotion." McNamara handed over the MSP's lab results from the fire scene. "They found marijuana and cocaine residue next to the burned area, but no evidence to point to any one person as the owner."

"Enough nutters around the site to give you lots of suspects, though."

"Put another way, there are enough inconsistencies in the Overton family's behavior to warrant our interest. The father disappears with an expensive rental car, and his wives insist everything's fine. And then there's the film company's representative, a smooth young man who's one DUI away from se-rious jail time. Seems like an unwise choice for a liaison to a family with eleven children."

"Sawyer Renne."

The Chief nodded. "The garage would be easily accessible to him, yet isn't his property. No one else was using it, but it was padlocked, and he had a key. If that's where he stored his inventory, it would explain why he ran into a burning building and stayed so long. He'd have saved what he could carry and made sure the rest burned before the fire department arrived."

"That works," Banks said. "Hallie'd already called 911. The pole sirens would have been going off, and Renne probably thought the Marines would come through the door any minute." It wouldn't be the first time a new-comer had mistaken the village's ancient fire and ambulance notification system for a civil defense end of the world warning.

"The adults claim they didn't use the garage and didn't know it was locked. Renne told you he'd locked it to keep the kids out because it wasn't a safe place for them to play. He unlocked it when he saw it was on fire to make sure none of them had found a way in. He had no good reason for staying inside long enough to suffer smoke inhalation."

"If he had smoke inhalation," Banks interrupted.

"All of which adds up to nothing."

"That we know of." Banks made the comment reflexively, but he knew it was true. Something was right in front of him. But what?

"Do you think either of the women or Hallie knew about the drugs?" McNamara asked.

"Not Hallie," he said without hesitation. "I mean, that's not the feeling I get."

The feeling Banks got was that the Chief was allowing him to continue to work on the case because Hallie and Melanie talked openly with him. It was ridiculous to feel disloyal to the Overtons, but he did.

McNamara was studying the half cup of cold coffee he held, but Banks knew the signs. The Chief was working something out, and Banks was afraid he'd caused whatever was about to happen. Hoping to redirect his boss's thoughts, he said, "It might have been Renne's personal stash. There's no way to know how much there was, and he didn't have anything on him when the paramedics treated him."

"We'll see." McNamara rose and stretched. "You can do the grunt work for Grace when we get back. Let's go see the Overtons and ask to interview the newest wife about her missing husband. That'll get us in the door, and then you can work your magic. Who knows what we'll pick up."

"There's no magic. They just like me."

"Exactly. Let's go."

"Why are we bothering with them?" Banks persisted. "Let's pick up Renne and see what we get from him."

The Chief hesitated, then said, "Desi's team handled it. There were trace amounts of both drugs in the trunk of Sawyer Renne's car. Naturally, he doesn't know how it got there, and his uncle has an excellent attorney. I'm thinking the Overton women will be outraged at this news and might talk to us. Now, are you coming?"

Banks stayed where he was. "I can't see Melanie or Whitney having anything to do with drugs around their children, and Hallie's a nice kid."

"And you're a nice guy. I can handle it alone." McNamara left, but Banks caught up to him and slid into the passenger seat of the Explorer.

"Good choice," McNamara said.

Chapter Twenty-One

They could hear the yelling before they were halfway up the front walk. Two young girls sat on the porch steps eating apples. McNamara figured whatever was happening inside was either commonplace or not as bad as it sounded.

"Good morning, ladies," he said. "I'm Chief McNamara. I was here the other day with Corporal Banks."

"He*llo*, *Ai*dan," the girls chorused.

"Ah, yes," McNamara said, grinning at Banks. "Your fan club."

A woman yelled, 'You little bitch!'

Both girls gasped, jumped off the porch, and ran for the backyard.

"All of you kids are out of control." The front door flew open, and a tall woman came out, stopping as soon as she saw the officers. Her height and sleek, streaky blonde hair matched the description they had of Felicia Jones, but the ill-fitting clothes she wore were a surprise. She didn't look like the rag-bag type.

McNamara made their introductions and showed her his badge.

"Oh, come on. We aren't that loud." She went back into the house, leaving the door behind her open.

"That sounded like an invitation to me," McNamara said.

Melanie and Whitney Overton were shocked into momentary silence when the men walked into the living room. Several children made a bee-line for Banks, who returned high-fives and managed to lower the emotional level of the room by half. McNamara explained that they'd come to get Felicia's statement about their missing husband.

Banks offered to help Hallie with the children and ignored McNamara's nod of approval. However this turned out, he wouldn't do anything to hurt her. If it cost him his job, so be it. He figured he wasn't losing much.

"The kids are pretty hyper this morning,"

Melanie said. "That's why we didn't hear you arrive."

"The little hellions were so loud I have a headache," Felicia interrupted. "There's no discipline at all in this house."

The women had taken seats around the kitchen table, leaving McNamara the chair at the head. He wondered if the gesture had any significance and decided it didn't. They were too angry at each other to care where he sat.

"How old are your children?" McNamara asked Felicia.

"Sean is four, and Rebecca is two. If I'd realized how the behavior in this family had disintegrated without Heath in charge, I'd have never allowed them to stay here."

McNamara said, "Two and four are pretty young to live away from their parents. How long has it been since you gave your children to the Overtons?"

All three women looked alarmed.

"It wasn't like that," Felicia said and was immediately supported by a chorus of agreement from the sisters.

"We're family," Melanie said.

"Especially now that Heath and I are married," Felicia added, splintering the fragile peace. "And, no, Melanie, I will not keep quiet about it. Heath is my husband. I won't deny it."

"Is that what the yelling was about?" McNamara asked. "They asked you not to say that you were married to Mr. Overton?"

Before Felicia could answer, Whitney said, "Nothing of the kind, just a family squabble. You said you wanted Felicia's statement about Heath, so why don't you move on to that?" She gave Felicia a look that could have been a warning or a threat.

Not waiting to be asked, Felicia jumped in and said, "I don't know where my husband is. I thought he was here. I would have come up here sooner, but I was trying to respect their privacy. Heath said they needed some time to adjust to the news that we were married."

McNamara couldn't imagine any of them ever thinking a four-way marriage of these personalities would work. "When was the last time you heard from him, Ms. Jones?"

"Mrs. Overton," Felicia said, and then leaned across the table toward the sisters. "He left me Sunday morning and flew here to tell both of you. I never heard from him again. One of you knows something. Maybe we should get Hallie in here. She doesn't seem as quick to lie as you two."

McNamara said he'd like to see Hallie, too, then sat back to observe the arguing and threats that rocketed around the table. When the women wound down, he asked Felicia why she was staying with the family if she didn't like them.

"Because my credit cards are maxed out, and I've got nowhere else to go," Felicia said.

"You're killing any chance we have of saving the show if you keep talking like that," Melanie said. For once, she was dry-eyed, but McNamara didn't expect it to last.

"You'd rather I said because we're family?" Felicia said, pronouncing 'family' like it was a different F word. "Well, if you want me to stay on script, then give me some cash, sister wives. I'm not wearing your castoff leggings a minute longer."

Whitney got up and took a small leather backpack off the top of the refrigerator. She fished out a wallet and handed Felicia a credit card.

"Knock yourself out," she said. "There's a Walmart in Easton." She picked up a set of keys off of a rack by the back door. "You can drive the green van, but have it back here by noon. Unless you want to do the grocery shopping while you're out?"

Felicia radiated anger but only said 'later' as she snatched the keys and left.

McNamara said, "That was uncomfortable,

but I'm glad she left. I was hoping to talk with you both without her."

"Uncomfortable?" Whitney said. "You can't imagine."

"We have nothing to say to you without our lawyer," Melanie said.

"Understood," McNamara pulled his notebook out of his pocket and flipped it open. "I have some information for you about Mr. Overton, but I can wait until you find Ms. Reagan if you'd prefer."

"Tell me right now," Melanie said before he could finish the last words.

"Since I'm the oldest girl, I'm another mother, really," Hallie said.

Banks had been giving her space and occupying himself by picking up the Lego pieces that were scattered around the room. Now he joined her, where she sat rocking a small girl. The child had fallen asleep despite the activity around her.

"This is Rebecca, Felicia's daughter," Hallie said. "Hard to believe, isn't it? Becca's so sweet."

Banks watched her cuddle the toddler closer.

The master bedroom suite had been turned into the playroom. The corner where Hallie sat was the quiet zone, so designated by the lettering artfully painted on the wall. Banks hoped Avril had gotten a hefty security deposit. With the older kids in a basement rec room watching videos, the upstairs was reasonably quiet.

The rocking chair was the only adult sized seat, so he sat on the rug and tried to ignore the uncomfortable tug of his gun belt. The old movie *Kindergarten Cop* came to mind, and he pushed it away.

"That's how you see yourself? Like another mother to all the little kids?" Banks asked. "You're a teenager. In high school, right?" She frowned, and he knew he'd said something wrong. "I mean, you're great at it, taking care of the children. I saw that right away."

Her expression lightened. "I love them," she said. "And somebody has to help Aunt Whitney. Mom's great and all, but she's not able to do much. And *Felicia*," she rolled her eyes in a perfect copy of Whitney, "is an I-D-I-O-T." She whisper-spelled over the head of the child sleeping in her arms. "That girl is just useless. The only good thing about Dad marrying her is that Becca and Sean are ours now, and she can't take them away."

Banks hadn't thought about the new wife from Hallie's point of view. Felicia, in her mid-twenties, was closer to Hallie's age than Heath Overton's.

"And for your information, I already have my high school equivalency certificate. We're all home-schooled and can go at our own pace."

"Wow. You must be really smart." And have no social life, he guessed.

"Yes, I am. Not that it will do me any good anytime soon. I can't leave the family and go to college until the show's off the ground and money is coming in. I'm taking some courses on-line, though."

Banks imagined trying to study when all the children were at home. He'd barely made it out of high school with a room of his own and his mother at his elbow every step of the way.

"How about friends?" he asked. "It must be hard to be yanked up from your life in Atlanta and have to leave everyone you know."

"Friends. That's a good one. When you're as smart as I am and your family's famous, you don't waste your time with stupid stuff. Cheerleading and sleepovers are for losers."

Banks thought cheerleading and sleepovers might be exactly what Hallie would have rather been doing.

"Besides," she said, "I can get friends anytime I want them. I just don't have time right now."

"Is Sawyer Renne a friend?"

"I hate him." Hallie's words came fast and

angry. "And I didn't do anything wrong. Aunt Whitney and Mom said I can't talk to you without them here, anyway."

The toddler she held woke up. With a practiced move, Hallie flipped the child from her arms to her shoulder and rubbed her back. Becca popped a thumb in her mouth and settled again.

"Okay. I understand," Banks whispered. He got up — ungracefully enough to make her smile — and went back to picking up Legos. When she let several minutes go by without speaking, he said, "Can I ask another question, not about anything official?" He got a curt nod and continued. "I've wondered about your names. Most of your brothers and sisters have biblical names. How'd you get Hallie?"

She was so quiet, he thought she might not tell him. Eventually, she said, "Dad named all of us. Mom was out of it after I was born, but Aunt Whitney tried to talk him into a different name for me." She stopped and sighed.

"Why?' Banks asked. "I like Hallie."

"It's just a nickname, but thanks. Dad was a minister back then, and he says he felt called to set an example for others on how to honor God, and he started with our names. The oldest is my brother Abe — Abraham. Lucky creep got to take the older boys to California for the summer, to an acting camp because they're all clueless. Did you know that? Guess what I get to do? Change diapers and chase kids."

"Don't you enjoy anything about being here?" Banks asked.

"I don't hate it. I'd be doing the same thing at home, and at least here I can go to the beach, although going with a bunch of little kids is hard. Back home, Dad would take us up to Lake Lanier. Once, just the two of us went."

Her voice trailed off, and Banks could see she was getting upset again, so he got busy with the Lego collecting. "I'm not a fan, myself," he said. "Never learned to swim. You'd be surprised how many of us locals don't. We'll go out on the water, but don't toss us in."

She shook her head at him and smiled. "That's crazy."

"Finish your story. I want to know about your name."

"I was hoping you'd forget. Okay, the oldest boys are Abraham, Ezekiel, and Isaiah. The twins are Hope and Charity. Then there's little Faith. But I got the winner. Guess."

Banks tried to imagine what Hallie could be a nickname for.

"Give up? It's Glory. Glory Hallelujah. Good one, huh? Aunt Whitney made them call me

Hallie, and she broke the cycle of holy names when she had her babies."

Banks had been poised say something positive, but all he could manage was, "Ever think about changing it?"

"All the time. But Dad still likes it. We'll see. Maybe when I move out."

"When do you think that'll be?"

She kissed the top of Becca's head and sighed. "Not soon enough. I love them all, but I'm dying here."

"You know if you'd like to tell me anything — "

"I don't."

Inspiration struck. Banks said, "Are you scared of Sawyer?"

Hallie hesitated. "You've talked to Mom?"

He was just doing his job, Banks told himself. He was careful not to nod as he said, "The Chief knows all about it."

Chapter Twenty-Two

"Mr. Overton and Ms. Jones were married in Las Vegas on May third."

Whitney lost what little color she had, and Melanie hugged and twisted herself a bit tighter. Other than these small tells, it seemed to McNamara the sisters weren't surprised by the confirmation of Felicia's claim, so he continued with his news.

"We know from his application for the now-missing rental car that he checked into a hotel off Route 97 near BWI airport late Sunday morning. The manager confirmed that information and said he paid in advance for one night and left before the checkout the next day. He didn't contact the front desk or any other hotel facilities while he was there, and there were no charges to the room."

"Are you saying you didn't learn anything?" Whitney's disappointment was sharp in her voice.

"I did expect to turn up some trace of him before now. He was last seen here Sunday night." He let this sink in for a moment. "You may call your lawyer before you answer, but I have to ask you again, do either of you know where he is? If you have any information, I can understand you not telling Ms. Jones, but you need to tell me."

Maybe it was that he'd said 'Ms. Jones' instead of 'Mrs. Overton,' but the sisters seemed to thaw a bit toward him. Or maybe they were as tired of the subject as he was.

"My answer hasn't changed," Whitney said. "We had a nice visit with him on Sunday afternoon and evening. He flew up here to meet with Fred Renne at Lightning Strike. The trip to see us was a surprise. He went to Atlanta to complete the sale of our house and help Felicia pack up her apartment. They were supposed to drive up here together next week."

"He said all of that while he was here?"

Whitney thought for a minute, then said, "No. I mean yes, the part about why he was here was new, and he explained that. The rest of it, the next steps, that's what we had all agreed to. He didn't say any of it had changed."

"Did those next steps include him being married to Ms. Jones?"

"No!" the sisters said in unison.

McNamara said, "In that case, it was generous of you to give her a credit card."

"There was a miscommunication about the laundry. Some of her clothes were damaged," Whitney said, a ghost of a smile on her lips.

Melanie laughed, the sound harsh and without amusement. "Whit gave her the big kids' debit card. It has a fifty dollar a day limit for emergency gas and food when they're out."

"You didn't tell her." He could imagine the reaction when Felicia hit the limit, probably with her first purchase.

"She'll find out," Whitney said but didn't seem to be entertained by her own trick. "The Uber she took to get here from the airport wiped her out, and she expects us to pay for everything."

McNamara said, "I won't take up much more of your time, but have you been able to think of any reason Sawyer Renne would padlock the garage door?"

"You're not bringing up that ridiculous idea that Hallie started the fire, are you?" Melanie said. "Because we will sue you and don't think we won't."

"Understood. But I was asking about Renne, not your daughter. How well do you know him?"

Melanie looked at him with curiosity, but Whitney's face darkened. "I should have guessed," she said. "What's the little weasel done?"

"Residue from marijuana and cocaine were found in the garage," McNamara said. "Renne was the last person in there before the fire department arrived."

The sisters' shock seemed genuine.

"Sawyer was keeping drugs in there?" Whitney asked.

"Someone was." McNamara's voice was still mild, but his statement was a question.

"I said we needed a background check on him."

Melanie's only reaction was to ask for a glass of water as if she were in a restaurant and not her own kitchen. When Whitney was at the sink, Melanie said, "Was he selling it or using it?"

McNamara said, "I don't have proof that he was doing either, but those are excellent questions. Any information you can provide will be helpful."

Taking the water her sister offered, Melanie

rose and walked out of the room without further comment.

"We don't know anything, Chief McNamara," Whitney said. "But you'd better believe I'll be watching things more closely."

He took a business card and wrote a website address on the back before handing it to her. "The background check would have been a good idea. This isn't a substitute, but it's something you'll want to look at."

Whitney's hand trembled as she read the card. "The Maryland Judiciary Case Search?"

"Records of arrests, charges, trials, and their resolutions. All public information. Just type in his name. It's an interesting read."

"Drugs around our children. I'll kill him."

"Mr. Renne's occupied with some legal problems of his own at the moment, so let us handle him. In the meantime, I have to interview Hallie. Either your sister cooperates, or I'll have to get a warrant."

"I can get her to cooperate. We've overreacted, I can see that now. We're not handling things very well at the moment." Whitney glanced around before continuing. "Felicia showing up here was the last straw, and we're stuck with her now. I can't see any of us working with her, so even if Heath comes home, we might lose the show."

"If he comes home?" McNamara asked. "Why the change?"

"My sister has the luxury of denial, largely because I don't indulge in it. One of us has to be practical. He'll come back to us if he can. And if he does, all I want is our old life back."

Banks could feel the answers about to spill out of Hallie's mouth in response to his lie. He tried to feel pleased with himself.

"I can't make any more mistakes," she was saying. "Mom says Dad can take care of everything that's happened so far, but I can't do anything else wrong."

She was rocking faster, and Banks wanted to tell her to talk quickly before she woke Becca. "What's your Dad going to do?" he asked.

She looked surprised. "Get rid of Sawyer, of course."

Banks could think of several reasons a father would make Renne leave his teenage daughter alone.

"But I don't need him to do that," Hallie went on. "I'm old enough to make up my mind about men. If I hadn't gone out to the garage the day of the fire, and acted so silly he wouldn't have assumed, you know."

Banks wanted to hit something. Something named Sawyer Renne. "Did he hurt you?"

"What? No! I only meant he wouldn't have thought I knew about the drugs. I feel so dumb about how I freaked out. It's not like he uses it. It's for clients; a professional service."

"But he kept drugs in your garage." Banks tried not to make it a question and hoped he'd guessed right.

"Only one packet of joints and only because he was staying overnight at the Egret and didn't want to keep it in his room."

Banks remembered how anxious Renne had been until he'd seen the burned area of the garage. He doubted a few joints were the cause. "Good thing it was just marijuana," he said, hoping to keep her talking. If she didn't know about the cocaine, she might have thought Renne wasn't breaking the law.

But his first instincts had been right. Hallie was very smart.

"You didn't know, did you? You lied to me."

Banks was caught fair and square. He stood holding a bucket of tiny plastic blocks and was shamed by the glare of a teenage girl. Left with no other honorable option, he told her the truth.

~

"I'll hand over my badge and gun when we get to the office," he said as the Chief pulled away from the Overton house. "Do you want a written resignation, or am I fired?"

There'd been yelling and the ubiquitous tears from Melanie when the sisters learned that Banks hadn't been in the basement with the younger kids, but upstairs with Hallie and a sleeping toddler. Then Hallie told them how he'd had gotten her to confess that she'd known Sawyer was using the garage to store his drug supplies. Threats of lawsuits had followed them out the door.

"Do you want to quit?" McNamara asked.

"I'm not a cop." Banks knew that much was true. He wasn't just bad at his job, he was in the wrong place, doing the wrong thing.

"Work out a two-week notice," McNamara said.

Banks nodded but wondered if he'd last that long.

Chapter Twenty-Three

Wrapping up the Overtons' work was easier said than done, but it offered Grace a temporary reprieve from the tension in the office. Ernie's Royal Rides hadn't responded to the letter she had sent by fax and email, and she decided not to wait for the car rental agency to ignore the snail mail version. She might not learn anything helpful, but it would get her out of Mallard Bay for a few hours. That was enough incentive to drive over the bridge and into Baltimore County traffic.

She'd missed the worst of the morning congestion and tried to enjoy the expansive views across the Chesapeake Bay from the top of the bridge. Unfortunately, once she was on the western shore, there was plenty of less exciting landscape that allowed her mind to wander. The conversation she'd had with Mosley made her sad, but pushing it aside took her back to the breakfast with Niki and from there to the argument with David.

His demand that she return to Washington sent fresh spurts of anger through her every time she thought about it. It had been his fastest reversal, ever. He'd jumped from 'we can live wherever you want' to 'come back to DC, or else' in three days. Grace had opted for 'else'. While satisfying at the moment, there was too much unanswered, and she knew David would only double down.

She made herself eat a pack of stale cheese crackers she found in the bottom of her tote and drink a bottle of water. She felt better afterward and tried to think about her trip to France.

Travel had always been a passion for her, but life had other plans. College led to law school. Law school led to work. Work to David. Her mother's death brought her to Mallard Bay. And here she was at thirty-eight, coming into middle-age and desperate to start over on her own terms. Terms that kept changing.

She'd wanted a commitment from David for years, and here he was, ring in hand and a waterfront estate for a wedding gift. Three years ago, she'd have had a better shot of winning the

Powerball. Today, the thought of David on forever terms made her panic.

She'd wanted to give her mother her last wish, to see Delaney House restored to its former glory. She'd used all the skills Julia had taught her and sunk most of her money into the project, fully intending to make a sizable profit. Now, the house was not only renovated; it was worthy of its place in history. But at some point in the long process, the old building had gotten under Grace's skin and burrowed into her soul. She had to sell it or be cash poor for the rest of her life. But not selling it was fast becoming an obsession, and was the reason she'd let Niki talk her into using it as an inn.

And then there was the overriding want that had been in her heart since childhood, but the possibility of a real, complete family wasn't realistic, and she needed to let it go.

By the time she'd followed the GPS navigation system to the rental agency, she was berating herself for deciding to drive into Baltimore. The clipped British accent of the voice she'd named Nigel usually made her smile. Today it was just irritating as it directed her up Route 2, then took her along a rat's nest of run-down streets and construction zones. When she arrived at a concrete block building with a hokey castle facade, Ernie's Royal Rides turned out to be only two miles from I-97. Nigel had saved her ten miles and cost her thirty minutes.

Ernie Sherman was as unpleasant in person as he had been on the phone. Grace waited for him to finish with a couple renting a Mercedes convertible, and watched him argue with the man, ogle the woman, and in general, act like an ass. When he finally turned his attention to her, she abandoned her plan to ask for Heath Overton's rental contract.

"What's a cutie like you lookin' for?" Ernie asked as he maneuvered his beach ball belly in her direction.

Having not been called 'cute' since she was five, Grace had to un-bite her tongue before answering. Her hesitation prompted Ernie to add, "Sweet Thing, I got a Mustang over here with your name on it. All tricked out and ready to go."

She gave him what she hoped was a smile and said, "Sounds fun for someone else, but I have my heart set on a Land Rover."

"Land Rover? Oh, darlin'. You're too fine for that. You need showy — "

"I *need*," she said, unable to simper a second more, "a Land Rover, preferably an HSE. Do you have one, or not?"

"Not. But I got something better. Look at the Jag over there. That baby screams class."

"Can you recommend another dealership? A friend of mine told me she'd had good service from you, but I'll tell you're not handling the higher end Land Rovers anymore."

"Don't do that," Ernie said. "It's just that the one I have is out right now."

Grace sighed theatrically. "So you do have a one? Is it new?"

"Almost brand new." Ernie's eyes all but disappeared into folds of fat as he winked. Or had a seizure; it was hard to tell.

"I can't wait long," she said and took out her wallet. "When can I pick it up?"

"You coulda walked outta here with it, but the guy who has it didn't return it on time. That's the problem, see? His wife says he'll be back any minute, so I can get it to you soon."

"My goodness! Can't the police find it for you?" Then, because he was beginning to look suspicious, she said, "Never mind, I don't want it after someone has stolen it."

"Oh, it'll be in good shape," Ernie assured her. "The woman with guy was nagging about him gettin' fingerprints on the finish. Drove the poor sucker crazy as they were loading their luggage. A real ball-buster, that one. She wanted to drive the Rover, but her license had more points than I could count and I said nothin' doin'. Well, didn't she give me a load of crap? She only shut up when he said he'd buy her one when they got home."

Grace struggled to hide her disappointment. This couldn't be Heath Overton. "Do you only have the one Land Rover?"

"Yes. And I'll have it for you soon if the wife is telling the truth. A' course she didn't know about the chickie who was hangin' on her husband while he was rentin' my Rover, and I didn't tell her. And, I didn't tell her that Little Miss Chickie was calling herself his wife, too."

Ernie Sherman and Baltimore traffic occupied Grace for the next two hours. She'd just cleared the worst of the congestion on Route 50 when Whitney Overton called.

"How bad do you think this is?" Whitney asked after describing the morning visit from McNamara and Banks.

"It's hard to say. I'll talk to Chief McNamara," Grace wished she could do anything else but that. She was running over the points she'd make to him when she realized Whitney was crying. While she would expect Melanie to cry over a grocery list, hearing the soft sobs from Whitney shocked her.

"None of this makes any sense," Whitney

said when she'd collected herself. "Heath wouldn't do this to us. To me. He never makes me feel as if I'm second to anyone, and he never shuts me out. I love my sister, but her story about her last conversation with Heath changes every time she tells it. Something bad happened that last night he was here, but she won't talk about it. I don't think Melanie has ever successfully kept a secret from me before, so this is scary. Maybe Heath's in danger, or he might be hurt and can't get to us."

Grace searched for something soothing to say. She had to find out if Ernie Sherman's 'chickie' was Felicia. If so, Felicia had lied to the sisters. If not, there was a fourth woman connected in some way to their husband. In either case, she wanted to be with her clients when she told them.

She settled for, "Don't do that to yourself. Heath married Felicia without telling you and then abandoned all of you. Whatever the reasons, whether or not he comes back, that's what he did."

"I guess it seems that way."

"Because that's how it is."

"Look," Whitney said with a sigh. "I have to get through today and then tomorrow and every day after that. If I looked at Heath the way you do, I'd just lay down and die. I'm not stupid, or in denial. I'm doing the best I can, and I need your help."

Cyrus would be furious, and she couldn't avoid Mac if she continued to work for the Overtons, but Grace agreed anyway.

"Thank you," Whitney said. "It's such a blessing to have you to talk to. I have to measure everything I say around Melanie just to keep her functioning."

"Do you think it's wise to have Felicia remain in your home after this morning's incident?"

"Wise? Good Lord, no, it isn't *wise*, but I can't make her leave. Yesterday, we thought the best thing to do was to have her with us so we could keep an eye on her, but we'd never been around her without Heath at least nearby. We're seeing the real woman now. If she's mad, she says she and Heath can't wait to leave us. Then in the next breath, she says we have to fire you, so we don't look guilty to the police and Lightning Strike. She kept us up past midnight last night talking about new storylines that Lightning Strike might buy if Heath wants out of the film deal. I've never seen her like this. She might be on something."

"Do you mean illegal drugs? Could she be involved with Sawyer?"

"I not sure. I'm so naïve, Hallie had to tell me she was smoking. Even Mel knew that. And I didn't know Hallie was trying to start a romance with Sawyer and that he was going along with it. Or that he was supplying other clients with marijuana and cocaine."

"Yeah, about that," Grace said. "You should keep him well away from your family and tell his uncle as soon as possible. While it's true that marijuana has largely been decriminalized in Maryland, what he's doing will land him in prison and cause you no end of problems. If you're worried Hallie's involved, I can recommend a lawyer who specializes in that area of the law."

"No. No more new people in the mix. This nightmare has to end, and we're not starting over with a stranger."

They agreed that Grace would talk with both the local and state police. If Hallie was under suspicion, she'd get in touch immediately. If not, she'd call Whitney on Monday with the latest information on Heath.

"Heath promised Mel and Felicia that he would take care of everything," Whitney said. "I don't mind doing the heavy lifting while he's gone, but he should have said those words to me, too. I want my husband wherever he is. I want to bring him home."

Chapter Twenty-Four

Grace used the rest of the drive to make the calls she knew she'd avoid once she got back to Mallard Bay. Some days she regretted the hands-free phone system she had in the car.

She made the easy call first. Desiree Marbury said there was no news related to Heath Overton. The MSP detective was short and to the point with her no information message. Aidan Banks answered the phone at the Mallard Bay Police Department and was just as uninformative as Marbury. Mac was out of the office.

Stymied for the moment, she decided to put all the Overtons out of her mind for a few hours. She'd call Mac later to discuss Hallie, but she needed time to think.

After a quick stop on Kent Island to pick up

a few things, she returned to the office but didn't stay long. She shocked Marjorie by saying she would work from home until Monday. It was petty, but Cyrus had made it clear he could do without her if he had to.

The nausea that had been nagging her wasn't any worse, but wouldn't go away. Whether it was nerves, or a bug was hard to say. Between David, Cyrus, Niki, and the Overtons, she was proud of herself for not being in bed with the covers over her head. Which, now that she thought of it, was an excellent idea. There were two things she had to do before she could give in and pamper herself, and she tried not to over-analyze either.

She reprogrammed Nigel with the address of the house David had picked out. She wanted to see it, and at the same time, she needed to pretend it didn't exist. Mostly, she was ashamed that the man could give her a panic attack from ninety miles away.

"You'll be double-crossing your legs and twisting your hair next," she said out loud. The thought of being Melanie Overton's emotional twin straightened her up.

The house was on a long spit of land that could only be reached by driving east out of Mallard, turning north and then west to circumvent a tributary of the Wye River. The property was only five miles from Mallard Bay, but, thanks to Kingston County's twisty shoreline with its many inlets, it was a twenty-minute drive from her office — almost enough time to change her mind and turn the car around.

She didn't turn around.

She was furious with herself and growing angrier every day. She'd drifted back into a relationship she didn't want because it was easier than standing up to David. And now she had to break up with him — again. If she was going to live the life she'd planned, she had to start acting like the person she wanted to be.

A van came up fast behind her, and Grace realized with a start that she'd slowed to thirty miles an hour. She sped up and gave an apologetic half wave to the van's driver. As she blew past farmland and large estates, she waited to feel happiness, relief, *something*. She'd made a life altering decision, but felt nothing. It had taken her much too long to do the right thing.

When she saw the van in her rearview mirror, she said, "If you think my driving's bad, you ought to be in my head."

"In eight hundred feet, you will have arrived at your destination." Nigel's chipper announcement was even more exasperating than it had been in Baltimore. And he was still wrong. There were no houses in sight, but sure enough, a glance at the map display on the BMW's console showed a red blinking dot straight ahead.

Despite her mood, she was curious to see the house that David wanted. Shaking her head at her own mixed signals, she slowed as she approached a three-way intersection and realized where she was. Mallard Bay was to her left, Queenstown to her right, and the Wye River would be directly ahead on the other side of the woods. A large Realtor's sign with a bright red 'SOLD' sticker slapped across it sat at the edge of a newly paved road that disappeared through the trees. Grace's first thought was that someone had bought David's dream house while they'd been arguing over it, but she knew that wasn't how it worked. David had been out here with an agent on Tuesday, and the 'sold' notice wouldn't go up until settlement.

She'd felt bad before, but the idea that David may have already bought the property made everything worse. She stepped on the gas and hurtled down the macadam lane.

After two twists of the road, she was out of the woods and facing a wide expanse of water. She pulled the brochure out again and read the fine print. Nine and a half acres. She sat for a while, lost in the realization David had bought the entire point of land along with the enormous house. She couldn't imagine why he would do that.

A tap on the driver's side window nearly gave her a heart attack. Felicia Jones stood beside her car, arms crossed, and an unfriendly look on her face. For a moment, they just glared at each other.

"I've been looking for you," Felicia said when Grace lowered her window. The van that had been behind her now blocked the driveway. Hallie was in the front seat, watching them.

"You mean you've been following me." Grace pushed her door open, making Felicia move back to avoid being hit. If the newest Mrs. Overton wanted a fight, she'd come to the right place. Once out of the BMW, she mirrored Felicia's aggressive stance. "What do you want?"

Felicia was off balance but didn't back down.

"Your secretary told me you were out, but luckily, I saw you drive past us. We need to get some things straight."

"Really? Here, with Melanie's daughter?" Grace nodded toward Hallie, who seemed to take the attention as an invitation. In the next second, she was out of the van.

"I told you to stay put!" Felicia yelled.

"I told you to go to hell, but you're still here," Hallie said. "I'll do what I want. And you should know, that ice cream you had to have is melting, but by all means, talk." With that, she walked past them, and down to the edge of the water.

Felicia clenched and unclenched her fists but finally said, "My stepdaughter is right, we have to go, so I'll make this short. You're fired. I told Whitney to handle you, but she isn't any better at following instructions than the kids are."

Behind Grace, her cell rang. She grabbed it from her purse, saw the call was from Mac and hit 'decline' as she slipped the phone into her pocket. "You can't fire me. I don't work for you."

"You've been encouraging Whitney. Telling her Heath's in danger so she'll pay you to find him. But here's a news flash — she and Melanie aren't in charge of the family anymore. I am, and we aren't paying you a dime, understand?"

Grace wondered how she could have ever thought Felicia was pretty. She wore heavy makeup, but the bruise on her cheek from Melanie's slap was still visible. Anger-pinched lines around her eyes and mouth foreshadowed the older woman she would one day be. Would Heath Overton think she was worth it when that was the face he saw every morning? Or would there be a new model to take her place?

"If that's all you wanted, you need to leave. This is private property and you're trespassing."

Felicia threw her hands up in frustration. "Listen to me. We can't have you spreading the news that Heath's missing. You're stirring up the police and that's the last thing we need. My husband is fine, but he wanted a break from the whining and nagging those two old women subject him to."

"Do you know where he is?"

"Of course I do," Felicia said, and then looked over Gracie's shoulder at Hallie before moving closer and lowering her voice. "He's taking a few days off, that's all. But if I tell the sisters that, they'll fall apart, and Heath and I need them to make the show. Understand? Nobody's missing. This is just a family squabble."

Grace was only inches from the car door. Felicia was planted in front of her, hemming her in. "Back up." she said and stepped forward.

Felicia smiled but didn't move.

"Why did you lie about Heath leaving you behind in Atlanta?" The shock on Felicia's face told Grace she was right. "Did you think Ernie would forget you?" Grace went on, pressing her advantage. "He told the police about the woman who was with Heath, and he described you perfectly."

"That's a lie." Felicia was loud, but she sounded far from certain.

"Chief McNamara told me himself." Grace sent a silent apology to Mac for the lie. "Now, back up and give me some room."

But Felicia moved in so close, Grace felt more than heard her next words. "Or what?"

A second later, Felicia was three feet away, yelling, "You shoved me!"

Hallie materialized next to Grace, asking, "Are you okay?"

"Is *she* okay?" Felicia was incensed. "What about me? I'll press charges — "

"No, you won't," Hallie said. "I saw the whole thing, and she didn't touch you." To Grace, she said, "I'll tell Mom what happened, and I'll tell her that Felicia's been lying."

"I'll call your mother," Grace said, raising her voice over Felicia's squawking.

"Nope, I've got this." Hallie trotted to the van and climbed in. "I'm driving, Felicia," she yelled out the window. "If you want a ride, get your butt in here."

"I'm not finished with her." Felicia said, not looking away from Grace. "Now get out of the driver's seat, Hallie."

Appalled at how the situation had devolved, Grace stopped the back and forth by reminding Felicia she was trespassing. When her warning had no effect, she threatened to call the police.

"Grace?" McNamara's voice boomed out of the phone in her pocket.

Felicia turned and ran for the van.

Chapter Twenty-Five

"I told you not to come," Grace said.

"And yet, here I am," McNamara said.

They were on the patio, looking out over the lawn that rolled down to the riprapped shoreline and gently lapping waves. The humidity was high for May, and the temperature was pushing ninety, but the breeze off the water was like a silky caress. It would have been peaceful, if not for the tension between them.

Grace didn't know what to say. Mac was such a sweet man. A good man. A man who usually made her happy. Today she felt ungrateful and selfish. And angry — couldn't one thing in her life go right?

"It bothers you that I came out here, doesn't it?" he asked.

And damn him for always seeing right through her.

"I hit 'decline' on your call, not 'accept.'" Her words came out sharp and angry. "It shouldn't have connected. Why didn't you tell me you could hear us?"

He frowned. "Yes, you hit decline, and five minutes later, you called me. I heard a scream and arguing, and you said something about calling the police. I thought you needed help."

She remembered holding onto the phone in case she needed it. Needed him. And then she'd dropped it into her pocket. She could have accidentally called him at almost any point. "I guess your number was still up on the screen. I didn't mean to call you."

It was a lame non-apology, but he nodded. "I was only a few minutes away. It was easy enough to check on you after you gave me the address."

She couldn't tell if he was hurt or only irritated, but he wasn't happy. And why shouldn't he be? She'd ruined his afternoon. "I told you I was fine," she said, not able to let it go.

"Understood. Next time, I'll listen."

She wanted to say there wouldn't be a next time, but he deserved the truth. "Yes, it bothers me that you felt you had to come and save me, and it bothers me that I let you."

"You're assuming you could stop me."

Grace focused on the small waves rolling in, slapping the stone shoreline. *Take it back, please take it back.*

He didn't.

Hating the nervous tone in her voice, she said the first thing that came to mind. "Felicia Jones ordered me to stay away from Whitney and Melanie. I didn't cooperate by staying at the office where she could reach me, so she came after me. It was bizarre. She had Hallie with her and groceries. She couldn't have been planning to visit me, just acting on impulse."

"How did Hallie react?"

"Most of the time she was down at the riprap, looking at the water."

The memory of shoving Felicia and Hallie offering to cover for her was embarrassing now. Then she remembered how quickly Hallie had reached them. Had she been close enough to hear Grace say Felicia had been in Baltimore with Heath when he rented the car? Was that why she'd called Felicia a liar?

McNamara interrupted her worrying by making it worse. "You're right to be concerned. The woman's exhibited some anger issues today."

"Yeah. I heard about this morning, too. Whitney called and filled me in."

"Is that why you're mad at me?" he asked. "I

told your clients I'd wait to question them if they wanted to call you."

She had to laugh. "You offered to let them call me after you dangled information about Heath in front of Melanie."

"All in a police officer's arsenal." He smiled briefly at her, but the awkwardness was still there.

"It's okay. Even if I'd been there, it would have been difficult to shut Melanie up. Whitney said you asked Felicia about Heath, and after she left, you were asking about the fire. Is there new information on either situation?"

"Your clients didn't tell you about the drugs?"

Grace sighed. "Yes. And about Sawyer and Hallie. If you and the State Police are interested in Sawyer, that's fine, but no one talks to Hallie without me."

"Yes, ma'am. Same thing go for Heath Overton?"

"What does he have to do with the garage fire and the drugs?"

"Don't know, but I'd like to ask him. When he showed up in Mallard Bay that last day, he stayed a few hours, and then disappeared right before we found the evidence of illegal drugs. APBs were issued for the Land Rover he rented and for Mr. Overton. This isn't a case of a late return, anymore. The lease restricted the car's use to Maryland, but it was caught on a speed camera in South Carolina over a week ago."

Grace tried to make all the pieces fit. She needed to tell Mac about Felicia being with Heath in Baltimore, but she had to tell her clients first.

"Are the Overton women hiding their husband?"

She was so surprised by the abrupt change; she looked directly at him for the first time since he'd almost made her heart stop. Shading her eyes from the sun, she tried to read his expression. "No, but nice try."

"I'm not playing games, Grace. Not anymore."

He was angry, and she didn't have a chance to catch up before he changed the subject again.

"This place," he gave the house a dismissive glance. "This is the property David was talking about last night, isn't it?"

"Yes," Grace said, grateful to get off the subject of the Overtons. "He's quite pleased with himself."

"You must be, too. Isn't that why you bought it?"

"Not me. This is all David."

Her answer only seemed to make him angrier.

"When you told me where you were, I called the address into dispatch. Your name comes up as the owner."

"Oh, no," she whispered. "Only my name?"

It was his turn to be caught off guard. "Sole owner," he said.

Grace looked embarrassed as she explained what David had done.

"The man doesn't fool around, does he?" McNamara said. "When do you suppose he'll tell you he bought it?"

"Soon. It's probably a bribe to give up the trip to France."

"How's that going to work out for him?"

Judging by her expression, he thought Farquar would be lucky to survive the argument they were going to have.

"Think the inside looks any better?" he asked, hoping to make her smile.

Grace shook her head, then looked up to take in the expanse of glass and jutting angles that had been some architect's masterpiece. "Let's find out," she said and walked over to look in the nearest window.

The oversized windows and glass doors gave them a good view of the first-floor rooms. Somewhere between the sterile living area with its polished concrete floors, and the stainless steel kitchen, he relaxed. This house would never appeal to Grace.

"Why would David buy this?" she said. "I hate the interior more than the architecture, and neither is his style."

McNamara could think of two reasons, but he kept them to himself and followed her around to the front porch. Through the glass-paneled door and the windows that flanked it, they saw more empty rooms in need of decorating. "I guess when you have water views on three sides, you want a lot windows, but I'd hate to wash them."

"When you have water views on three sides, you generally don't wash your own windows," she said, then blushed.

McNamara didn't need the reminder that Grace and her obnoxious boyfriend had been together for fifteen years in a world very different from his own. And Farquar was literally banking on that history since he couldn't get his money back if she called the wedding off. It was a brilliant hook that would stop her from making a knee-jerk decision. She would want to be exceedingly fair.

When she asked what he was thinking, he was sorely tempted to tell her.

"I was wondering what a place like this cost," he said. It was true, but that hadn't been *all* he'd been thinking.

"Three-point-eight."

Now he had to turn and look at her. Whether or not she was aware of it, she'd braced herself against his reaction, with her arms crossed and feet planted apart. Curls had crept out of her French braid and framed her much-too-serious face. She was beautiful, but her expression made him sad, and he searched for a response that wouldn't upset her.

"Million?" he asked. "You could buy a sizable chunk of Mallard Bay for less. This is waterfront, but still."

"David's big on making statements," she said, dryly. "This property is worth more than mine."

McNamara pointed to the other side of the river. "And it's three times the size of mine."

"You live over there?"

This time her blush was red and splotchy. He had no idea what that meant.

"I thought you knew," he said. "That's my beach just before the bend. I recognized this place when I saw the brochure last night."

"Well, that's just perfect." She stood, looking across the water. When she spoke again, it was under her breath, but he heard her say, "It ticks all the boxes for him."

"So, you do know why he bought it."

"I have a good idea," she said, giving him a half-smile. "This is a classic David move. It's what he does when he's in a battle. He's never met a fight he didn't like."

"Is that why you're marrying him?" His head was telling him to walk away, but it was too late. If she liked a fight, she'd get one. "You can't make me believe you enjoy tricks likes this. And if you do love him, why are you constantly telling me you don't?"

"I've never said that to you."

"You show it in the way you hold yourself when you're near him and in the look in your eyes when you talk about him. Let the poor son of a bitch go for good. You deserve better, and so does he." He took a breath. "So do I, Grace."

He reached for her, and in less time than it took her to jerk away, he regretted it all.

He watched her leave, the rear wheels of her BMW shooting crushed shells and gravel at the Explorer. When she was gone, he stared at the Mallard Bay Police Department seal on the car's door. It looked as out of place as he felt.

He gave her a good head start before following David Farquar's fiancée down the long country lane.

~

When Grace reached the end of the road, she turned left towards Queenstown. She wasn't going to have Mac sitting on her bumper all the way to Mallard Bay. She drove past farms without seeing a single thing she'd remember later. She'd have driven around longer before turning back, but the queasiness that had tormented her all morning had returned.

She couldn't remember the last time she'd been sick. Traumatized and battered, but not sick. The absurdity of the situation would have been comical if she hadn't been so miserable. How had she screwed things up so badly?

Mac thought David deserved better. He had sympathy for *David*.

David thought he could buy her.

Cyrus was replacing her with someone still in law school.

Niki wanted her out of Delaney House.

Mac had ruined their friendship. Or had she?

As she entered Mallard Bay, David called. Sending him to voice mail didn't save her because he left a very long message that played through the car's sound system. His words rolled over her, leaving only shock, and then relief in their wake. David thought he'd won, but he'd just set her free.

Chapter Twenty-Six

Delaney House was blessedly quiet and empty. She made it to the third floor, ate a handful of saltines, and fell across her bed. A brief nap helped until a shrill 'Graa*cie!*' sent her running to the banister on the landing.

Niki stood at the base of the staircase in the front hall. "Get down here. The delivery truck's just arrived. We have to tell them where to put the furniture."

Once an elegant mansion furnished in elaborate excess, the house had been stripped of its finery over the past half-century as pieces were sold off to shore up the family's finances. Everything of value Grace's grandmother had managed to save, her son had stolen. Even items bequeathed to Grace's late mother were gone long before Grace could claim them.

As tables, chairs, sofas, and a huge French sideboard were unloaded, the large downstairs rooms once more became welcoming spaces.

"I don't remember buying all of this," she said when a walnut inlay dining room table appeared in the doorway.

Niki laughed and said, "That's my surprise. The big pieces are on loan from a dealer in Cambridge. We'll keep the ones you like and, in the meantime, I can photograph the house for the brochure. The dealer gets a mention, and everyone is happy." She hugged Grace. "Smile, isn't this fun?"

Grace wasn't having fun but thought she might be having a panic attack. It was all moving too fast. She couldn't adjust to the suddenly furnished first floor before the movers brought in the pieces for the bedrooms. From the entry hall, she watched beds and dressers, chairs, and sofas move up the cantilevered staircase to where Niki waited, clipboard in hand, to direct their placement.

A lethargy came over Grace as she watched the activity. It was as if she wasn't a part of this stage of the house's transformation. The crew and Niki were in motion. Chatter, laughter, and hurried footsteps swirled around her and made her dizzy. She leaned back against the wainscoting and closed her eyes.

"Gracie?" Niki's voice was soft, then louder. "Gracie. Look at me."

How had she gotten on the floor?

"I'm fine," she said, but it was an automated response that no one believed. The last thing she remembered was deciding she would rearrange all the furniture. "I didn't eat much today, and it's hot. Sorry, everyone." She let two of the delivery men haul her upright, relieved to find she was steady enough to remain standing without help.

Niki brought her a glass of orange juice and peanut butter crackers before returning to the unloading. Grace remained on the sidelines and watched as the last of the furniture snaked up the staircase.

Her house was very close to being the inn of Niki's dreams.

When she felt steady enough, she distracted herself by calling Whitney Overton. The sooner she told the sisters that Felicia had been with Heath in Baltimore, the better. The call went to voice mail, as did the one to Melanie. She left messages for both women telling them to call her as soon as they could, then wandered into the front parlor where she found Niki.

"There you are. Doesn't everything look beautiful?"

The delivery crew was gone, leaving them alone in a house that was furnished for the first time in decades. All Grace could think of was how much it cost. The sight of Niki dancing around the room sent warning signals to her overtaxed nerves.

"For God's sake, be still." She hadn't meant to shout, but it felt good. Not whining, not suffering in silence. Shouting. Maybe she should do it more often.

Niki, however, didn't seem to appreciate the change. "Well, goodness, you don't have to be so mean. I know you're sick, but really."

Climbing the stairs was more than Grace could manage, but she made it to the big rocking chair in the kitchen. To a piece of furniture she'd chosen in a spot she'd reclaimed from ruin. Once in the chair with her head resting against the carved back and her eyes shut, she willed herself to calm down. It couldn't be good for her heart to race this way.

"Is it David?"

Never one to leave well enough alone, Niki had followed her. And she'd gone right to the heart of what was wrong. David. He was no doubt in his beloved office doing what he wanted while she sat here watching her cousin happily spend her money.

"Here. Drink this." A worried Niki stood over her with a glass of water.

In a fit of anger, Grace grabbed the glass and threw it across the kitchen, knocking over a vase of peonies she shouldn't have left on the edge of the table. She decided throwing was more fun than shouting.

"What are you doing!" Niki cried as Grace jumped up, steadied herself, then grabbed David's favorite coffee mug.

The bright red cup had *Superior Specimen* in gold letters around the rim. She'd bought it for him as a joke on their last trip together — a conference where David was the keynote speaker and she the unacknowledged speechwriter. She let the cup fly.

"Stop it now!" Niki grabbed a broom and seemed to be deciding whether to hit Grace with it or sweep. "What the hell is wrong with you?"

"I'm not getting married," Grace said, feeling better until she looked at the mess she'd made.

"Okay. Should I say 'sorry'? What did the jerk do?"

Grace winced at the memory of David's voice over the BMW's speakers. "He booked the

National Cathedral for the wedding and Karloff's for the reception."

Niki stepped back from the hug she was giving Grace and stared up at her. "That sounds exquisite. I'd love a wedding like that. But I didn't know you'd set the date."

"Neither did I."

"Oh. But, the National Cathedral! You'll have a princess wedding. The dress can have a long train, one of those that you'll need half a dozen little girls to carry. And I'll be your Maid of Honor and…" The look on Grace's face penetrated Niki's wedding dreamscape. "If you're this upset, I guess he just told you?"

"Yes, but I've been upset since I found out he bought me a house."

The house took a while to explain. Then a while longer to convince Niki she didn't want the architectural monstrosity and no; Niki couldn't use it for an inn.

"It isn't fair," Niki said when Grace would not be swayed. "You keep getting what I want, and I have to watch you throw it away. If you just tried to appreciate what you had, you'd be happier. I'd give David a second, third, and fourth chance if I were you. Handsome, rich men don't show up every day."

"Why didn't you stay with your husband?"

Grace felt better. She was on solid ground with this argument.

"Bob didn't love me, he *wanted* me, two different things. He also wanted a couple of girls on the side for when he got tired of little, blonde and perky." Niki struck a comical pose somewhere between Shirley Temple and a stripper.

Grace didn't let her stray off topic. "He was unfaithful, and you wouldn't put up with it."

"You know he was; I've told you all of this — oh."

"Now you see my point," Grace said.

"But that was years ago. You forgave him and took him back."

"And look how happy I am."

While they swept up the broken glass and tattered flowers, Grace described life with David, a man who was there one minute and gone the next, all without leaving the room. A call from a client, a deadline for a brief, or an idea for an investment, and David's attention evaporated like so much smoke. And there were other absences, ones she never investigated. Ignoring obvious signs of dalliances had been the price for having the man she wanted in a relationship that didn't interfere with her growing career and still left her time to care for her mother.

"It doesn't sound like you. And the man you're describing sure doesn't sound like the guy who's buying houses and obsessing over a wedding."

Grace returned to the rocking chair. "You're not looking at it the way he is. He has to marry me to win — don't ask 'win what.' David's life is one long competition. Win one game and move to the next. Right now, I'm the prize, but that won't last. He can't give in to me, he has to come out on top. And how does a wedding benefit him?"

"He's getting a wonderful woman and a business partner?"

"Not even close. This Disney-inspired extravaganza has to be worth the investment, so his major clients are invited. It's good for business, and he can't understand why I'm upset. He keeps reminding me of the fabulous gifts. Last week when he dragged it all up again, I was tired and didn't want to argue, so I told him I'd think about it just to get him to drop it. Today, he called to surprise me with a fully arranged wedding and a guest list of two hundred people. He was thoughtful enough to leave room for ten guests of my choosing."

Niki picked up the broom again and swept the already clean floor. "Well, okay. I think you're cracked, but that's not new. Other than an epic wedding that he's paying for and a mansion

— *another* mansion in your name, why aren't you going to marry him?"

"Because I don't love him anymore. Even though this time around, he's made an effort to be…" she searched for words to describe the complicated man she'd once adored. "Attentive, even thoughtful. But it doesn't come naturally to him. David's driven, hard-wired to go bigger, better. With every milestone, I think, this is it — he'll be happy now. But he always wants more. He's a controlling, pig-headed, insensitive, conceited, ungrateful…" she wound down and put her head in her hands.

Niki continued to sweep, but for once said nothing.

"I wasted fifteen years on him," Grace said.

Niki put two undamaged peonies into a water glass. "We're both idiots where men are concerned. It's time for me to dump Aidan, too. We'll be the spinsters of Delaney House with little Leos and Louises for our children. Dogs are a lot less trouble than men, anyway."

That thought sent a shiver through Grace, but it was still better than feeling smothered and hopeless with David. She was the only person who could make herself happy, and she wouldn't marry a man she didn't love.

Chapter Twenty-Seven

FELICIA

"Get used to it. I'm your sister wife! In fact, I'm first wife now, no matter what you say."

Felicia's French twist was sliding down the back of her head, giving her the look of a bedraggled Barbie doll. A Barbie dressed in off-brand jeans and picked knit shirt. After a very unpleasant scene at Talbots, her brief foray into Target only netted her one change of clothes, so she was still wearing Whitney's castoffs around the house.

She demanded again that they replace her ruined clothes, but no one, least of all the sisters, paid any attention. Just as they hadn't cared when Faith and Hope added the contents of Felicia's suitcase to the family wash — the hot *bleach* wash — while she was in the bathtub trying to soak away the humiliation she'd suffered in that bitch of a lawyer's office. And now they were acting as if she should be grateful they'd gifted her with fifty dollars in compensation. All the pretty clothes Heath bought for their honeymoon either had holes or were small enough for Rebecca. Her shoes would probably disappear next.

They'd all be sorry. The lawyer would eventually drop them when she didn't get paid, and without someone to tell them what to do, Felicia could take charge. In the meantime, she'd left messages in Sawyer's voicemail.

"First wife! Do you hear me?" She yelled to make herself heard over the bedlam.

Afternoon snack and cartoon time rolled on with Whitney, Melanie, and Hallie pretending to be engrossed with the children and oblivious to Felicia. They were ghosting her, and she was so angry, she couldn't think straight. Hot tears burned her eyes, but she'd be damned if she'd cry like Mel.

Heath had told her he needed a strong woman, a woman who knew how things were in the real world. He'd said that together they'd build a business and fabulous careers. She understood he adored Melanie and always would, but it surprised her to find he also loved his second wife. She'd seen his face soften when he looked at Whitney.

Felicia couldn't understand it. Melanie's older sister was just average. She was sturdy in a way that Felicia worked hard to never be, and she rarely spent any time on clothes or makeup. When she did, the transformation was remarkable, and Felicia guessed that was the image Heath held in his mind when he took Whitney to bed. He never had to use his imagination with Felicia. She made sure of that.

For all the good it did her now.

If she'd just let him talk Sunday night. Helped him work everything out. If she'd kept her eye on the finish line and been patient. But he was a fool, and she'd lost her temper. Now look where she was.

She couldn't stand the chaos another minute.

"I *said*," she yelled, "It's time to talk."

Chapter Twenty-Eight

McNamara and Banks wrapped up the day's work without their usual banter. Banks didn't change his mind about quitting, and McNamara didn't mention it again.

"Have you checked on Grace this morning?" Banks asked as they were leaving.

McNamara locked the door of the station and followed the corporal out into the small parking lot. Muggy air enveloped them and, for a few seconds, felt good on their artificially chilled skin. "I don't do daily checks on Grace," he said and wondered if Banks knew where he'd been earlier.

"I asked because Niki called and broke our date for tonight. Said she had to stay home with

Grace because she was sick. Some kind of bug. She passed out this afternoon."

"Grace passed out?" McNamara stopped walking. "Did they get her to the ER?"

"Nik said she hadn't eaten anything today and then got overheated. Don't worry, she's fine." He stopped talking, but it was obvious he had more to say.

"What?" McNamara demanded, irritated at Banks for making him ask.

"Nik also said Grace and David had a major fight, and that's why Grace feels bad. You know Nik — she'll want to be right there, digging up all the details." Banks added a mock salute, then got into the patrol car for a last ride around the village for the day.

By the time he was home, McNamara had decided he was finished with women. Whatever Grace did as a result of what he'd said, was on her. She was a big girl, and he was tired of pretending that he thought her life choices were fine. Not that she'd ever asked him. Not that it was any of his business who she married. Who she loved.

"Not my problem," he said out loud and winced as the words bounced around his empty house. He'd missed a call from Ashley when he was racing up and down Route 50 after Grace.

He'd ignored it all afternoon but played it now as he rooted around in his freezer for dinner. He set a container of chili in the microwave to defrost and listened to Ashley explain why she needed to cancel their dinner plans. He didn't remember making any dinner plans, but it was her reason for canceling that stopped him short.

"I hope you don't have me on speaker," she paused. "I'm a coward doing this on voice mail, but I've finally gotten my nerve up, so I'm just going to get on with it. I like you, actually more than like. I think I've made that clear." There was another pause where he was horrified to hear her sniffling. Had he managed to upset two women in one day? Three, if you counted weepy Melanie Overton. A stellar personal best.

"This isn't working for me, Lee. I would say it's me, not you, but we both know better. You're a great guy, but you're not *my* guy. If you ever figure out what you want, and it happens to be me, get in touch. But for now, let's call it done, okay? Take care of yourself."

For a man whose workdays were rife with drama and crisis containment, McNamara maintained an even keel in his personal life. Usually. He stood next to the beeping microwave and asked himself how everything had gone so wrong. The introspection didn't sit well. One word covered all of his problems. Women.

There wasn't a damned thing he could do about any of them.

The Nats' game did nothing to improve his mood and staying up after midnight to see the last heartbreaking minute of play started Saturday morning off with a headache and a rare temper. As he was leaving for work, an explosive thunderstorm opened the sky, driving him back inside for rain gear.

It had been weeks since he'd taken a whole day off, he grumbled to himself. A man ought to be able to sleep past five and read the paper in peace on a Saturday. But the paper was at the end of the driveway, wet.

He should retire. The thought surprised him so much that he stopped, raincoat in hand, and watched the rain pound the front steps. Retirement. Where had that come from? He'd turned out in hurricane conditions, and snowdrifts up to his waist. He'd held dying people, and then their grieving loved ones. On his worst day, he'd never considered doing anything but police work. What the hell was happening to him?

Staying home wasn't the answer. His house, a nineteenth-century waterman's cottage, was usually a safe harbor in an uncertain world. Everything he loved was in this house. Or had been. Today it felt empty.

His cell rang, ending his unhappy thoughts,

and reminding him he wasn't retired yet. Suddenly he couldn't wait to get to work.

Chapter Twenty-Nine

Grace woke early to sirens. She barely had both eyes open when the house phone and her cell erupted at the same time. Minutes later, Grace, Niki, and a not even slightly embarrassed Aidan Banks raced out the kitchen door and ran through the wet woods toward Avril's house.

They found her standing at the edge of her garden, huddled under a huge umbrella. She was facing the Overton house, but for once, she wasn't elbowing her way into the action. "Someone's dead," she said and pulled the neck of her robe up tight under her chin.

That much they already knew.

Avril grabbed Aidan's arm. "Lee made me leave. You get over there and make sure they don't traumatize those poor children. They shouldn't say anyone's dead where the kids can hear." Avril shook her finger at Banks. "You take care of them."

Banks asked Niki to stay with Avril and waved for Grace to follow him. McNamara had summoned both of them — Aidan to work on his morning off, and Grace to tend to her clients.

~

The den was packed with Overtons large and small, but it didn't take Grace long to determine that Felicia was missing. Whitney and Melanie settled the children they were holding, told Hallie to start breakfast, and pulled Grace into the dining room to talk.

"Thank you so much for coming," Whitney said. "I was worried about asking the police to call you, but I was more worried about doing something wrong. Do you think it makes us look guilty that I asked Chief McNamara to call you?"

"Of course, it does!" Melanie snapped, then glanced over her shoulder and lowered her voice. "You keep calling her as if she's your fairy god-mother or something. You're always saying you'll handle everything, but you don't."

"I'm also your neighbor, Melanie," Grace

said. "So, it's okay. But somebody needs to tell me what's happened."

"You mean your police friends didn't fill you in?" Melanie's terrified-of-everything persona was gone. Anger, or fear, had transformed her. "I thought everyone knew everything around here. Felicia's dead."

"Lower your voice, Mel," Whitney begged. "I'm sorry, Grace. I'm pretty sure we'll need a lawyer. We think Felicia died in her sleep, but since she's so young, there are questions."

"Tell her about the argument we had while you're at it," Melanie said. "Felicia told us how you hit her and then called the police on her. You're supposed to be our lawyer, not make trouble for us."

"No, that's not what happened," Grace said, then stopped, hard-pressed to explain what actually had happened with Felicia. "She didn't want me involved with your family."

"I'm not sure I do, either," Melanie said. "She didn't talk about anything else after she and Hallie got home, and last night she was unbelievable. The windows were open, and I'm sure that old biddy next door heard everything."

Whitney groaned. "Stop it. I mean it. Just shut up, Mel! Every word out of your mouth makes us look worse. And I swear if you ask for a death certificate one more time — "

"*What?*" Grace stared at Melanie. "You didn't, did you?"

"Well, we'll need one," Melanie said. "Each of the adults has a life insurance policy payable to the other three to compensate for the loss of income. It was actually Felicia's idea. She said we'd lose the show if one of us died, and five million split three ways really isn't that much. I'm only being practical. Our show is as good as gone, and we have to face facts. Lightning Strike could stop our money today, and what will we pay the bills with? Felicia's insurance may be all we have if Heath doesn't come back."

"Mrs. Overton?"

They all turned to see that McNamara and Banks had joined them.

"What happened to Felicia?" Grace asked before Melanie could say anything else.

"That will be up to the Medical Examiner to determine," McNamara said.

"But do you have any ideas?" Grace pressed. "If there's any danger, we need to know."

"There's no obvious cause of death, and that's all I can share with you. However, we might learn something when we take your client's statements." The brief smile McNamara aimed at her clients held no warmth at all.

~

It was Desiree Marbury who took their statements with Banks standing by for assistance.
After seeing the proceedings underway, McNamara disappeared. For the next hour, Grace
didn't have time to process why things were un-
folding as they were. She was busy representing
first Melanie, then Whitney, and finally Hallie as
each met with the MSP Detective Sergeant.

At first, Grace was impressed with the
change in Aidan as he stood behind Marbury
and took notes. He still wore the rumpled tee
shirt and jeans he'd thrown on before racing out
of Niki's room, but everything else about him
said *COP.* It soon became clear that the soft-
hearted man who'd soothed the children and
tried to avoid assignments from McNamara had
changed. There was nothing comforting about
his presence.

Melanie trotted out her trademark tears but
changed tactics when Marbury just rephrased
and repeated her questions until she got answers.
A dozen versions of 'I was asleep' was all
Melanie would say about Felicia's death. She was
forthright about the arguments with Felicia, but
not as descriptive as when she'd been with
Grace.

"Are you finished?" Melanie demanded when
Marbury paused to confer with Banks. "I want
to see that all the kids eat, and I need to make

some calls. Oh, and don't forget about the death certificate. I know you're supposed to give it to our husband, but I'll see that he gets it."

Marbury's only response was to give Grace a pitying look.

It was Whitney who broke under questioning.

"How many times do I have to tell you?" she said in a shaky voice when Marbury repeated a request for details about the discovery of Felicia's body. "Using different words doesn't change what happened. Felicia was supposed to get up with the children and start breakfast. The kids woke me, I went to get Felicia and couldn't wake her."

Grace put a supportive hand on Whitney's shoulder and found herself caught up in a bear hug.

"Help me!" Whitney hissed into Grace's ear before releasing her.

"Unless you have something new to ask my client, I'd like to bring this to a close," Grace said. "Mrs. Overton needs to lie down." She expected Marbury to refuse, but instead she asked Banks to escort Whitney to her room.

Hallie's questioning didn't go any better.

"It's not my fault," the girl said before she was even asked anything. "It was my turn to sleep in. Mom and Aunt Whitney said Felicia had to be on the schedule and put her on break-fast duty. I told Mom she'd do something to get out of it."

Marbury nodded and said, "She did that a lot? Pushed her responsibilities off on other people?"

"On me? All the time. Back in Atlanta, when she came to our house, she'd order me around like her personal maid. She doesn't dare do it to Mom, and when she tries it with Aunt Whitney, you should see the fireworks, but me? I have to be polite."

"And are you?" Marbury asked. "Polite, that is?"

"Sure." Hallie's tone said she was anything but.

"What happened to your mouth?"

Hallie gingerly touched her swollen bottom lip. "It's stupid. One of the little kids bopped me a good one when I was trying to dress her. Why do you care?"

"Looks like it hurts," Marbury said. On the surface, the MSP detective seemed sympathetic, a friendly shoulder for an upset girl.

"Desiree," Grace interrupted, deliberately using the detective's first name. "Do you have any more questions about this morning's events for Hallie?"

"Oh, stop it," Hallie said. "You work for

Aunt Whitney. I can talk to whoever I want. Aidan's here, and he's my friend."

It was a toss up as to who was more surprised, but Grace jumped in before Banks could respond. "I'm your attorney, and Aidan is a police officer. We need to have your Mom join us."

"I don't need my Mom."

"Then you have me, and that's the end of the discussion," Grace turned back to the officers. "If we're all on the same page, I want to speak to my client for a moment."

Hallie looked annoyed but kept silent while the officers stepped out of the room.

As soon as they were alone, Hallie said, "I'm sorry. I mean, you're cool and all, but I don't need you. Felicia's horrible, and if she's overdosed or something, well, at least it'll get her out of here for a while."

"You think she overdosed?" Grace asked.

"There are pills by her bed. Maybe she took too many? She's certainly dumb enough to do that. Aunt Whitney said she shook Felicia hard, but she was too out of it to wake up."

Was it possible? Grace got up to find Melanie. She or Whitney could just climb out of their own drama and handle this child. She checked the kitchen and den and saw only children.

"What?" Hallie demanded. "What's going on?"

Grace couldn't decide how much to say. "What have you heard?" she asked.

"You're acting as if I did something wrong, but this isn't my fault. It isn't! I'm not responsible for Felicia, or any stupid thing she does."

"Hallie, at some point during the night, Felicia died. I think everyone assumes you know that."

Grace wanted to hug the girl, but didn't think it would be welcomed. It turned out that no one managing the morning's crisis had thought to tell Hallie her tormentor was dead.

Chapter Thirty

By noon, medical and police personnel were gone, and Whitney and Melanie had closed ranks, packed up all the children. In what Grace thought might be their last act of professional courtesy, Lightning Strike agreed to put the Overton brood up in an Easton hotel while Melanie and Whitney faced their corporate sponsors and tried to save *The Plurals Next Door* from cancelation.

"Maybe they can get a show called *Two Women, Eleven Children, and No Prospects,*" Lily said.

Grace groaned. She'd come into the office hoping for something resembling peace, only to find both Lily and Cyrus working.

"It's raining, so no golf," Mosley said. "Be-sides, what choice do I have but to be here on

Saturday?" He eyed Grace's denim shorts and Parrothead T-shirt critically. "I have work that isn't getting done."

Grace was surprised he had any work at all after the last load he'd dumped on her, but she let it go.

"He doesn't suffer alone," Lily muttered.

"I can hear you, young lady," Mosley said..

Grace left them picking at each other, wondering when her work life had gone as screwy as her personal one. She made a large mug of peppermint tea and took it to her office. The Provence lavender fields greeted her on her monitor screen. She sipped her tea and waited for the picture change. Up next was the Paris sidewalk cafe shot. The Musée d'Orsay followed, then the cathedral at Rouen. She would be there soon.

"You're drinking herbal tea?"

Grace looked up to see Lily in the doorway, and after waving her in, found Cyrus was right behind her. They took chairs and appeared to be waiting for a response to the tea question.

"It's mint, and I'm a grownup. I'm allowed," she said to Lily. "But I should bring both of you up to date."

"Thank you for the consideration, but there's no need," Mosley said. "Avril called me right after you got there, and I called Lily."

That explained Cyrus' snit, Grace thought.

"Do you know yet if the young lady's death was natural?" he asked.

"No. There'll be an autopsy."

Grace had an appointment at three to give her statement at the police station. Marbury had agreed to the delay only because she and McNamara had their hands full.

"And before you ask," Grace continued, "I'm not dropping the Overtons as clients, but they may not be needing me much longer. I don't see any way to salvage the film contract, and I'm sure they'll return to Atlanta as soon as the police let them."

"If the police let them," Mosley said. "But I agree. They don't need you anymore. I, however, do. Jake can't start for a month."

It was all Grace could do not to groan. Lily's glare was hot enough to scorch her boss's bald head, but Mosley talked on as if both women were on board with his plan.

"I need this place ship-shape when he gets here. I'll have my hands full with my own work and mentoring him, and I don't want any oddball cases to gum up the works."

Grace couldn't contain herself. "Cyrus, this is a law firm, not a factory. The law is all about oddball cases." As soon as she said it, she saw she'd given him his opening. The law Mosley practiced was all about factory-like efficiency. It was Grace's cases that were odd and Grace herself who gummed things up.

Mosley rarely ignored an invitation to argue. "I don't want this firm tied up in a lurid murder case — *another* lurid murder case — when you're gone. And, as I've already said, this Overton situation is not the kind of work I handle." It was a long statement for him, and he stopped for a deep breath. "Grace, you will remove yourself as the Overtons' counsel immediately, please." With a brief nod, he left the room.

Lily said, "I quit."

On the desk, the monitor changed to a shot of a long narrow riverboat gliding past a crumbling medieval castle. Grace felt it was more of a taunt than a promise. She nodded and said, "Me, too. Let's go to the Egret, and I'll buy you a drink."

"Yeah, right." Lily stood and turned away, saying, "Not such a good idea, is it? You should stick with tea."

Grace followed Lily into her office. "What's wrong? Talk to me."

"I am *leaving*." Lily rounded on her, hands on her hips. "Just like you are. Gone. Quitting. I got another job. I was willing to work after hours and weekends here to help Mr. Mosley out, but he's been impossible. And I'm not breaking in a new lawyer. Not even Jake." She hesitated, then added, "Especially not Jake. This is insane."

It was hard to argue with her about that.

"Okay. I'm sorry I've been so dense. How did all this Jake business start, anyway?" Grace asked, watching Lily yank open a desk drawer and grab her purse.

"Stupidly. And all my fault. Jake and I were at Scossa in Easton for our six-month anniversary. Mr. Mosley came in with some friends and joined us for a drink. That's when I should have made Jake leave. The next thing I knew, he and Mr. Mosley were one-upping each other with golf stories. Then Jake started talking about night school and his long-range plans, and that ran through dinner. Mr. Mosley picked up the check, which pissed me off, I can tell you, and Jake didn't shut up about the great man until we got home." She stopped and sank back in her swivel chair. "They clicked."

"Hard to believe," Grace said, trying to image the handsome, thirty-something Jake being buds with Mosley.

"Not really," Lily said. "Jake's like a puppy. He likes everyone and has the energy of ten people. He can talk to a wall and learn something new. And we know what Mr. Mosley wants."

"A partner who'll do what he's told," Grace

said, realizing yet another reason for Lily to be angry with her.

"Yes. And he's certainly not getting that from you, is he?"

Grace almost apologized. But she was only sorry Lily was being hurt by the changes. Anything truthful she said would sound patronizing. Life was moving on for all of them, and it never paid to stand in the way of a celestial steamroller. She knew this firsthand and had the scars to prove it.

Grace was exhausted and ready to leave by three. She picked up Leo from Avril's, went home, and for the second day in a row, took a nap, only to be awakened an hour later by barking. She sat up to find David standing in the doorway of the bedroom.

"I wish you'd make up your mind," she snapped as she tried to control her racing heart. "Either stay mad and stay gone or get over it. This arguing then showing up unannounced isn't working for me." She picked Leo up and tucked him under her arm. "And while we're at it, I want your key back."

"Well, someone's grumpy." David hugged

her as she passed him and was rewarded with a none-too-gentle shoulder punch. "Ow!"

She showed no signs of hearing his complaint as she moved into the kitchen area and settled Leo in his crate with a fresh chew stick. When the little terror was corralled, David tried again to act like they were having a normal conversation.

"I heard about the latest mysterious death in your client circle and decided I'd come help. Let's go out to dinner." He watched her fill a glass with ice and open a Coke. "That's not your speed, babe," he tried, but still got no response.

When hovering over her got him nowhere, he settled on the sofa and waited for her to land somewhere. It took an inordinately long time, and when she finally sat in the chair across from him, her face was grim.

"What's wrong?" He gave her a hurt look, the version with puzzled eyes, and a defeated slump of his shoulders. This was a go-to staple of their conversational fencing. If telling her didn't work, and coercion and yelling failed, he usually doubled back to Prince Charming. Wounded Little Boy was the Hail Mary pass.

Grace started to respond, then stopped herself as she realized she didn't care what he wanted or how he felt. It was over. She couldn't go back, and he wouldn't change. There was a new feeling growing in her heart, one that would take some getting used to. She thought it might be pity. Wherever she ended up in life, he would always be a part of her. It was time to find out how big his role would be.

Half an hour earlier, she'd been asleep, a tangled series of stressful dreams working away in her subconscious. The actions she'd taken and decisions she'd made, even the events she couldn't control, all seemed to have led here, to the third floor of Delaney House with David.

She said, "I need a few minutes alone, and after that, we'll talk."

Chapter Thirty-One

"They aren't home."

The voice appeared to be coming from a holly hedge to the right of the Overtons' front porch.

Talking to shrubbery wasn't the oddest thing McNamara had done in his career as a police officer. "When will they be back?" he asked the hedge.

"I'm observant, not nosey. You may as well come on over for coffee."

He crossed the lawn to find Avril weeding a bed of Hosta on the far side of the hedge. Her rental property was neat and well maintained, but Avril's residence was a showplace. The interior of the house was a jumble of mid-century modern, but the exterior was a *House and Gardens* example of late Georgian architecture.

Avril got to her feet and stood next to Louise, whose only response to McNamara's appearance was a slow wag of her bushy tail. The shepherd looked ferocious unless you knew she'd lost half her teeth and used Avril for protection. McNamara was glad they'd found each other.

Once they were in her avocado green kitchen, he watched her make coffee in a battered aluminum French press. He knew where the Overtons were and could call Desiree Marbury for an update, but talking to a friend was more appealing.

"I can't keep up with that family's antics, and I'm rather disappointed that you have to ask me," Avril said.

The coffee smelled amazing, and McNamara wondered if it was the kind she used or the old pot she made it in. He accepted a cup and declined cream.

"There's a Kingston County Sheriff's cruiser parked at the curb," he said, "so I stopped to see if they needed a hand. Finding you and being invited for coffee was a bonus. And," he added when her snort made clear she wasn't buying the flattery, "I'm always interested in your observations, Miss Avril."

"Only what any reasonably observant person would. Bobby Nelby rode up to Baltimore with the Medical Examiner. Someone will be along eventually to get the car."

McNamara didn't bother to ask how she knew the Sheriff had sent one of his officers to accompany Felicia Jones' body to the morgue. That was the thing about Avril. She knew everything that happened, and most of what was going to happen. Once you accepted that irritating fact, you could make use of it.

"What's your theory?"

"Took you long enough to ask," she said and got up to top off their cups. "They had a big row at dinner time and another around eight o'clock last night. I was out on the screened porch and heard a good bit."

She gave Louise the second of three small brown cookies she'd lined up along the table's edge. Training treats, she'd called them, but she hadn't said which of them was being trained. McNamara decided it was Avril since Louise had mastered sitting quietly and staring at the food until she got it. Her human, on the other hand, seemed antsy. McNamara thought Avril had probably lived on the porch next to the rental house since the Overtons had moved in.

"What was the fight about?"

"The usual thing three wives with one husband and eleven children fight about." Avril's laugh took years off her face. "Not that I'm anyone to talk about things like that. As you well know, I was a scandal in my day."

McNamara knew. A gay woman openly living with her partner, if not a scandal, was an anomaly in Mallard Bay during the years Avril and her beloved Glenda had been together. He remembered Glenda Grant as a beautiful woman who'd taught music and lived in this big, fashionable house with Avril Oxley. They were 'too — *too*,' according to his mother, who counted them among her closest her friends. What he remembered best from that time was Halloween. The 'ladies at Oxley House' gave out great treats — full-sized candy bars, the good stuff — and they'd let kids trade in raisin boxes and jaw breakers from lesser houses for Snickers and PayDays.

"Hello? You just going to ignore that?"

McNamara pulled himself out of the late sixties and refocused on the wizened face across the table. "I was remembering how beautiful Miss Glenda was. You, too, as I recall."

A glint of moisture appeared briefly in Avril's eyes and was quickly blinked away. "You don't play fair," she said, but there was a smile with the words.

"I only tell the truth." And then, because it

was Avril, he added, 'usually' and made her laugh. "Seriously, my father said you looked like Kathryn Hepburn. Used to make my mom jealous."

"I'm a foot too short for that comparison, and your mother was an angel. But thank you for your bullshit. *Seriously.*"

"Your turn," he said. "What were they arguing about?"

"Money."

"Not their missing husband?"

Avril shrugged. "It sounded to me like he *was* the money. The young new one said they had to stop asking people to find him because it kept the police stirred up, and that was bad for their deal. There was a lot of 'who do you think you are' back and forth. Then one sister told the upstart she was bankrupting them. And the other sister — I can't always identify them by their voice — anyway, she said if Felicia knew Heath was dead, she had to tell them so they could file for his life insurance."

After Melanie's performance during her interview, he wasn't surprised but tried to look as if he were. It didn't pay to disappoint Avril.

"So, you already knew that part, huh?" Avril shook her head. "It's so hard to keep anything quiet around here."

McNamara nearly choked, trying not to laugh.

"Anyway," she continued, "that's when the new wife said it was Whitney and Melanie who were causing all the problems by keeping Grace around. Well, I really started paying attention at that point."

"I'll bet," McNamara said. "You got out the binoculars and microphones, and then what happened?"

"You want to make jokes or find out what they said about Grace?"

"My apologies. Please continue."

"The new one started yammering about getting rid of Grace. She said having an attorney poking around made them look guilty because an innocent family wouldn't need a lawyer to manage their lives."

"What did the sisters say?"

"Melanie agreed with Felicia, which set Whitney back, I can tell you, until Felicia said she'd met with Grace and told her to leave the family alone. She said they had a good deal however the situation with Heath turned out, if they just didn't screw it up. She did not, however, say 'screw' if you get my point."

McNamara nodded, but he wasn't thinking about Felicia and her F-bomb; he wanted to hear more about the good deals. "Give me the rest," he said when Avril's dramatic pause went on too long.

"Felicia said they could wring their hands all they wanted, but like it or not, Heath had married her. Had chosen her over them. I couldn't hear much after that. They were standing sort of bunched together, and it was getting dark, so I couldn't see as well through the bushes."

"The bushes? I thought you were on your porch."

"I had to get a little closer when they started talking about Grace, didn't I?"

He let it go and hoped Avril wouldn't have to retell her story on the witness stand. The women's argument was interesting. It was also a reason to question the Overtons further, but words didn't kill. Not directly, anyway. "Anything else?"

Avril looked thoughtful but didn't answer.

He changed direction a bit, hoping to jog her. "I've seen you with the Overton children. Have they won you over?"

To his surprise, Avril didn't have a sarcastic comeback.

"I've gotten used to them. They're nice kids. They come over when they can get away from the asylum over there. First, they dared each other. The whole family seems to think I'm deaf. When the kids discovered Louise and Leo were friendly, and I had cookies, I started having regular guests every time I was out in the yard."

"Where is Piglet, anyway?" McNamara asked, looking around for Leo.

"Grace took him home when she finished next door this morning. She thought he was too much for me after all the excitement." Avril's tone said she didn't appreciate the consideration. "She needs to look after herself and leave that poor dog here where he'll have company. I barely get his diet straight and his digestive tract under control before she takes him and gets him all riled up again."

McNamara wanted to ask why she thought Grace needed looking after, but Avril wasn't finished.

"Since we're on the subject, maybe you and Ashley would take the little guy. Leo, I mean. Grace says Niki will keep him while she's traveling, but a vet would be a better choice. Grace is going to be too busy when she gets back to handle a dog with dietary issues."

He wasn't going to discuss Ashley with Avril. And while she'd grabbed his attention with the comments about Grace, that subject was off the table as well.

"Did the Overton kids tell you anything interesting?" he asked.

Avril's evil smile said she knew she had him worried. "Only the little ones. And I'm not sure how reliable they are. The bigger ones keep family matters to themselves. Doesn't stop them from accepting cookies, though. They're concerned about their dad. The older ones are bored and want to go home, wherever that is now, and the little ones ask a million questions and give me tidbits like the new mommy yells a lot, and they don't need any more babies. Faith said her mommy cries a lot. I'm guessing she's Melanie's. I explained to Faith that nobody likes a weak woman, but I think she's too young to grasp the concept."

"Indoctrinate early and often," McNamara said with a smile.

"Don't be snide. And in that woman's case, it's just so much show. All that crying and wringing of hands and the 'Can't somebody do something?' whining. Some people genuinely need to be cared for, but that little schemer isn't one. If she had to, she would mow down anyone who stands between her and what she wanted."

"We're still talking about Melanie, right?" McNamara asked and earned a snort from Avril.

"Yes. Melanie, the crier. The other one is the enabler."

"The other one being — "

"Oh, good grief. We're gossiping, Lee, not laying out directions for brain surgery. The weak sob-sister is the manipulator, the real power. The other one thinks she's in charge and keeps everything running. The third woman is dead, so I'm not sure she's important to this topic. I met her just after the kids ruined all her clothes. Which, I have to tell you, is very hard to talk about and keep a straight face."

"Do you even try?"

"Of course not. It's a waste of energy."

"What's your opinion of the Overtons, overall?"

"It's interesting, isn't it?" she said. "If you removed emotion from the mix, practically speaking, they have a workable situation. They have the large family they all seem to want and enough hands to handle the work. Children always thrive with more people to love them, and if the adults could get along and follow a sensible schedule with sex, it should work."

McNamara set his cup down, thankful he hadn't taken a sip of coffee before that last part.

Avril didn't miss his discomfort. Dozens of wrinkles bloomed into a brief but bright smile. For an instant, McNamara saw the pretty woman who'd traded him a giant-size Mars Bar for a three-stick pack of gum.

"Emotion rules everything, Lee," she said. "You'd do well to remember that. All three women were in the same boat, but none of them wanted the same thing. You understand what I'm saying?"

He didn't, so she told him.

Chapter Thirty-Two

Power. Love. Money.

McNamara thought about Avril's theory as he drove back to the station. The argument she'd overheard could be the answer to everything or mean nothing at all. He needed to find out what the women had done when they left the porch.

He pulled into the parking lot behind the station and lowered the Explorer's windows. The rain had blown out to the Atlantic, and the early afternoon sunlight carried the heavenly smells of roses in full bloom and the latest offering from the bakery. It wouldn't do to rest his head on the seat back and close his eyes, but that's what he wanted to do. He was tired. No good reason for it; he hadn't exerted himself unless you counted emotional athletics. But there was no point in brooding over that. He took out his notebook and jotted down details of his conversation with Avril. If he waited until he was in his office, any number of distractions might waylay him.

When he looked back over his notes from the past week, he thought how easy it was to form opinions about the Overtons based on generalities and social norms. The truth was more elusive. Truths. Fifteen people were involved in this family drama. Four of them were worth five million dollars each, but only if they were dead. Right now, the sisters could be five million ahead and closing in on ten. Not the worst motive he'd ever heard for murder.

He called the Office of the Chief Medical Examiner in Baltimore. As a former head of the regional office of the Maryland State Police Criminal Investigation Bureau, he had a little more pull than the average small town police chief. He hoped one of his old colleagues had drawn Sunday duty. The voice that answered sounded young, but the officer recognized his name.

"Major McNamara! Major Brixson asked me to call you, sir. I was just about to do that."

McNamara heard the salute in the nervous tone. "It's not Major anymore, but I appreciate the courtesy." He rarely pulled rank outside of his official duties and tried never to step back into the MSP world unless he had to. To his mind, nothing said 'fool' more than someone pretending to be who they no longer were.

"Are there any preliminary results on the body we sent up from Mallard Bay this morning?" he asked.

"Yes, sir. But that's not why I was supposed to call you. We have another body Major Brixson would like you to have a look at. He wanted to know if you could come in today?"

Some things you never forget.

Memories, pleasant and disturbing, can be recalled in an instant with a visual or verbal trigger, a smell, or a touch. The sterile autopsy room and its grisly contents offered all four. McNamara hoped he wouldn't have to touch the body in front of him. Looking at it, listening to Jeff Brixson and smelling the significantly deteriorated corpse through a double mask was bad enough.

"You said you have a video of the Overton family. Anything in it that might help us make a preliminary identification?"

"I have it on my phone. I'll send it to you," McNamara said. "It's possible this is Heath

Overton, but you'll need to work your magic to know for sure." He looked up at his friend of more than thirty years. They had closed many cases together, and McNamara knew he was being asked to identify the body out of friendship, as well as professional courtesy. Brixson could easily have obtained the film and studied it himself, but he'd given his friend a place on the front line of the investigation. Not that McNamara wouldn't have some heavy lifting to do.

"You'll notify the family?" Brixson asked.

McNamara nodded. "They moved up from Georgia recently. Overton was only here for two short visits, so if I can't get anything with his DNA, we'll need samples from his children."

"I'll send a tech with you."

"Sounds like a plan. So, what happened?" McNamara gestured toward the table between them. "Looks like any of half a dozen injuries could have killed him."

The corpse known only by a long string of numbers had been in a refrigerated drawer for the past four days. The autopsy reported a fatal head wound and numerous post mortem injuries. As bad as the head looked, it was the mangled hands that made McNamara queasy.

Brixson said, "If this is Heath Overton, he skipped his trip south and took the scenic route to a west Baltimore landfill dump. Most of the damage to the body was post-mortem and consistent with being cycled through a trash truck compactor."

McNamara winced. "Any idea when death occurred?"

"It's a fairly wide window, but since you say he was last seen alive on the evening of May 6, I'd estimate within a forty-eight-hour period after that. He'd been dead at least a week when we got him."

McNamara held up a hand as Brixson made a move to recover the body. "What ties this guy to Heath Overton?"

"Despite the damage, he's about the right size. But what got our attention was this." Brixson handed McNamara a small plastic bag containing a misshapen gold ring.

McNamara looked at the corpse again and asked, "Where was it?"

"Crushed into the left stump."

McNamara studied the pulpy mass that had once been part of a hand. "Overton is reported to have worn a wide gold band with three inter-twined circles engraved on it."

"You can't make out much through the plas-tic, Mac, but the engraving is still visible. Only it looks like there might be four circles." He handed McNamara a second bag. "It matches the pattern on the one I took off the woman you sent up here."

McNamara nodded and looked down at the ravaged face of the dead man. A murder investigation would put a hold on at least half of the sisters' insurance payout.

"Can you tell what caused the fatal injury?"

Brixson pointed to photographs that hung behind them. The back of the dead man's head was caved in. "I only know the what, not the how, but I'm working on it."

"What's the call on Felicia Jones Overton?" McNamara asked as Brixson returned the corpse to its drawer.

"Moved her to the front of the line when we made the ring connection. I think you've got another murder on your hands."

"Murder?" McNamara said. "Not suicide?"

"Not unless she smothered herself. Why did you assume suicide?"

The question caught McNamara off balance. Why was he surprised at the swift and unequivocal answer? Because the suspects were Grace's clients? Or because one of them was a teenage girl? Thirty years of police work told him this would be the outcome, but he was off-kilter these days.

He said, "Open pill bottles on the bedside table pointed to a possible overdose. I sent them up with the body. It was a classic setting, and she was in a stressful situation."

Brixson said, "We checked it out. They're heavy duty sleeping pills, all right, but they didn't kill her. There's something else you should see."

McNamara and Brixson stepped out into the hallway, where they shed their protective coverings into a bin. "The testing will go on for a while, as you know, but Mrs. Overton suffered an interesting antemortem injury."

Brixson led the way into a small office and picked up a file from the desk. Handing it to Mc-Namara, he said, "I'll give you any copies you need."

This time the corpse was easily recognizable. Brixson pointed to Felicia's face, but it wasn't necessary. McNamara saw a large greenish bruise on her cheek.

This time McNamara knew the assailant was an Overton. The only questions were, which one, and was she also the killer?

Chapter Thirty-Three

"You aren't going to see Grace, are you?" Avril stood at the edge of her yard, arms crossed, glaring at him.

McNamara had interrupted her gardening again, this time to collect a key to the Overton house. He was tired after the long day and needed to check in with Brixson. The last thing he should do was drop in on the suspects' attorney.

"It's hot as blazes out here, and it's getting dark," she went on when he didn't respond. "Give me your arm and walk me into the house, please."

If she'd asked him to loan her money, he wouldn't have been any more surprised. Then he realized she was playing him. Her arthritic fingers still had a grip that could deaden the nerves in his arm. She didn't need his support; she wanted to keep him on her side of the woods.

"Why don't you want me to see Grace?" he asked as they walked up the steps.

"Because I was over there earlier, and she's resting."

Resting? Grace?

"Is she okay? Banks said she fainted yesterday, but it was the heat."

"Oh, yes," Avril said, sarcastically. "All women fall over when the temperature hits ninety."

"Are you saying she's sick?" he wasn't in the mood for banter.

"David was here, but he's gone." Her tone said 'gone' might be permanent.

He tried not to be hopeful about her non sequitur, but his heart lifted a little. "Idiot," he said under his breath.

"They're a *pair* of idiots," she said and squeezed his arm before letting him go. "Try not to make it a threesome. Come on in and have a drink with me."

When they reached the kitchen, she sank onto a cafe chair with a red plastic seat, told him to find something good, and bring her a double. He thought it was too late for her to have coffee, but water seemed inadequate. A box of Lipton tea bags sat on the counter, neatly answering his dilemma.

"I bought that tea for Grace," she said when he filled the kettle. "There's some bourbon in the sideboard. Far right side on the bottom."

"None for me. It's only — " he looked at his watch, surprised to find it was well after eight. "Oh, why not." He found a small juice glass, poured himself an inch of bourbon, and then saw Avril glaring at him.

"I meant for *me*," she said. "But, please join me."

He got another glass and splashed a bit of bourbon in it only to have Avril switch with him and drink the larger portion with one swallow.

"Better," she said and burped.

He laughed in spite of himself.

"You take things too seriously, Lee. It's just life." After a second, she added, "And death. And in either case, bourbon helps."

He swallowed the scant ounce he'd poured for her and was pleased to find her watching him in her usual hawkish way. Some color had returned to her face, and he decided he could call the bourbon medicinal.

"There's ham in the fridge, and a half a brick of cheddar. Get that and some gherkins, and let's have dinner."

"No veggies?" He teased as he got up to do her bidding.

"Damn things tear up my insides, so I puree them and drink a glass in the morning. It's delightful if you'd like a sample. And yes, I'm fine, just old, so don't even get into it."

He put the bourbon away, assembled the 'dinner,' and they ate in a companionable silence for a few minutes.

"You see anyone next door since we talked this morning?" he asked when her eating slowed. She'd had enough food to absorb the alcohol, he reasoned, but he got them each a glass of water.

"Bring the cookie jar, too," she said before answering his question. When he'd complied, she took an oatmeal cookie and said, "No one's been over there unless they came while I was at Grace's. How's it going with Ashley?"

Bourbon, pork, and sugar worked wonders for Avril, McNamara thought. She had perked right up while he was floundering for an answer. He decided what the hell and answered her. "Ashley isn't the one."

"Are you ready to find The One? I mean another One, of course."

He smiled at the old woman across from him, grateful there was someone left who knew his heart. "It seems so," he answered.

"Grace isn't Meredith, Lee," she said, referring to his late wife.

"We were talking about Ashley."

"And now I'm not. You're a man. A good man, but nonetheless, you're a man, and you have no idea what you're doing."

Hard-pressed to come up with a response, McNamara sat back and let himself be lectured. Like he had a choice.

"Meri was a good woman," she said. "She was cut from the same cloth you are. Grace is different. A good person, but not for you. She'll lead you on a wild ride, and I'm not sure either of you will survive."

"I'm not discussing Grace," he said, knowing he was wasting his breath.

"You don't have to. Just listen to me." Avril waved one of her semi-lethal index fingers at him. "She's refusing to believe that she loves you, and she's bound up in something big right now. David stormed out of there today, and if she's lucky, he'll stay gone. But you have to know that girl's never been able to recognize her good fortune. It's a curse with those Delaneys. Always in the middle of something and trying to fix everything. She can't leave anything alone, and she'll drive you crazy with her constant crusades and causes that she calls clients. Nothing she ever settles on is exactly right for her, and I'm afraid that will include you. I'm worried about both of you."

McNamara said he understood and kissed her cheek before telling her not to worry and taking his leave. He behaved as he always had, but Avril knew he hadn't absorbed a word she'd said after 'she loves you.'

Chapter Thirty-Four

McNamara arranged for a search warrant and coordinated the details with the MSP. On Sunday morning, while the Overtons were waking up in an Easton hotel, search specialists from the MSP and the Kingston County Sheriff's Office joined McNamara and Banks in going through the family's home. They entered the house at seven, their actions closely monitored by the property owner who watched from her side porch.

Brixson had given up his Saturday evening to complete Felicia's autopsy and confirm the cause of death. Among the first items to be bagged for testing were all the pillows and bed linens.

The women and children had left in a hurry the day before, leaving clothes, unmatched shoes, and less favored toys scattered in a haphazard trail from the bedrooms to the front door. Relegated to outdoor duty, Banks spent the first hour sulking as he photographed and bagged toys, an assortment of flip-flops, and the occasional Lego block. His instructions were to catalog and collect anything unusual or out of place outside the house. He spent some time deciding whether shoes and toys should be considered out of place, but this only earned him a sharp rebuke from Marbury, who was in charge of the outside search area.

Red-faced and furious, Banks picked up speed and photographed everything he could see. He was so intent on looking as professional as the state officers that he almost missed the bright pink plastic phone case. One of the drop-proof, water-resistant kind that might have survived the events that landed it under a leafy nandina and within range of the sprinkler system.

He called out, "Found something," then stood back and let the MSP techs do their thing. When McNamara joined him, he accepted the Chief's 'good work' without comment.

"That solves one mystery," McNamara said after he'd conferred with the tech. "Hallie Overton couldn't produce her cell phone when I asked to see it."

A veteran of dropped, dunked, and sat-upon

phone emergencies, Banks itched to attempt the resurrection. Instead, he followed McNamara to the rear of the house where they watched as another team emerged from the back door carrying sealed boxes and bags.

His pleasure at making the find vanished and was instantly replaced by worry for Hallie. He might not be a good police officer — sometimes not even a competent one — but he felt sure she was innocent. He couldn't explain the gut reaction he'd had when interviewing her, but Banks knew whatever had happened to Felicia had also swept Hallie up and dropped her in dangerous territory.

He'd connected with the girl, and understood her yearning for order, for things to be *right*. He'd felt the same at her age. He recognized her determination to be the fixer, and he knew disappointment was waiting for her. Had already found her. Whatever was left of her family when this current soap opera was over, Hallie would never be the same. None of them would, but he worried Hallie might lose the most. Her childhood would be over, and the sense of rightness that had driven her would be crushed under the weight of adult reality.

No one gets out free.

"What?" McNamara was looking at him with a quizzical expression. "Who doesn't?"

Banks shook his head, embarrassed to have spoken his last thought out loud. "It's nothing," he said and was saved from further questioning by a shout from inside the house.

Once blood was discovered on clothes in the closet of the room where Felicia died, the intensity of the search ramped up. More officers were called in, and luminal lights were used to sweep every inch of the house. Closets were emptied, and drawers that had been sight checked were now unloaded in order to scan each item they contained. Furniture cushions, curtains, and loose rugs were flipped, unhung, and shaken out, but nothing more of interest was found.

"Somebody in that house was stoned or stupid or both," Banks said when he and McNamara met up as the search teams dispersed.

"And you're making this determination based on what?" McNamara asked.

"Finding the dead person's bloody clothes on the closet floor?"

"You don't know they belonged to Felicia."

"But, they were in her closet," Banks protested.

"No, they weren't." McNamara had no patience for Banks' argumentative attitude. "I thought you were in the interviews with Marbury yesterday."

"I was — oh. Felicia took Hallie's room."

"Hallie's room, Hallie's closet. The clothes could be hers, too. Or they might belong to anyone who lives there. We can't make assumptions with that many people in the house." They needed to get back to work, but McNamara let the next few seconds pass in silence.

When Banks started again, he spoke more deliberately. "Someone either put the bloody clothes in the closet because she didn't consider them incriminating evidence or because she did and wanted them found where they were."

McNamara was impressed, but only said, "A woman?"

"You see any men living here? Hell, yeah, the person who dumped those clothes is a woman, and I think it's Whitney Overton."

"Why?" McNamara was astounded that somehow, despite Banks' jackrabbit reasoning, they had reached the same conclusion.

"Simple," Banks said, somewhat mollified. "She's always the loudest. Whitney, I mean. She's the one who jumps in to correct people. Interrupts them when she thinks they're getting off track, tries to explain what they really meant to say when she thinks they're looking bad, that kind of thing. The opposite of her sister. Melanie is all fluttering hands and hugging herself, and God almighty the crying. The woman is a leaky faucet, isn't she?"

McNamara said nothing but was still listening, so Banks plunged on.

"Heath didn't abide by the rules. They had a game plan, but he and Felicia ditched it, and Melanie and Whitney were left looking like fools. Maybe they could have saved the TV series, maybe not. The point is, Heath and his new wife —Jesus, can you imagine any man wanting *three*? Anyway, the newlyweds did what they wanted to, and the family be damned.

"Now, Whitney might have accepted and adjusted if she'd been the only one hurt, but she wasn't. The whole family was hurt. And because she's a fixer, a protector, Whitney couldn't let that stand."

"What do you think she did?" McNamara asked.

"Felicia killed the dream, so Whitney smothered her and somehow had bloody clothes and…." None of it made sense, and Banks didn't want to say anything else wrong. But McNamara was waiting for an answer, and once more Banks was coming up short. "I don't know," he mumbled, defeated.

"Me either," McNamara said. "Let's go find out."

Chapter Thirty-Five

Grace's only goal for Sunday morning was to eat. The pounding pressure in her head and nausea had both evaporated overnight, and she wanted to eat the French toast and bacon she'd just made.

Niki appeared as she took the first bite. "Thought I smelled something good."

Grace got another plate and forked half the stack of toast onto it and added a piece of bacon. She handed it over and said, "I haven't eaten anything substantial in ages, please let me get this down."

"Go ahead and eat. I'm not stopping you."

Niki pulled a stool to the opposite side of the kitchen island and made a show of reading her phone as she ate. Before her arrival, the little apartment at the top of Delaney House had been a haven. Now it was becoming uncomfortable.

Grace got up and nudged the AC control down a notch. "I'm not up to talking about anything negative, okay? With everything that's happened this week and David's visit last night, I need some peace and quiet."

"Jeez. Quit yammering at me and eat. It's not like I came up this early just to ruin your Zen, but we have to make a decision on the furniture this morning, and we have to get a photographer to do the shots today."

Grace groaned. "After I eat. I mean it."

"Why? It's not bad, I promise. The gallery owner decided to ship whatever we don't take to a show in St. Louis, and he wants to pick everything up tomorrow, that's all."

"Easy," Grace said around a mouthful of food. "The only pieces I like enough to buy are the sideboard and the dining room table. How much are they?"

"Not the settees for the parlors and the writing desk? What about the — "

"The sideboard and table?" Grace repeated, recognizing a misdirection when she heard it. "How much?"

"Twenty-two."

"*Thousand?*"

"For the sideboard. The table is only ten." Niki's shoulders went back, and she sat very, very straight on her stool. "They're authenticated pieces and are priced very well. We could sell them for more at any time."

Grace tried to force down another bite. If she spoke now, it would not go well.

Niki raced into her sales pitch, words tumbling out as she tried to stem the explosion she saw coming. "I know it's a big number, but we need to furnish the common areas in keeping with the house and the image we're selling. Now, I also found a solution for the shortage in the decorating account. We haven't been taking in to account function rentals. I'm working on brochures to send out to local businesses and groups advertising the first floor for meetings and party venues. The brochures will only run a couple thousand and — "

"Stop. For the love of all that's holy, please stop."

Grace's headache was thumping again. Six months ago, she'd had one enormous house she couldn't sell. Today she had a half-furnished inn and a cousin for a partner in a business she didn't want. All because she hadn't said 'no' at the outset to the one person she considered to be her family. She carefully placed her knife and fork on the table beside her mostly full plate and tried not to panic.

"I knew you'd be okay when I explained it all," Niki said as she dug into her breakfast. "And if you want to stay here for a while when you get back from Europe, you can share the apartment with me while you decide what to do next. It'll be fun."

Grace pushed her plate away. The toast was a greasy mess, and the bacon fat was revolting. She smoothed out the paper towel she'd used as a napkin and draped it over the food.

This seemed to get Niki's attention. "Jeez, you weren't kidding. I guess I should have let you eat before pouring all this out. You should go to bed."

"A bit late for you to catch on, don't you think?" Grace's rational side was saying 'slow down' and other warnings that her emotions ignored. She grabbed both plates, and dumped the still fragrant food into the trash can. "Happy?" she yelled and ran for the bathroom.

"Why didn't you tell me?" Niki asked. The plastic stick lay between them on the bedspread, its bright blue plus sign telling her what Grace couldn't. "I'm so sorry."

"About which part?" Grace removed the wet washcloth from her forehead and tried to lay back on the pillows, but sat up again when her stomach twisted. She wiped her face and gestured to the stick. "Or about pushing me out of my own house? Or about being so damned insensitive, I could die right here and you'd still be spending my money?"

Niki flinched, but reached over and took Grace's hand. "All of it," she said. "I was just so excited about the inn and about us having a business. I'll return all the furniture, and I promise, promise, promise the inns will be successful. I'll repay every penny of your money and help you sell this place in a couple of years if you still want to give up a gold mine."

Grace didn't respond, but she didn't pull her hand away, either.

Niki looked at the stick with its life-altering message. "How do you feel about this? Has it ever happened to you before?"

"No."

"Me, either. It's just not fair when you're this close to going to Paris. But I know a good doctor. You don't need to tell David. It can all be over in a few days."

Niki spent a long time listening first to retching and then to water running. She'd washed the dishes, remade the bed, and answered a dozen emails when Grace finally joined her in the sitting room.

"You'd do that?" she asked without preamble. "Get it taken care of and not tell Aidan?"

"Yes. No. I mean," Niki took a deep breath. "I made tea. Sit."

Grace sat on the edge of the love seat as if poised to run. Niki could see the tremor in her hands from ten feet away. She brought a half-full mug of Earl Grey to her cousin and said, "Sip it slowly. I put lemon in to settle your stomach."

"It's going to take more than lemon," Grace said and set the mug down. "Tell me what you'd do. The truth, Nik. There's only one answer for me, so you won't influence my decision."

Niki was scared, and she felt guilty. She didn't have a truth to tell on the subject of pregnancy, and if she said the wrong thing, Grace might go off again. "I think it would depend on when you asked me. I've never wanted children. Look at the train wreck our family is. I'd never subject an innocent baby to my parents."

Wrong, wrong, wrong. Maybe Grace wanted the baby. She regrouped and tried again. "But, Aidan's good with kids. He's a goof-ball and everything, but he's a good man. I might have his baby, but I wouldn't marry him." She didn't know what else to do, so she shut up, and they sat in silence.

After a while, Grace said, "I'm going to DC tomorrow to see my doctor."

"What about David?"

Grace shook her head. "I told him yesterday. He needs time to take it all in. And drop it, okay? Keep this to yourself until I tell you otherwise. I'm serious, Nik. Nothing to anyone. Can you do it? If you can't, tell me now."

"I'll go with you tomorrow, and I won't tell a soul."

"No, I can handle this."

"Yes, you can, but you're not going to. You have me." Niki stood, for once able to look down at her cousin as she spoke. "You're not alone, Gracie."

Grace closed her eyes and leaned back on the sofa. Minutes later, Niki was saying, "Here, try this."

"Cinnamon?"

"Basically, just hot sugar water with cinnamon. See if you can keep a few sips down."

After a mug of the cinnamon water and a piece of toast, Grace had to admit she felt better.

"I'm making a pitcher of this," Niki said. "Keep sipping it all day. It's the most important thing, staying hydrated, so concentrate on that. The sugar keeps your energy level up a little, too. Of course, you've got to eat real food whenever you can."

"You know all of this because, why?"

"Always the helpful girlfriend, never the preggo one," Niki laughed, then winced. "Sorry. I'm nervous, and the wrong things keep popping out. At least I can make a mean hot water, huh?"

Grace's phone chimed, ending the conversation, and not just for the moment. Whitney Overton didn't waste words easing into the reason for her call.

"Can you come to me?" Whitney's voice was steady, but an octave higher than usual. "I'm in Easton, in a shopping center off the bypass. I'm parked in the Target parking lot near a bank and — "

"I know where it is," Grace said. "What's happened?"

"Something bad. I think the police are looking for me."

Chapter Thirty-Six

Armed with a sleeve of saltines and a bottle of Niki's cinnamon-sugar water, Grace raced down Route 50 toward Easton. The distraction from her immediate personal problems seemed to banish the remaining tendrils of discomfort, but did nothing to push the baby out of Grace's thoughts.

God Almighty, a baby.

Tomorrow she'd be driving in the opposite direction on her way see a doctor who would tell her what she already knew. She was pregnant. She'd gone through her calendar, matching memory to dates, and realized she was at least two months along. How could she be so blind to something so obvious?

Unless it was menopause. She'd never had

regular cycles, and now she had early onset menopause. Or a disease. A disease that made two pregnancy tests read positive and caused her to throw up everything she ate.

Her mind twisted back and forth between the possible reasons for her symptoms and David's initial reaction to the stick with the bright blue stain.

Whose is it? She would never forgive him.

She was a mess from top to bottom, and it was in this fine state that she reached MD 322, the short bypass that rounded the western side of Easton.

When she found the green van in the Target parking lot, she barely had time to pop the locks before Whitney was at the BMW's passenger door. Once inside, her client said 'thank God,' in a small voice and closed her eyes.

"Take it easy. It's going to be okay," Grace said. Trite words which were rarely true, but saying anything else seemed cruel.

"No, it isn't," Whitney said. "Were you followed? I forgot to tell you to be careful about that."

"Who would follow me? The police?"

Whitney nodded. "A patrol car just drove through the parking lot. Look, Mel and I talked all night about what to do next. We decided to take the family home to Atlanta. I was on the way to Mallard Bay to pack but didn't get far before Mel called and told me the police were at the house. I was afraid to go back to the hotel in case they were there, too."

"And how did Melanie know that?" Grace asked, wondering why she didn't know it herself. News of police at the Overton house would have flown all over Mallard Bay in minutes. Had she missed any obvious signs as she left town? She'd heard about Baby Brain, the muddled mental state that sabotaged pregnant women. Did she have it already?

Or maybe she had Alzheimer's. With morning sickness.

"Avril Oxley called Hallie. They're friends, of sorts. I understand Avril's a friend of yours, too, but she's been a royal pain to Mel and me. Now I guess I owe her an apology. I would have driven right up to the house and been arrested on the spot."

Grace checked her phone and saw three calls and a voice mail from Avril that must have come in while she was barricaded in the bathroom.

"Why?" she asked. "On what charge?"

Whitney dug into a diaper bag, which was doing double duty as her purse. "Do you take checks? Or, I can make a call and transfer the money to your firm. The point is, I want to give you another retainer. I want to be sure you'll continue to represent our family, all of us. How do we do that?"

"What happened, Whitney?"

"It's bad, and that's all I can say until you agree to represent us no matter what happens."

Grace grabbed the bottle of cinnamon water and sipped it, buying herself a moment to assess the situation. "Okay. Here's what I can do. You and Melanie and your children are my clients already. The first retainer you gave me still has a credit balance. You don't owe me anything right now. I may not be the best attorney for you. I'm working for Mr. Mosley temporarily for about another month, and then I'll be away for a while. Mr. Mosley isn't taking new clients. If I can help you, I will, and if I can't, I'll help you get new representation. Everything you've told me will remain confidential, even when I'm not representing you. Does that sound fair?"

A greenish-blue vein pulsed at Whitney's temple. Dark circles under eyes testified to her sleepless night, and she clutched the diaper bag like a life vest. Her eyes were shiny with tears, but unlike her sister, she held them in. "You're a nice person, you know that?" she said. "We could have been friends. I would have liked that."

Touched, Grace said, "I'll do all I can for you, and I won't leave you without good legal representation. And when this is all over, we'll be friends."

"I don't think so." Whitney reached for Grace's hand. "I may have killed Felicia."

"May have?"

"That's the first thing you need to do. Find out how she died. If she didn't overdose, I smothered her, and I'm pretty sure the police know."

~

"She ruined everything," Whitney said. "You saw how Felicia was, but Friday night was unreal. All she talked about was keeping the family away from you and the police so that Lightning Strike would still work with us. She kept talking about doing the show without Heath, and the children were getting upset."

A small sports car took the turn into the bank parking lot too fast, causing horns to blare and making both Grace and Whitney jump.

"I'm so scared, everything makes me flinch," Whitney said. "I've never been as angry as I was with Felicia. In our real life, we're happy people. In Atlanta, I had the life I always wanted — a big family, children, and Mel was as happy, too. She's actually a lot of fun most of the time. Heath was sweet to me. He and Mellie were closer as a couple, but Heath and I loved each other, too. The three of us were a team. I never thought either of them was unhappy. If we'd had enough money for the lifestyle they wanted, Heath would never have wanted a third wife and a TV show." She scanned the lot, then sighed again. "This is so hard."

Grace had let her talk without interrupting, but now she said, "If time is as short as you say, let's skip to the part that will concern the police."

Whitney cleared her throat and sat up. "It's been such a horrible week. Heath. The fire. Mellie slapping Felicia in your office. The awful fights and yelling. That's not us. We're… we're *peaceful.*"

"What happened Friday night?"

"Felicia had been horrible all afternoon, but after dinner, she completely lost her grip. She pulled Mel and me out onto the porch to yell at us again about the fight with you. I couldn't believe she'd taken Hallie with her when she followed you out of town." She gave Grace a tired smile. "You're a rock star in that kid's eyes, by the way."

Grace felt her cheeks warm. "Oh, good. That's the sort of influence I want to have on the next generation. What happened after that?"

"I said I'd have called the police on her, too, if I'd been you. I had to end the argument because the kids could hear us, and we needed to get the littles into bed. Mel and I rounded them up and left Felicia downstairs. We thought Hallie was with the big kids, but she waited until we left to confront Felicia. She told Felicia to leave for good, or she'd tell us that Felicia had been with Heath when he'd rented the car in Baltimore." Whitney reached out and patted Grace's shoulder. "Is that why you left those messages on Friday afternoon?"

"Yes." Grace was glad to have it off her chest. "I'd hoped Hallie hadn't overheard that part of my argument with Felicia. Yesterday wasn't the right time, but I need to tell Chief McNamara soon, and I wanted you and Melanie to hear it from me. I'm sorry."

"For what? That Felicia lied, or that Heath did? So many horrible things have happened, I don't even know where to rank that one on the scale of awfulness."

"I hate to add to the list," Grace said. "But now the police can't question Felicia. She said she knew where Heath was, but she wouldn't say where."

"That sounds like her," Whitney said. "You may as well tell him, the Chief, I mean. What if it wasn't Felicia? They need to find out if there's a fourth woman."

Grace drank her cinnamon water and didn't

respond. She'd never felt less like judging anyone else's craziness.

It took several minutes for Whitney to pull herself together, but eventually, she said, "Back to Friday night. We heard Felicia and Hallie yelling all the way upstairs. When we came down, we saw Hallie doubled up and Felicia standing over her. Felicia said Hallie had fallen and bitten her lip and thrown up. While we were taking care of Hallie and getting all the kids back in bed, Felicia slipped upstairs and locked herself in Hallie's bedroom."

"Why would she do that?"

"Because after she tried to spank Faith for ruining her clothes, I'd told her if she touched one of the children again, I'd kill her. When Hallie could talk, she told us Felicia had hit her in the stomach. Hard. And she also told us why. I wanted to call the police, but Mel wanted to handle Felicia without publicity. We were afraid to say anything yesterday when the police were there, and later it didn't seem important anymore."

The car was heating up, but Grace turned on the air conditioning instead of opening the windows. The parking spaces on either side of them were empty, but she wasn't taking a chance on someone walking by and overhearing whatever was about to come out of her client's mouth.

Whitney angled the side air vent to her face before continuing. "It was all up to me, as usual. If I didn't stop her, Felicia would ruin our lives and turn Rebecca and Sean into mini versions of herself. After everyone was asleep, I went into Hallie's room to have it out with Felicia, but she didn't wake up, and I saw the pills on the table beside the bed. I hoped she'd overdosed, but I couldn't take a chance, so I picked up a pillow, and you know the rest."

Grace's mind raced with the implication of Whitney's words. "Where was Melanie during all this?"

"I told you. They were all asleep. You believe me, right? And you'll do it? Find out if I killed her, and take me to the police, so I can confess? I mean, if I need to."

"Let me think for a minute. There's no rush. If the police show up here, we'll deal with it."

"No. The sooner the police get the answers they want, the sooner we can take the kids away from here."

There was no dissuading Whitney. Grace drove to Mallard Bay trying to remember everything she knew about arrest procedures for violent crimes. When she was parked behind her office, she turned to Whitney and said, "Who unlocked the door?"

"What?" Whitney looked dazed.

"You said Felicia locked herself in Hallie's bedroom. Then you said you went in the room. Who unlocked the door?"

After a moment, Whitney smiled and reached out to clutch Grace's hand. "Thank you so much," she said. "That could've really messed me up."

Chapter Thirty-Seven

Whitney accepted her offer of tea but said no to food, leaving Grace with no way to nibble on the saltines without an explanation.

"Sorry. This is rude, but I haven't eaten. These keep me going."

Whitney smiled. "I know. Mel guessed right away, but I didn't agree with her until yesterday. Congratulations. When are you due?"

Grace froze, a saltine halfway to her mouth. "What? No. I just didn't get breakfast."

"Please. Between us, Mel and I've been pregnant nine times. I'm a novice compared to her, though, and if she says you're having a baby, you are."

Grace was saved from having to respond

when the rear entrance buzzer sounded. She found Mac on the back stoop.

"We need to talk," he said without preamble.

"I'm with a client. Can it wait?"

"Sorry. No. I need her, too."

"Ten minutes."

He nodded but said, "If she tries to run, I'm arresting her."

Whitney listened to Grace's instructions and answered her questions without verbal wandering or embellishment. If she had to have a client confess to murder, Grace was glad it was Whitney. Melanie would have sobbed the entire time asking, 'why me?' But then, Melanie might not have been lying.

By the time they faced McNamara, Whitney was resolute. She hadn't argued when Grace accused her of covering for someone else but had sat silently, wearing a sad smile. When McNamara read her Miranda rights and asked Whitney if she understood them, she looked him in the eye and said, "I do."

"You weren't entirely honest in the statement you gave yesterday," McNamara said.

Grace shook her head at Whitney.

McNamara said, "She needs to cooperate. Certain information came to light in the autopsy."

"Then ask a question. She can't read your mind."

McNamara nodded and turned back to Whitney. "Who smothered Felicia Jones-Overton?"

It went quickly after that.

~

McNamara couldn't remember anyone ever thanking him for arresting them, but Whitney came close. She looked so relieved, he thought she'd have hugged him if he hadn't been putting handcuffs on her. She confessed, talking right over Grace's objections.

The arrest had the added benefit of keeping one of the sister wives out of the way, even for a few hours, as they investigated Heath Overton's death. The situation seemed agreeable to everyone except Whitney's attorney.

"What are you charging her with?" Grace demanded as she followed him from the booking area into an empty conference room in the State Police Barracks in Easton.

"Your client fell all over herself confessing to smothering the woman who'd broken up her family."

"I was there, Mac! You could see she's half out of her mind with worry over her husband

and would confess to anything to keep the police away from her family."

McNamara thought Grace looked sick again. Sick and angry, a combination he was learning could be dangerous. He didn't want to think about how she'd react when she heard the information he wasn't sharing on the missing husband. He'd decided when she finally went off to France, he was going on a long fishing trip. Alone.

She yanked a small laptop out of her leather tote before slinging the bag onto the table. "For God's sake, listen to the tape of your conversation with her. She confessed to killing Felicia and then asked you how she died!"

"That was odd," McNamara agreed. "Good thing she has legal counsel."

"Funny, funny man. You show me the coroner's report that says conclusively, beyond any doubt, Felicia didn't overdose on sleeping pills and was alive when the smothering happened, and I'll agree you have cause to arrest someone for something, but it won't be Whitney Overton. She's — " Grace stopped and tried to look engrossed in her laptop screen. Mac had made her so mad she'd almost done just what she'd forbidden her client to do.

"She's protecting someone?" McNamara supplied in a helpful tone.

She pounded the laptop keys as if they had offended her. "It won't take me long to get her out of here, and what will you have gained?"

He didn't answer because she didn't stop talking.

"You could have at least had the courtesy to contain this farce to Mallard Bay instead of dragging her in here. The press will send you a thank you note, I'm sure."

"The Easton Barracks serves Kingston County, too, as does the Talbot County Department of Corrections," he said, telling her what she knew very well, and winding her up further. He wanted to keep her here and occupied until the techs were finished at the Overton house.

"She's not going to jail. I'll petition for a release for a medical evaluation."

"Which can be done in jail."

"What else has happened?" she demanded.

"Undoubtedly a lot, but you'll have to be specific. I'm not a mind reader." Throwing her own comments back at her didn't go over well. He'd dropped the artificial politeness and stood, arms crossed, waiting to end the argument. He hadn't expected to fool her for long, but another hour would have been nice.

"Let's start again," she said. "I am the family attorney, Mac. *All* of the family. That means everyone named Overton living in Mallard Bay, in case you're about to split hairs about the definition of family."

As if on cue, her cell buzzed. Even standing four feet away, McNamara could hear Melanie's squawking. Grace glared at him and jabbed a forefinger in the direction of the door. He'd barely cleared it when she slammed it behind him.

He checked his messages and made a call, which led to two other calls. While he and Grace had been wrangling over Whitney, the medical examiner's office had issued updates on the autopsies, and the search of the Overtons' house had wrapped up.

Saliva and mucus on a pillow at the foot of Felicia's bed and bruising inside her nostrils confirmed homicide by smothering. Whitney's confession wrapped up that investigation, or would if she proved to be telling the truth. He wouldn't admit it to Grace, but if she believed Whitney was lying, he'd have to consider it, too.

The State Police were at the hotel with Melanie, delivering the news of the John Doe and asking for DNA samples from the children.

Grace had a real problem now, he thought as he walked back to the holding cells to check on Whitney. Even a very good attorney couldn't be in two places at one time. It would be interesting to see which of her clients got her.

~

Cyrus Mosley, Esquire, did not do criminal work, and on the rare occasions when he had to attend to a client facing the police, he was off-stride and irritable. But despite his determination not to represent the Overtons, it took Melanie less than a minute to win him over.

First, there were the tears in her big blue eyes. The trembling of her slight body and delicate hiccuping completed the picture Mosley saw when he arrived to find her huddled with Hallie in a small conference room of their Easton hotel. Melanie didn't argue when he introduced himself as her attorney, and the MSP detectives looked relieved to see him, which in his long experience was never a good sign.

Mosley's last century manners and Melanie's 'save me' personality connected like magnets. Hallie wisely followed her mother's lead and stayed quiet while Mosley absorbed the news that Whitney had been arrested for murder, and Heath Overton's wedding ring had been found on an unidentified corpse.

In short order, Mosley dispatched the detectives by promising to keep the family available and had the Overtons on their way to the Egret Hotel in Mallard Bay. An hour after that, Melanie and the children were settled into the two suites on the top floor of the venerable old hotel, and outside security was engaged to make sure no one breached their privacy without a warrant. A private duty nurse arrived to serve as a nanny, and the hotel's room service began making regular runs to the larger suite's dining room.

The success of her decision to pair Mosley with Melanie was a relief for Grace, but she still had her hands full with Whitney. She broke the news about the John Doe as gently as she could, but Whitney's silent grief was so profound, all Grace could think to do was hold her hand. After a few minutes, Whitney gathered herself, and when she did, she was more determined than ever to take responsibility for Felicia's murder.

All things being equal, she'd have left Mosley with Whitney, which on the surface only involved keeping her quiet and riding out the arraignment process. But stopping Whitney from confessing to everyone who came near her wasn't easy, and there was the unpleasant matter of Grace's raging nausea. She tracked Lily down and offered her triple time to pick up the suit Grace kept at the office and bring it to the Easton Barracks. Once she'd changed from the jeans and tee she'd thrown on that morning, she was at least dressed to handle a crisis.

"We're a fine pair," she said to Whitney as she reentered the small room where she and Lily were conferencing with their client. "You won't stop incriminating yourself, and I can't stay out of the bathroom."

"Still insisting you aren't pregnant?" Whitney asked. "Keep sipping that water. You're retaining some of it, and that'll help. But you should see a doctor."

With a pointed look at Lily, Grace said, "It's a twenty-four-hour bug."

"It's a nine-month bug," Whitney said. "I'm guessing you have about seven months to go."

"God help me," Grace groaned and briefly lowered her head to the table before remembering where she was and jerking upright again.

"Are you sure we aren't being recorded?" Whitney asked.

Grace mustered the best 'do not lie to me' glare she could manage. "Why? Are you about to confess to being on the grassy knoll in Dallas?"

"No. I'm about to tell you the truth."

"The truth-truth, or your latest fairytale?"

"You're supposed to be my lawyer and believe me." Whitney looked at Lily and said, "You, too."

"I believe we've established that I'm not on my A-game," Grace said. She knew she was in no shape to assess her client's behavior or determine how to help her. She might have another five minutes before she had to run to the restroom again. "My legal spidey-sense is a little woozy right now, and I refuse to act on anything you say that isn't in your best interest. Don't spin another load of crap that you think will confuse the police and stop them from finding out what happened to Felicia."

"Please try to understand," Whitney pleaded. "If they don't have a suspect in Felicia's death, they may take the children from us. Even removing them temporarily would be terrible. They need their mothers, but one of us has to make the sacrifice. If the police believe me, they'll leave the family alone."

"You're saying you didn't do it?" Grace asked.

"If she died from an overdose, no. If she was smothered, you'll get me off."

"Now wait a minute — "

"I could hear you yelling at Chief McNamara. You'll save me, I know it. But I'll cast enough doubt with my confession to make them think twice about charging anyone else in our family."

Grace reread Whitney's statement. "You're saying you smothered Felicia."

"Yes."

"But in your statement to the police yesterday morning you said you went in to wake her. Why would you do that if you'd smothered her?"

"I lied."

A knock on the interview room door interrupted them. A young officer whose shiny brass nameplate said 'DFC Blanc' announced that they had fifteen minutes before the room was needed. Upset at hearing she'd be returning to the holding cell, Whitney demanded that Grace do something.

"I am doing something," Grace said as she stood up. "I'm leaving."

"You can't. Please," Whitney said.

"You've insisted that I represent your entire family. Why would you do that if you were the only one who was guilty? I've done all I can here if you won't tell me the truth."

The stubborn set of Whitney's face said any further argument was a waste of time. She was determined to save her family by condemning herself, and Grace knew nothing she said would make a difference.

Chapter Thirty-Eight

Grace decided if Whitney wouldn't tell the truth, her best move was a plea of temporary insanity. She spent the drive from Easton to Mallard Bay trying to decide how to lay the groundwork. When she and Lily arrived at the office, they met with Mosley and compiled their notes and information into an unwieldy narrative with more holes than a sieve. The only good news was that Whitney's arraignment wouldn't take place until Monday afternoon.

Mosley didn't react well to learning she would be out of the office in the morning on a personal matter. Lily had been quiet since witnessing Whitney's announcement of the pregnancy, and Grace was in no mood for sharing confidences. She left them both and went home, where she fell into bed and slept straight through the night.

A chronic insomniac, she grudgingly admitted that whatever was wrong with her had some nice side benefits. She managed toast and tea, but even a full application of makeup couldn't make her look like someone who should be on her feet at six a.m.

"Who are you?" she asked the woman looking back at her from the bathroom mirror before re-checking the positive sign on the plastic stick. The third plastic stick in thirty-six hours.

She could wait a few more weeks. See what happened. Early menopause was sounding better and better. Surely that would cause hormones to go haywire. Maybe she'd missed a news report about defective pregnancy tests. Maybe she was delusional.

When Niki knocked on the apartment door ten minutes later, Grace was still in the same spot, and the stick still said 'pregnant'.

"Why aren't you ready?" Niki asked. "We need to leave."

"I told you I'm fine, and I'm going alone."

"Not happening, sweetie. Now, move."

Niki drove, swearing for all she was worth as she negotiated bridge traffic on Route 50 and later on the Washington beltway. By the time they'd reached Arlington, Grace had agreed to switch to an OB/GYN on the Eastern Shore if she was pregnant, which she still insisted wasn't possible.

Two hours later, the return trip was quiet. Traffic was bad leaving Arlington and only increased on the beltway. When they hit a standstill at the Route 50 exit, Niki tried to start a conversation, but Grace lowered her seat back and closed her eyes. She didn't open them until they arrived at Delaney House.

"Okay, give it up," Niki said as she turned off the BMW's ignition. "There's no more road, and you can't ignore me forever."

"I can try." The car seat was comfortable. She could lock the doors as soon as Niki got out.

"You're gonna need a bathroom sometime. I can wait."

"You're a witch." Grace scrambled to get out of the car. "You and my bladder are conspiring against me."

A few minutes later, Niki set a pot of cinnamon tea on the kitchen table. "Think you can keep some down?"

"Let's see if those anti-nausea pills work," Grace said, reaching for a cup of the fragrant tea. Minutes ticked by, Grace reliving every moment in the doctor's office and her cousin, for once, mercifully silent.

Niki had insisted on going into the appointment with her. At the last minute, Grace had pulled her into the doctor's office to hear the exam and ultrasound results. It had been Niki, not David, who'd held Grace's hand as the doctor had explained that yes, she was pregnant, but there were problems. The baby had attached in a precarious location in her uterus and was small for a ten-week pregnancy. There were other issues, too, all of which bounced off Grace, who was too numb to process them. She'd have to wait another month, assuming she was still pregnant in another month, for the tests to give her answers.

The information wouldn't sink in, and she'd argued with the doctor. "I saw it moving," she'd said, waving sonogram photographs that looked like Rorschach tests. "It's possible that everything could work out, and I could have a healthy baby." She didn't know why she'd said that so emphatically. She'd meant it as a question.

Dr. Goulden was a gentle woman whose array of family photos said she might empathize, but would never understand how the unwillingly childless portion of her clientele felt. "Anything's possible," she said. "But not likely. I'm sorry."

Possible, but not likely. The words would not go away.

But now she was back home and needed to refocus. It was a beautiful May afternoon, and even inside the house, she could hear birdsong. It was the kind of day where anything should be possible.

Possible, but not likely.

"I don't have any words," she said to Niki. It was true. She couldn't think of any way to express the weight of this awful turn of events.

"I know," was all Niki said. No arguments, no nagging, no in-your-face 'talk to me'.

Eventually, tea and saltines stayed down, and Grace moved to the old high-back rocker. Niki went upstairs and, finally alone, Grace let the doctor's words sink in.

Possible, but not likely.

Murder investigations aren't scheduled, and a double-booked lawyer is rarely an excuse to delay an arrest. She was on her way back from Easton, where Whitney had been arraigned and delivered to the Talbot County Detention Center when she received a call from Mosley. The news that the State Police wanted to interview Melanie and Hallie wasn't a surprise. While

Mosley agreed to run interference with the police and act as the Overtons' fairy godfather, he'd made it clear that would be the extent of his involvement. He was waiting for her at the Egret.

At the office, she briefly conferred with Lily, outlining her plan for handling their clients to the extent 'handling' was possible. If Lily seemed cold, Grace was grateful no questions were raised about her absence. She was trying hard to wall off the morning's events and just be thankful that the prescription the doctor had given her seemed to work. She was even beginning to feel hungry and found a packet of gingersnaps in her tote bag. Niki to the rescue again.

"Cookie?" Grace said, holding the bag out to Lily.

Without looking up from the briefcase she was packing, Lily said, "No, thanks. Wouldn't want to catch that twenty-four-hour bug you've got."

"You know I haven't got a bug."

"Now that you mention it, I did hear that from a client," Lily said. "Congratulations. We need to get going. Mr. Mosley is waiting."

～

Mosley met them in the lobby of the Egret, looking both tired and exhilarated.

"Ready for some golf, Cyrus?" Grace asked and gave him a hug, surprising herself as much as Mosley, when she found it hard to let go.

"The boys can get along without me for a while," he said, referring to the trio of octogenarian golfers who usually commandeered the lion's share of his days. "The mother and daughter upstairs are a handful, but I don't think they killed anybody. Proving it will be a challenge, but we're up to it."

Breaking her silence, Lily said, "But, sir, you said you wouldn't represent them. And you," she gave Grace a dark look, "are leaving. Are you just going to prop these people up for right now and then drop them? That seems to be the operating plan these days."

Mosley frowned and said, "I don't care for the tone, Lily, but you have a point."

"She has an attitude, is what she has." Grace was ready to drive home her point, but the tea she'd been so grateful to keep down was ordering her to find a restroom. When she returned, she found Mosley and Lily sitting in a quiet corner of the lobby, briefcases open, and papers spread out between them.

Mosley stood as she approached them, and this time, he hugged her. "Congratulations, m'dear," he whispered in her ear. "What can I do to help?"

"She told you." Grace pulled away from him and got a legal pad and pen from her own bag. She was furious with Lily, but this wasn't the time to sort it out. At least the problem of how to tell Cyrus was solved. "We have clients upstairs. This conversation needs to wait, okay?" She made herself look Mosley in the eye until his smile faded and then turned to Lily. "I'd appreciate it if you keep what you think you know to yourself. The Overtons aren't going to be put off by a lawyer with morning sickness, and other than frequent bathroom breaks, I'm fine."

"Now, Grace," Mosley interrupted. "Let's not argue. Your condition — "

"It's a baby, Cy, not a virus. I'm not incapacitated, I just need short breaks at inconvenient times." She told herself it wasn't a lie; she was feeling better. Better and tired of trying to manage other people's feelings. "Who's going to understand the situation better than Melanie Overton? She knew I was pregnant before I did."

Mosley still looked worried but quit arguing. He briefed her on the current situation while Lily kept her head down, reading and sorting the paperwork they were discussing.

"I've arranged for Melanie and Hallie to be

interviewed here," he said. "All I got from Detective Marbury is that results are in on the autopsies, and there are questionable circumstances surrounding both deaths."

"What does that mean?"

Mosley shook his head. "That's all I have. I've told Melanie they're coming, but try to prepare her. Marjorie found a second certified nanny. I hope having two professional caretakers will forestall the removal of the children by Social Services. Unfortunately, if they arrest both Melanie and Whitney, I'm sure that will be the result."

"Have you heard anything to make you think that's imminent?" Grace asked.

"You mean other than Whitney's repeated confessions? Not yet. Melanie says Whitney will fix everything."

Grace groaned. "Any idea what that means?"

"Just wishful thinking, I'm afraid. But in better news, the three older boys arrived this morning. At least for now, they're distracting their mother and sister. They're polite and well-spoken and make a good impression. In fact, all the children seem to be taking their unstable circumstances more or less in stride."

"We should be so lucky with the adults. What about Felicia's children?" Grace asked.

"DSS arrived without notice last night and

collected them. They're together in a temporary foster home until Ms. Jones' parents can be found. Apparently, there are no fathers named on the birth records." Mosley stopped for a breath, and his phone rang before he could continue. His end of the conversation consisted of a string of acknowledgments and a short 'thank you'. He disconnected and motioned for Lily and Grace to move in closer.

"I have a connection in the medical examiner's office. I've never had to call in this particular favor before." He shot Grace a look that said *before you*. "Test results prove that the John Doe in the morgue is Heath Overton. He was killed by a blow to the head that appears to result from a fall. He may have hit the edge of a dumpster."

Grace winced and asked if the fall was accidental.

"Unlikely, according to my source. And while the unfortunate man died on impact, he was also damaged rather severely after death by a trash truck compactor."

Lily accepted the information without flinching, while Grace gave a prayer of thanks for the anti-nausea pills.

"Are you up to telling Mrs. Overton and her daughter?" Mosley asked.

Grace stood and gathered her things. "I'll do

the best I can. But you know they will talk, especially now."

Mosley offered to stay, but Grace insisted she could handle things. She tried to send Lily with him but was secretly glad when she lost that argument. They rode the elevator to the fifth floor in silence.

Chapter Thirty-Nine

Grace expected to find bedlam on the penthouse floor, not the laughter that filtered down the hallway between the two suites. A door burst open, and several small children in swimsuits ran out followed by a tall young man and two shorter boys, each of whom scooped up a giggling child before nodding to Grace and Lily and trotting off to the elevator. An efficient looking woman carrying an armload of flippers, goggles, and bottles of sunblock hurried after them.

"You've met the big boys and Nanny Williams, I see." Melanie held the door for them. Her face had a grayish cast, and there were shadows under her eyes. Grace and Lily followed her into a surprisingly neat living room.

"We can talk over there," Melanie pointed to the far end of the room where a dining table sat next to a window with a view of the town square and the harbor. "I can't possibly describe how grateful we are for your partner's generosity. Lightning Strike officially notified me this morning that as of today, we are off the payroll and the series is canceled." She handed a Fed Ex envelope to Grace. "We do still have money, but not enough to pay for all this and whatever else is coming. We're fortunate that the rent on the house in Mallard Bay was paid in advance. We can stay there until the end of June. The only good thing is Sawyer's gone. No need to be nice to him now."

"How are the children handling everything?" Grace asked, then regretted it when Melanie looked like she would dissolve.

"The three oldest boys know their dad is missing, but not about the man in the morgue and that he might, you know."

"And how are you and Hallie," Grace said, hoping to forestall the hysterics that appeared to be a heartbeat away.

"We're beside ourselves, naturally. Did Whitney stick with her story?"

Grace could feel Lily glaring at her, but there was no time to lecture Melanie on truthfulness.

"Let's handle your police interview now. We'll work out the rest later. Where's Hallie?"

"She's napping — "

"No, I'm not," Hallie said as she came into the room. Slumping into a chair next to her mother, she tossed a credit card onto the table. "When have you seen me nap? I signed up for another SAT prep course. Dad said I had to keep my skills up."

"And I told you we need every penny to make it through the next few months. What part of 'no money' don't you get?"

"What part of 'insurance settlement' do you think I don't understand?" Hallie snapped.

Melanie froze, then glanced at Grace before answering her daughter. "You must have misunderstood everything I said about that. Felicia's policy won't pay out until the insurance company has delayed every way they can. And your father's policy is still up in the air."

"Dad's policy?" Hallie said slowly, looking from her mother to Grace and back again. "You said the police made a mistake. Dad's alive. You promised."

"Oh, of course he's alive," Melanie said. "They're wrong about that poor man they found."

She didn't have time for a soft spin of the truth. Grace said, "Melanie, I'm sorry, but the identification was confirmed. The police will give you the details."

Hallie didn't seem to need a translation of the conversation. She sat motionless as tears rolled down her cheeks. Melanie untwisted herself and put her arms around her daughter.

Grace let them have a moment and then reluctantly interrupted. "Ladies, the police will be here soon. When they leave, one or both of you might leave with them. I'll do everything I can to prevent that from happening, but you have to help me, okay?"

Hallie nodded. Melanie just looked blank. Grace decided it was the best she was going to get.

"Detective Marbury will interview you. You've met her, so that will be helpful. She'll want to ask about Heath, and about Felicia's death. You have to accept that she was murdered. She didn't overdose, and she didn't die in her sleep. The police have arrested Whitney, but they want to know if she had help."

"They suspect *me*?" Melanie gasped.

Grace let that image sink in, then added, "We have to assume so. You and Hallie."

"But why?" Melanie wailed.

Grace hung onto her temper, but she saw Lily roll her eyes.

"The marriage, Felicia's behavior, your arguments, her attack on Hallie — take your pick. If Felicia was the woman who was in Baltimore with Heath, they'll consider it another motive for you to kill her. We don't want to add to their suspicions, so let's discuss what you'll say when they ask you about the night she died."

"Whitney's handling that," Melanie said. "So, we aren't saying anything, right, Hallie?"

Hallie nodded.

Grace tried from a different direction. "They'll ask where you were and what you were doing between the time you last saw Felicia and when you called 911 on Saturday morning."

Melanie didn't hesitate. "We were asleep, right, Hallie?"

"Stop it!" Grace shouted and was glad to see both mother and daughter jump. Even Lily was startled. "This isn't make believe — it's real. What happened to Felicia?"

Melanie hugged herself tighter.

Hallie looked lost for a moment, then said, "Felicia caused all of it. She deserved to die."

"Oh, shut up." Melanie got up and went to the wet bar, took a bottle of vodka out of a cabinet, and poured herself a healthy slug. When she came back to the table, she said, "This is all wrong. Grace, you and this girl," she jerked a thumb at Lily, who gave her a 'no you didn't' look, "work for me, not the other way around. Now, what do I need to do to get my children out of here?"

Grace checked her watch. She'd been talking for a half hour, apparently to no avail. She had to find a way to get her clients through the MSP interview without incriminating themselves. "When the police come, don't speak to any of them unless I tell you to. Not even Chief McNamara or Corporal Banks. Understand?"

Melanie nodded, but Hallie said, "Aidan wouldn't do anything to hurt us."

"No one's trying to hurt you," Grace said. "But the police have to find the person who killed Felicia. Corporal Banks has taken an oath to uphold the law, and yes, *Aidan* would act on anything you said. You're a minor, so unless they have cause to arrest you already, they can't interview you without your lawyer and your parent's permission. They can't make you talk. All you have to do is to be quiet unless I tell you to say something."

"I don't want them to talk to her at all," Melanie said. "I want her out of here. Hallie, go pack your things. You," she pointed at Lily, "can make yourself useful and take her somewhere safe."

"No," Grace said. "Detective Marbury has a

warrant to interview her. We can only control how you handle the questions. You both had motives to kill her, and the police won't stop until they have answers."

"I did it," Hallie said. "Make them leave Mom and Aunt Whitney alone. It was me."

"Oh, don't be ridiculous," Melanie said, dismissively. "Grace, why are the police even bothering with Felicia? She took too many sleeping pills, so anything Whitney did to her is irrelevant."

"But it wasn't Aunt Whitney. Tell the truth, Mom. Tell her how you found me with the pillow — "

"Stop it." Melanie was speaking to her daughter but looking at Grace. "I will not lose a minute's sleep over that woman's death. Do you understand me?"

"I'm not asking you to," Grace said. "I'm simply trying to keep you both from being arrested."

"And Aunt Whitney?" Hallie asked. "She — "

"Not. A. Word." Melanie said. "Remember?"

A knock at the door ended the argument.

Grace rose and looked at the mother and daughter, once again huddled together. "Listen to me. No matter what the police say, wait for me to tell you to answer, then only answer what they ask you. No explanations, no side comments, no questions. Understand?"

"And then it will be okay, right? They'll leave us alone?" Hallie still held onto her mother, but she sounded stronger.

"I don't think so, honey," Melanie said with a gentleness Grace had never seen in her. "You're my big, strong, beautiful girl, and you'll be able to take care of things. Just remember what I told you."

"No, please," Hallie begged. "I can't."

"You'll do fine," Melanie said.

The knocking was getting louder. Grace had no time left to find out what her clients were up to. She gave them a last stern look and opened the door to Marbury and McNamara.

"Come in," she said, moving back and waving them inside. "I'd like to set the ground rules first thing — "

"I did it!" Hallie was on her feet so fast her chair flipped sideways and crashed into a small glass table with a sound like a gunshot. "I killed Felicia."

"No, no! Not like this." Melanie reached for her, but Hallie twisted away.

"I did it," she said again, backing away from her mother but watching the police.

Detective Marbury said, "You have the right to remain silent..."

Hallie heard her mother crying as the detective talked on, Grace's objections rising over the perfunctory words. She also heard her own pulse pounding through her head, a rhythm that had been growing louder the past few days, synching with a litany of her father's last words to her.

Hallie, how could you?

It's your fault.

You never listen.

Help your mother.

"... do you understand these rights as I have explained them to you?" Marbury finished.

Hallie understood everything.

"You can't do this to her," Melanie cried. They were all watching her when Hallie began to run.

"Stop!" Marbury shouted.

The next moments would replay over and over again for all of them in the days and weeks to come. Desiree Marbury would feel the pistol in her hand, her only thought to keep it away from the girl charging toward her. Grace would remember being frozen where she stood, watching Lily moving to stop Hallie. McNamara would see them slam into Marbury, and all of them fly backward into Grace before he could pull her to safety.

Melanie would hear Marbury's gun go off and realize her dreams were over.

Hallie would only remember was that it was all her fault. Again.

Chapter Forty

The police had a field day with a hysterical Melanie and her non-stop talking daughter. Hallie was arrested but released into Melanie's custody the next morning. Court ordered psychological evaluations would be considered in determining the outcome of the charges. Whitney held steadfast in her claim of killing Felicia. She agreed with Grace's proposal of a temporary insanity plea until she learned she'd also have to have a psychological evaluation.

Lily served a one-night sentence in Easton Memorial Hospital. The bullet had gone through her thigh, miraculously doing little damage, but resulting in an impressive bandage and a month's paid leave from an apoplectic Mosley.

Grace met Jake Briard over Lily's hospital

bed. The strain of being polite to her showed plainly on his face. She was making an awkward apology to Lily when they were interrupted by the delivery of a massive bouquet of roses.

Lily read the card out loud — Whitney and Melanie were grateful and sorry and keeping Lily in their thoughts and prayers.

"Those two should save their money," Lily said and sent the flowers out to the nurses' station.

"No roses for marines?" Grace asked, but her attempt to get a smile from Lily fell as flat like every other thing else she'd said. A reference to Lily's military career usually went over well, but all she got in response was a curt 'I don't want anything from them'.

It was easy to leave after that.

Getting Melanie, Hallie, and the children home took the combined efforts of Grace, Mosley, and Avril, who morphed into a grandmotherly person no one recognized as she entertained kids and organized meals.

When Grace and Mosley met with Melanie and Hallie on Tuesday morning, they were all tired, and the Overtons were in varying degrees of denial. Melanie insisted that although Felicia had viciously attacked Hallie, they had nothing to do with her death. Hallie ignored her mother and repeated her confession.

Grace read Whitney's statement out loud to the group. It was short, with just her admission to smothering Felicia. Melanie nodded and said, "Yes. That's what we agreed on."

Hallie immediately contradicted her.

"Can we leave?" Mosley asked Grace. "We can't keep them out of jail forever, and this is hard on my nerves."

Mother and daughter fell silent.

"All right. I'm asking one more time," Mosley said, his voice weak with exhaustion. "Hallie, from the beginning."

"But, I — " Melanie started.

"No," Mosley said, but this time his quivery, old man voice filled the room. "*Hallie.* From the beginning, the truth, please."

"Thank you," Hallie said. "I did it."

The morning ended as it had begun, with three clients, two confessions, one tearful Melanie, and no progress at all.

It was almost noon when Grace returned to a quiet Delaney House. Niki's car was gone. They hadn't talked much, but Niki knew all about the shooting by the time Grace had gotten home the night before. Her only question had been, "Are you okay?" and Grace loved her for it.

Louise greeted her when she opened the front door.

"Is this where you guys have been stashed?" she said as she rubbed the shepherd's ears. "Where's your BFF?"

The scrabbling sounds of toenails on old wood floors heralded the arrival of Leo, who assessed Grace's state and wisely decided his mistress didn't look capable of catching him mid-air. Both dogs accepted her hugs and kisses and followed her to the big kitchen at the back of the house.

The dogs got kibble, and she ate an egg, toast, and hot tea. All of it not only stayed down but felt good as her body absorbed the food. She lingered over the last of the tea and let her mind drift over the memories of yesterday's events.

The doctor's sympathetic words. *Possible, but not likely.*

Hallie's tears as she begged for reassurance that her father was alive.

Marbury's hand moving under her jacket.

Hallie running, crying, *I did it! I did it!*

Lily coming from nowhere, the gun's roar, the screams.

And Mac kneeling beside her on the floor,

cradling her to his chest. Grace had been more stunned by his embrace than by the fall.

She placed a hand over the hollow of her belly. Everything was still okay.

"I'm sorry," she whispered. "I'll be more careful. I promise."

Concern for the baby sat like a cold weight in her heart, something she couldn't push away, yet nothing she could fix. Only time and nature could determine the biggest issue of her life, and no amount of planning, or arguing, or research or tears would change it. She would be careful and hope for the best. But for now, lunch was over, and she had to go back to work.

She drove to the office, keeping her mind firmly on the work ahead of her and away from emotional ramblings.

Mosley met her in the kitchen. After asking if she'd eaten and suggesting she have a glass of milk instead of a cup of tea, he invited her to join him in his office. They had to prepare for a four o'clock appointment with Whitney.

Mosley said, "I had a call from Avril a few minutes ago. Hallie was with her and wants to meet with us alone. Avril is coming in with her."

Grace frowned. "What happened after Hallie and Melanie left this morning?"

"Apparently, a lot."

"What do you think, Cyrus? They look guilty — all of them, frankly."

Mosley said, "Yes, they do, and I think that's because they all are. Of what, I don't know, but each of them is hiding something."

Chapter Forty-One

"I'm old enough to do what I want," Hallie said. "And I don't want to stay in the house with my mother. Miss Avril says I need to make sure you'll still represent me if I move out."

"You're sixteen years and nine months old," Avril said. "You cannot do what you want. Your mother gave permission for you to spend some time with me, and for us to come here."

Hallie looked mutinous but didn't argue.

"And," Avril continued, "what I said was, you should ask about leaving your mother's household. You don't want to make your situation with the police worse than it already is."

"Whatever," Hallie said. Then, after a glance at Avril, she blushed and said, "Sorry. I appreciate your help."

Grace thought the girl looked like Melanie, talked like Whitney, and had flashes of her father's reported charm.

"It's not only that I want to move out," Hallie said. "I'll get there, eventually. Right now, I need a break and some rest. But I also need help with the insurance company. Our big problem is money. I've been reading a lot online, and I'm worried that the policy on Felicia won't pay out. Since Whitney and I confessed, I mean. We'll have to pay a lawyer," Grace and Mosley got a hopeful smile, "and that will eat up a lot of the money we get. Mom says Dad's insurance might not pay on him, either, at least, not right away, and once we've paid you, we won't have much to live on."

"I've told her not to worry about that," Avril said. "You'll wait to get paid, right, Cy?"

Mosley looked nonplussed. "Well, I — "

"Because," Avril cut him off, "if you bring the insurance company to heel and take a percentage of the payout on the policies, you'll be fully compensated, and the Overtons will get their money and can move on."

"And if the insurance is void on both individuals?" Mosley asked.

"Are you saying you can't win?" Her lower jaw jutted out. Avril was in full bulldog mode.

Mosley had been sparring with her for half a

century, and he wasn't cowed. "Hallie and her aunt have both confessed to murdering one of the insureds, and the family may have been the last people to see to the other one. Perry Mason couldn't get those policies to pay out."

"I'm not asking him to," she snapped. "You'll do it, won't you, Grace?"

"Mr. Mosley's been good to us." It was Hallie's quiet voice that ended the argument. "None of this is anyone's fault but ours. Mine, really. If I'd done what I was supposed to even half the time, we wouldn't be in trouble, and Dad would be here."

Grace and Mosley looked at each other. Neither had to look at Avril to know what she was thinking.

"Why don't you tell us what you mean?" Mosley asked with the air of a man who'd just capitulated.

"That's better," Avril said. "I'll wait out in reception and catch up with Marjorie." She stood, stretching herself to her full four feet, eleven inches while giving each of them the stink-eye. "You have a good attorney, Hallie. You can trust her. And him, too."

"No," Hallie protested. "I want you to stay with me."

Avril patted her shoulder and stepped away. "You want to be an adult; this is what it means.

You're responsible for yourself and your decisions. Tell them everything, young lady."

Hallie nodded but said nothing more as Avril left.

"I can call your mother," Mosley offered.

"No." Hallie said, looking troubled. "Why is it that when you get what you want, it's never what you expected it to be?"

"The law of life," Mosley said. "Now, tell me why you wanted to meet without your mother."

"Well, for starters, I'd like to talk without being interrupted."

Mosley's bark of laughter brought a genuine smile from Hallie and reminded Grace of what a charmer the old lawyer could be. The man who wanted no part of the Overtons now seemed on board for the whole ride.

"I have one rule," Mosley said. "No lies. If you lie to me, about anything at all, I'll not represent you nor any member of your family, and neither will Ms. Reagan. Do you agree with my terms, Miss Overton?"

Grace knew she shouldn't be surprised that Hallie actually had to think about her answer, but when she agreed, it was with a firm voice.

"Start talking, m'dear," Mosley said.

"You're going to think I'm terrible."

"No, I won't," Mosley said. "No matter what you've done."

Grace felt a rush of affection for Mosley as she watched Hallie settle down.

"When he left us here, Dad told me to help Aunt Whitney and take care of Mom. He said when everything was underway, he'd let me go to college. I tried, I did, but it was so hard without him. When Dad's around, everything's safe. We have rules, and everyone knows what to do. It's different being here without him."

Hallie sat very straight with her hands clenched. The blush spreading over her cheeks said she'd come to the point of her story.

"I'd never had a boyfriend, and Sawyer was around a lot after we moved up here, and — well, Mom caught us fooling around and called Dad. He was mad, and he yelled at me for a long time. I felt so bad, and I promised no more Sawyer and no more cigarettes. I didn't tell them about the marijuana, not even when I found out Sawyer was adding cocaine to the ones he sold. If I had, Dad might have come back, but he was already so mad at me. I was mad at him, too, because he wanted to be with Felicia, and he left us." Her chin came up, and some of her earlier defiance returned.

"What happened to your friendship with Sawyer?" Mosley asked.

Hallie dropped her head again. "His stash burned in the garage. He told me I had to find a way to pay him for it because I'd started the fire with my cigarette."

"When did Sawyer threaten you?"

"He didn't. He was right. I mean, I was careless with my cigarette. I owed him for his loss, but I didn't have any way to get that much money. I couldn't believe how mad he got."

"When?" Mosley asked again.

"Tuesday after the fire, when he came to the hotel. We met up in the lobby after he got away from Mom and Aunt Whitney. That's when he said the drugs had burned up."

"And since then? Did he ask you for money again?"

"Not directly. I told Mom everything on Wednesday morning, and I haven't seen Sawyer since. He left me a message on my phone, reminding me to pay up, but that was it, and he hasn't been around."

"Can you play it for us?" Mosley asked.

"No. I lost my phone. I swear I did," Hallie said. "I'd play it for you if I had it, but I lost it sometime after we left the hotel after the fire. That message from Sawyer was the last text I remember." She pulled a phone out of her pocket. "See, this one is Mom's. She's always losing hers, so I took it, in case Dad called." Her voice broke again. "I guess I can give it back now."

Grace said, "Hallie, tell us about Felicia. All of it."

"You mean why I did it? Friday and Saturday morning were horrible. Sometimes I think I remember all of it just as it happened, and sometimes I think I dreamed it all."

"Tell us what you know for sure," Mosley said.

"I smothered Felicia."

By now, an Overton confessing to murder didn't have much effect. Mosley asked her how she'd done it.

"How? With a pillow?"

"Is that what you used? A pillow?"

Hallie's eyes widened. "You don't believe me?"

"Are you telling the truth?"

"I said I would."

Mosley seemed to weigh this and then nodded. "How did you do it?"

Still indignant, Hallie said, "With a pillow."

"All right. What time was it?"

Hallie answered without hesitation. "Three-fifteen Sunday morning. I passed the hall clock on the way to my room. That's where she was, you know, my room."

"Don't wander with your answers," Mosley said. "Answer what I ask you."

Hallie turned to Grace, who shrugged. It was

the Mosley Show, and she was just the sidekick.

Mosley said, "Did you knock before you entered the room where she was sleeping?"

"Did I — " Hallie cut herself off and finished with a shake of her head.

"Was the door locked?"

"Yes."

"How'd you get in?"

"It's a push-button lock."

Mosley raised a bushy eyebrow.

"I used a bobby pin."

Grace wondered if Hallie and Whitney had rehearsed these answers.

Mosley said, "Did Felicia wake up when you went in?"

"No."

"But you're sure she was alive then?"

"She snored."

"Why did you go into the room?"

Grace thought it was Mosley who was wandering and was surprised when Hallie remained silent.

"Answer me, please," Mosley said.

"You said not to lie, and I don't want to tell the truth."

"I have a golf match in an hour. Tell the truth or call your mother and face whatever comes. Your choice, Miss Overton."

"No! Don't leave me."

"My terms, Miss Overton," Mosley said. "Your choice, but my terms."

"Felicia threw her shirt away," Hallie said abruptly.

"So?"

"She was wearing it when she hit me in the stomach. I bit my lip, hard, and it bled a lot, and I threw up. She was shaking me when I urped and she got messed up, too, and she threw her shirt away. I know it sounds stupid and gross, but I wanted the clothes she'd just bought to be ruined. I took the shirt from the garbage and sneaked into my room. Her new jeans were on the floor, and I wrapped them up with the shirt, scrunched them together, and threw it all in the closet."

"Go on," Mosley said.

"When I turned around to leave, I saw her lying there. All I could think of was that she was sleeping when I couldn't. When Dad might be dead."

"I went to the bed and picked up the pillow. It… it must have been horrible, but I don't remember. I swear I don't. Mom said she had to take the pillow out of my hands and take me to bed."

Mosley said nothing but nodded at Grace.

"Was Whitney with your Mom while this was going on?" Grace asked.

"No." Hallie looked confused. "I don't know. Maybe."

Grace could see the girl was becoming more agitated as she tried to remember smothering Felicia. She said, "What were your mother and aunt doing before you went into your room?"

"I heard them talking downstairs."

"How long did you listen to them?"

Hallie blinked and started to protest, but stopped when Mosley cleared his throat.

"I have to eavesdrop sometimes. I work as hard as the adults, but if there's a big decision to be made, I'm sent away with the kids."

"How long?" Grace repeated.

"Maybe an hour."

"What were they talking about?"

"Money. What we were going to do since they couldn't work with Felicia. Mom said it was a shame Felicia couldn't just die in her sleep."

Mosley walked Avril and Hallie out, saying he thought a nap sounded like an excellent plan for all of them. Grace said she was fine, but as soon as the door shut behind him, she yawned. Telling herself it was just for a minute, she stretched out on the sofa in her office and fell asleep.

For an hour, everything seemed possible.

Chapter Forty-Two

"You need to keep up with the evidence and change your thinking accordingly," McNamara said. He'd just given Banks a summary of the medical examiner's findings on Heath Overton.

"Well, you have to admit it's a surprise," Banks said. "I thought the nutter'd come to his senses and run off. Death by dumpster didn't even occur to me. Any idea on how it came about or is that why you're off to Baltimore?" He'd walked McNamara out to the parking lot, hoping for an invitation to tag along. Anything, even a garbage related death investigation, was better than the usual Tuesday morning routine.

McNamara said, "Brixson thinks the unfortunate Mr. Overton fell onto and then into the dumpster. The blow to his head killed him, and his body was eventually picked with the rest of the contents up by a garbage truck. Fortunately, we know where Overton stayed that last night and I've confirmed his room was on the back side of the hotel on the sixth floor."

"Balcony?" Banks asked, but he knew the answer was 'yes' before the Chief nodded.

"Brixson sent a forensics team out to go over it."

McNamara was getting in the Explorer, and Banks saw his chance to escape foot patrol evaporating. His departure from police work was forefront in his mind and, as usual, what he thought found its way out of his mouth. "Well, I guess if he was drunk enough, he could have fallen off a balcony. If they can prove that's what happened, that'll be one case solved before I leave."

The only reaction he got from the Chief was a reminder of the stack of reports that needed to be filed after foot patrol was finished.

Banks thought if death by boredom was possible, working another week and a half would be suicide.

The front desk manager was a nervous young

woman who escorted McNamara to Room 642, even though he assured her he could find it on his own. The Red Bird Inn and Suites had only been open a year, and if Brixson was right, Heath Overton was the first guest to die on the property. While they walked, DeNice Keel described Overton's stay.

"It doesn't seem real," she said, and she tugged at the bottom edge of her crisp white blouse as if trying to restore order to something she could control. "I checked him in, and I can't remember much about him, except he was very good looking. Older, but hot. As far as we can determine, I'm the only member of our team who interacted with him."

McNamara wondered when 'employees' had become 'teams.' Probably the same time 'staff' had become 'talent.' He felt old and cranky and told himself to snap out of it. He followed the team leader into the elevator.

"Mr. Overton moved his car after he checked in. I remember because he asked me where the safest place was to park, and he made a point of telling me he was driving a Land Rover, like I should be impressed. He must have reentered the building through the side doors because I didn't see him again. He left before checkout, and since he prepaid, and there were no charges to the room, it wasn't surprising that he didn't come back to the front desk."

The elevator bounced slightly, and the door opened on the sixth floor.

McNamara waited for her to step out first, but she seemed reluctant to move.

"I can find it from here," he said kindly. "Do you have the images from your security cameras for the period he was here?"

"The State police already asked. We only keep the data for a week. I'm sorry."

He thanked her and stepped into the hallway.

"This is a good job," she said. "I've been happy here, and the people are mostly nice. But now, I don't feel safe anymore."

McNamara wanted to say something to make her feel better, but nothing truthful came to mind. There aren't many professions where the formerly happy Ms. Keel would be safe from the darker aspects of human behavior, but he hoped she'd look for one.

He found Room 642 and introduced himself to the techs who were packing up their equipment. He slipped on protective shoe coverings before joining them. It had been over two weeks since Heath Overton's visit, but the room had only been rented to three other parties. They were all hoping the Red Bird's housekeeping staff was sloppy in wiping down surfaces.

He walked to the balcony, careful to keep his hands in his pockets. The room faced the woods that ran behind the hotel. It was a peaceful view if you looked straight out, but the second team of techs working on two dumpsters six floors below ruined the ambiance.

"Excuse me, Chief, we're about ready to leave."

McNamara turned to find the lead tech standing behind him. "No problem. Just getting a feel for the scene," he said and took a last look around.

"Major Brixson asked me to fill you in on what we've found so far, if you have time."

McNamara had an appointment at Lightning Strike Films in a half hour, but he was only five miles away. The report wasn't long, but when he left the Red Bird Inn and Suites, he had new information on both murders.

Fred Renne was not pleased to meet McNamara, although he managed a civil enough greeting.

The production company was a larger operation than McNamara had expected, occupying four large hanger-style buildings in a business park. Unlike the chatty front desk manager at the hotel, Renne's assistant had been silent on the walk from the security entrance of the administration offices to the CEO's office. Renne held a mug of coffee, but McNamara wasn't offered any and got the impression he was lucky to be sitting down. His presence was clearly an imposition.

"Let me save you some time, officer," Renne said. "I'm well aware that Heath and Felicia Overton are dead, but their deaths, about which I know nothing, do not connect in any way to my company. I should also tell you that LSF's contract to produce *The Plurals Next Door* is void. I've reassigned my staff and have no connection with the remaining Overtons. Out of sympathy for their loss, however, I'm allowing them to stay in the rental house in your town until the lease runs out next month. Now, if that's all, I have a busy schedule today."

It was a big speech from a little man. Fred Renne, who was even shorter than his nephew, was dwarfed by his outsized desk and a leather chair suited for the bridge of the *Enterprise.*

McNamara's interest was piqued. "Thank you," he said. "I'd like to know what you and Heath Overton discussed when he met you here on Sunday, May 6."

Renne looked surprised, and McNamara

wondered if he'd been expecting questions about Sawyer.

"My attorney wouldn't approve of this conversation, but I refuse to pay him to tell me to shut up. So, here's the deal: I gambled on the Overtons. If the show had worked, we'd have made a pile, but they were a long shot. I gambled and lost. It happens occasionally, and I move on. I own the rights to the show, though, and I have another family lined up to take their place. Not right away, of course."

"Is that what you told Overton when you met with him?"

"No. Heath was quite a salesman. He admitted he and Felicia had gotten married four months early and tried to make me believe they could keep it quiet and still meet the filming schedule. I said I'd think about it, but only because I don't make snap decisions, not because I thought I'd change my mind. I set a meeting with all four of the adults for this week. I intended to cancel the show."

"Did you know Overton and his wives each carried a five million dollar life insurance policy naming the other three as beneficiaries?"

"That so? Huh," The producer said as he leaned back in his captain's chair and swiveled. "Now, *that's* a story I can sell."

Banks couldn't believe the shirt from closet belonged to Whitney, had been last worn by Felicia, and was stained with Hallie's blood. He paced around the small police station, mad at the day in general, and McNamara in particular. The Chief had returned from Baltimore in an introspective mood and had dropped the news about the shirt almost as an afterthought. Did he think Banks wouldn't care that they were getting nowhere with Felicia's death?

He'd been pacing and fuming for five minutes before McNamara came out of his office and said, "Enough, already. Get past it and do some work."

Once, Banks would have at least pretended to do as he was told, but now he was a short timer and newly emboldened. "You're telling me Felicia kept Whitney's shirt *after* Hallie bled and threw up on it? And she and rolled it up with her own clothes? That's just sick, and it makes no sense."

"The risk you take when making assumptions," McNamara said, "is trying to make everything else you learn fit what you've decided has happened."

Banks dropped into the squeaky chair next to McNamara's desk and rubbed his head. When his blonde hair was sticking up in unruly clumps, he said, "Well, I'm not getting it, so tell me what happened."

McNamara said. "I don't know, but I'm going to find out."

"Right." Banks perked up. "What do we do first?"

"You complete the reports I gave you this morning and stand in for me at the Fourth of July parade committee meeting at three. The grunt work still has to get done." McNamara ignored Banks' expression. "I'm going to see Grace and the Overtons. And Aidan, see to your hair before doing anything. You need to pick a new nervous habit."

McNamara left, focused on seeing Grace, and without another thought for his disgruntled corporal. Banks, on the other hand, thought long and hard about the Chief.

Chapter Forty-Three

Whatever McNamara had expected to find Grace doing, it wasn't sleeping.

He stood in the doorway of her office and watched her, unable to make himself leave. He wondered if Marjorie had known what he'd see when she sent him back without alerting Grace, but he could hear his sister-in-law talking in the reception area. If she'd had set up an embarrassing moment for them, she'd have been front and center to enjoy it.

Grace lay curled up on the sofa, a hand under her cheek like a child. After a long moment, he eased the door closed. Returning to the reception area, he took a seat and checked his phone for texts and emails. "She's busy. I can wait," was all he gave Marjorie.

Twenty minutes later, Grace emerged with her leather tote and car keys in hand. She stopped mid-stride when she saw him. "How long have you been here?"

She was too pale and looked tired, but he didn't take the time to analyze the situation. Marjorie was laser-focused on them. He said, "Not long. You were busy, and I had time to wait."

"Come on," she said as she passed him on her way to the door. "You can feed me. I'm starved."

Food wasn't what he had in mind, but he followed her out of the building and down the block toward the police station. She said, "I only wanted to get away from Marjorie. I'm not hungry."

"Aidan has a stash of Doritos we could raid."

"Sold," she managed a weak smile, but he thought she was still off-stride.

The cabinet behind Banks' desk turned out to hold four varieties of chips, plus jerky, apples, and a sack of chocolate chip cookies.

"I'm going to take a pass," Grace said.

"You were starved five minutes ago."

She pinked up again and looked away. "My appetite comes and goes these days."

"Seen a doctor?" he asked as he closed the cabinet.

"Yeah. Just a thing, nothing contagious." She burst into giggles, and for a horrible moment, he wasn't sure she could stop. When she got herself under control, she said, "Don't mind me, I'm tired and there's a lot going on."

McNamara stared at her as she dabbed at what he hoped were tears of laughter. Unwanted thoughts were sliding into place, and he had no idea what to do with them. "The Overtons," he said with a touch of desperation in his voice. "We need to discuss your clients."

Grace nodded and pulled a Coke out of her tote bag. When she faced him again, her eyes were clear, and she looked resolute. "What do you think you can prove?" she asked.

He hoped she was only talking about the charges against the Overtons. "Not happening that way," he said. But he smiled at her audacity. "I have to interview Hallie and her mother, but I can't do it until six."

"Then why did you come to the office?"

"Just before you came out, I got a text that Desiree's replacement can't get over here from Reisterstown any earlier, but I thought we could talk."

He felt a tug of sympathy for Marbury. The detective's immediate admission that she should have handled Hallie's panic attack without freeing her weapon from its holster was the main reason the girl had been released. It could have gone much worse for the uncooperative teenager.

Grace said, "I was grateful she stepped up and helped us out. Is she in a lot of trouble?"

"Desi? It'll work out. But firing a weapon, even accidentally, always requires a thorough investigation. She'll be on desk duty for a while."

"What a mess. So, what's new? Something's happened, so let's have it."

"There's new information on both deaths, and I might be able to wrap up the investigation into the garage fire if your clients cooperate. We'll need to talk with Whitney, too, but it can wait until tomorrow."

"Let's start with the easiest."

He wasn't sure she should do anything but go to bed. She looked so fragile; he wanted to wrap her up and tuck her away until she could reemerge as his Grace and argue with every point he made.

"Mac." She was waiting. And looking just irritated enough to make him feel better.

"Nothing to do with the Overtons is easy. How about we start with the lesser charges?" he said. "I don't believe your clients were trafficking drugs, and I think the fire was an accident. We have questions for Hallie, though, and the outcome will depend on her answers. She has to talk, and it has to be the truth, or she'll be charged along with Sawyer Renne."

"If those are the easy charges, how many more are you contemplating?"

"Half dozen. Maybe more. It's time for the family to cooperate. The widows and children pass has run out."

"Is that all I'm getting?" she asked.

"Until we meet for the interviews, yes."

"In that case, I have some information for you. I went to see Ernie Sherman at Royal Rides. He told me that the day Heath Overton rented the Land Rover, there was a blond woman with him. He didn't describe her in a useful way, so I don't know if it was Felicia. I asked her, but she denied it."

He didn't comment immediately, but when he decided she'd worried long enough, he said, "How did Mr. Sherman describe the woman?"

"Well," Grace started, but he shook his head.

"I'd like his exact words, useful or not."

"Chickie." Grace stared him down. "He said she was blond, and he called her a chickie."

"How odd." McNamara wrote the word in capital letters on a notepad. "He called you a chickie, too. Said you were feisty and a real handful."

"Oh, for God's sake. How long have you known?"

"About an hour less than you." The laughter he'd been holding onto got away from him. "You did a number on the knucklehead, so he finally returned my call and dumped everything he knew, which I agree isn't much. He couldn't identify Felicia from her morgue photo. Said he hadn't been looking at her face while he was with her." He expected blowback from that, but she only shook her head.

She stepped outside to call Mosley, who dispatched Marjorie to make arrangements with Melanie and Hallie to be at the office at five.

"You can meet with them at six," she said when she returned.

"Think you can keep them from confessing to all my open cases?" McNamara asked as she sat down. "What's with that, anyway?"

"Many things, but I'm not discussing them with you. May I?" She pointed to the floor fan sitting near the doorway. "Is your AC out again?"

"Yes, sorry. I'll open the window."

Grace followed him to the single window in the office and watched people hurrying by outside. It was a beautiful afternoon, and a good forecast meant Mallard Bay was filling up with tourists. The view from the window was at odds with the conversation they were having.

"Come on, Mac," she said when he turned

back to face her. "Whitney's not a danger to herself or the family, and she certainly isn't a flight risk. She'd never leave them. They need her. Would you at least agree to release her on a reasonable amount of bail?"

"You know that's not how it works. It's not up to me."

"But, your opinion carries weight."

"One of the Overton women killed the new wife, and they all have motives. Whitney and Hallie are trying to cancel each other's confessions, and Melanie is a bona fide nut job."

"Your professional opinion?"

She gave him a real smile and erased his last doubts about the decision he'd finally made.

"Why waste words?" he said, wondering how to change the subject. "Anyway, how do you know one of them won't confess to something else? They might be at the state police barracks right now with a story you haven't even heard yet."

"Don't joke about that. It's not funny. Absurd, maybe, but not funny. They're odd and their circumstances — "

"Which they set up themselves."

"Agreed," she said. "But it's tragic all the same. All they wanted was a big family — "

"And a TV show."

"That's just rude. I don't interrupt you when you're talking."

"Really?" he laughed, pleased with himself. She was agitated and looking much better for it. "You're a constant interruption, talking or silent." They were back to the standoff, but this time he was ready for it to end. If she ran, he was going after her.

She didn't run.

"Do you like it?" she asked. "My interruption of your life. Do you like it?"

They were still in front of the open window in full view of the crowd on the sidewalk when he pulled her into his arms and kissed her.

"Before you do that again, I need to tell you something," she whispered, leaning back to look at him.

"Later," he said. "And, Grace, whatever it is, I don't care."

Chapter Forty-Four

Mosley sent Marjorie home at four and announced he'd help with the interviews. Grace didn't argue. She was finding it hard enough to stay focused without dealing with Marjorie's wrath. The village grapevine had beaten her back to the office, and only Mosley's unusual afternoon presence was keeping Mac's sister-in-law in check.

Mosley gave no indication that he knew Grace and the Chief of Police had made a spectacle of themselves in front of half the village, but she thought the odds that Marjorie had kept her mouth shut were slim and none. Which meant the old guy was having to adjust to her being engaged and pregnant by a man he disliked *and* involved in a new romantic relationship with one of his closest friends. She expected him to grab his chest with The Big One, but he seemed intent on work. In fact, he was so into prepping for the Overtons; he drove her crazy, mainly because she couldn't muster the attention or the energy level of an octogenarian.

But by the time their clients arrived, Mosley and Associate were ready.

"I know you've had a lot to deal with," Grace said. "But the police have questions for you, not only about Heath's and Felicia's deaths, but about Sawyer Renne and the drugs."

"We're not talking about that," Melanie said. "We can't burn our bridges with Lightning Strike. They may have canceled our show for now, but I have to consider our future options."

Mosley said, "The only future option you should consider involves staying out of prison. Once we accomplish that, everything else will fall in line."

"I'm not going to prison because I didn't do anything," Melanie argued.

"Perhaps not," Mosley drew it out, giving her a speculative look. "But your sister will be, if that matters to you. Do you understand what I'm saying?"

Melanie didn't seem moved, but Hallie said, "I understand. I'll tell the truth."

For the next half hour, they discussed how she could do that without going to jail.

Desiree Marbury's replacement was Sergeant Wes Everly. Unlike the occasionally aggressive Marbury, Everly was so laid back, he seemed bored. As soon as introductions were made, he relaxed in his chair, apparently content to watch the proceedings.

When McNamara had expressed his condolences to Melanie and Hallie, he told them how Heath had died. Grace thought she saw real grief in Melanie's eyes before she closed them and put her hands over her ears.

Grace patted Melanie's arm, and then gently pulled her hands down. "You have to listen. Hallie needs you."

"How did it happen?" Hallie asked. "Did he trip or something?"

"That's what we need to find out," McNamara said. "An accidental fall would be unlikely. There were no drugs or alcohol in his system that would cause him to be off balance. We believe he either jumped or was pushed over the railing."

Both of her clients looked ready to fall apart, and Grace glared at McNamara.

"Did he suffer?" Hallie asked in a small voice.

McNamara remembered the mangled body in the morgue. "No, I don't think he did," he said. He decided it was truthful enough. There'd have been no suffering after Overton's head hit the dumpster.

"And you're sure it's him?" she persisted. "It took you an awfully long time to figure it out. Isn't it possible someone robbed him and took his ring and the robber is the dead guy?"

"I'm sorry. We're sure. The DNA match is conclusive."

They waited as Hallie bowed her head for a moment.

"So, did he jump or not?" she asked when she looked at them again. "Did he commit suicide, or was he murdered?"

"Can you think of any reason for him to commit suicide?" Everly asked.

The question seemed to startle Melanie. "Absolutely not," she protested.

"We were all arguing the day Dad was home," Hallie said, turning away from her mother and Grace and focusing on the men. "The little kids were all trying to get his attention, and he seemed disconnected. Scattered, you know? Aunt Whitney got mad when he left her to go upstairs with Mom, and then I could hear Mom yelling, but I was the worst."

Melanie had been tugging at her daughter's arm while she talked, and now Hallie jerked away. "I said I would tell the truth, and I am. Leave me alone!"

Mosley suggested a break, but Hallie rolled over him as if he hadn't spoken. "I told Dad he needed to stay with us, and when he said he couldn't, I yelled at him, too. It was the last time I talked to him and I shut my bedroom door right in his face."

"What did you do after your father left?" McNamara asked.

"Watched TV for a while with the twins until they wound down. Then I went to bed, but stayed awake and read. I was waiting up for Dad to call, but he didn't."

"Did he say he would?"

"No," she whispered. "The last thing he said was that I disappointed him."

Grace looked to Melanie, who had her arms wrapped around herself and was staring into space.

"Let's take a little break," Grace said, leaning forward to touch the girl's shoulder, only to be immediately shrugged off.

"Were drugs involved?" Hallie asked. "With Dad or Felicia?"

Now they had Melanie's attention again.

"Possibly," McNamara said, waiting to see if she'd take the next step.

"So that's it, then." Melanie broke in, stopping whatever Hallie'd been about to say. "Can we take Heath to Atlanta for the funeral?"

"The Medical Examiner's office will release the body in a few days," McNamara said. "But for the time being, you must remain in the area."

"We can discuss the details later," Grace said.

"No, we won't," Melanie said. "I'm not accused of anything, and I didn't do anything. I can go wherever I want."

"Mrs. Overton has suffered a terrible shock, gentlemen," Mosley started, but Melanie ignored him.

Pointing a shaking finger at McNamara, she said, "I want my husband's death certificate, and I want to bury him in Atlanta, got it?"

McNamara decided he might prefer Heath's first wife twisted into a human knot and running a river of tears. "All yours," he said to Everly.

Wes Everly's smile wasn't nice. "Where's your cell phone, Mrs. Overton?"

"I haven't been able to find it," Melanie said. "I think one of you people stole it when you went through my house without my permission."

"Oh, Mom, stop it." Hallie stood and pulled

a phone from her back pocket and put it on the table.

Grace raised a hand to stop Everly's reach. Raising her voice to be heard over Melanie's complaints and Hallie's 'what*ever,* Mom,' she said, "Not without a warrant."

Everly didn't seem to be particularly bothered. Turning to Hallie, he said, "Do you often have your mother's phone?"

The exasperated looks that passed between mother and daughter gave the answer, but Hallie said 'yes' for the recorder.

"Why?"

"She's always losing it. When I find it, I stick it in my pocket and give it to her when I see her. If one of the littles gets it, they can mess it up."

McNamara said, "Hallie, you told us you lost your phone, too. Did you find it?"

"No."

"We did." Everly produced a plastic bag and removed a pink, rhinestone-studded phone.

Hallie looked at Grace and said, "They know."

Do you have it yet? Everly read aloud from Hallie's phone.

"What did Sawyer Renne mean by that?"

McNamara asked. He waited while Grace made her objection and instructed her client not to answer.

Hallie watched the exchange impassively while her mother glared her displeasure. Grace could tell the countdown to Melanie's next outburst was getting short.

"How many texts did he send you after the fire in your garage?" McNamara asked.

"It's not my garage," Hallie said, then listened to Grace whispering in her ear. She gave the Chief a sheepish look. "Uhm, two?"

"Two texts?"

"That's her recollection," Grace's usual sarcasm was gone, but she wasn't letting him get away with anything, either.

McNamara picked up the pink phone. "There are five texts from Renne." He looked at Grace over the top of his reading glasses. "They are all versions on a theme. Shall I read them to you or paraphrase?"

Grace held her hand out.

McNamara handed her a single sheet of paper. "Thought you might feel that way, so I had them transcribed."

She read the terse messages quickly, her heart growing heavier with each one. She handed the paper to Hallie, who took it and twisted away from her mother to read.

Melanie turned on the officers. "I have a right to see that!"

Everly said, "No. Actually, you don't."

"No, no, no." The words came out in a long sigh as Hallie returned the paper.

"Give us a minute, please, Mac?" Grace asked.

McNamara and Everly left and waited in the empty reception area, while Melanie yelled over her attorneys and shredded what was left of her relationship with her daughter. Eventually, things quieted, and there were only two low voices, Grace and Mosley.

"When was the last time you heard from Sawyer?" Everly asked when they reconvened.

The question was directed at Hallie, but Melanie said, "Those texts are all lies. He's trying to come between my daughter and the family."

"Do you mean you didn't pay him ten thousand dollars, Mrs. Overton?" Everly asked.

Melanie shot Grace an angry look, then said, "He told me he'd loaned money to Heath for our expenses, and his uncle wanted it back."

"Renne told you he gave money to your husband, not your daughter?" McNamara asked.

"Yes," Melanie said. "The texts are lies."

Far from relaxed now, Everly's impatience was visible. "He sent Hallie five texts over a five days. The first on the night of the fire. The last was early Saturday morning, approximately two hours after your ex-husband's wife was murdered in your home." He picked up a transcript of the texts and began to read.

Do u have it
WTF. 10K now
Time's up
MOS? Talking w her tom
Sorry kid

Melanie rounded on her attorneys and shouted, "Do something!"

Grace said, "Mrs. Overton explained that Sawyer demanded repayment for money he'd given her husband."

"He demanded repayment from Hallie," Everly said.

"Who informed her mother," Grace argued. "Further, Hallie told you she didn't see the final three texts from Sawyer because they were sent after she'd lost the phone. The person you should be questioning is Sawyer."

"I will, eventually," Everly said. "Mrs. Overton, how often did you talk to him?"

"Me? What're you talking about?" Melanie demanded.

Everly said, "It's right here in the next to last text. 'MOS' is 'Mom Over Shoulder.' Renne's asking Hallie if you're nearby and says he'll be talking to you the next day. Since Hallie so helpfully provided your phone for us, shall we see if he called you?"

"I told you, not without a warrant," Grace said.

Everly took folded papers from his jacket pocket, handed them to her, and picked up Melanie's phone. It didn't take long for him to scroll through her calls and texts. "Well now, Mrs. Overton, what did you discuss with Renne about on the day before Felicia Overton died?"

Melanie's eyes narrowed to slits, but she answered him. "Probably the show. He's our producer. Or he was."

"Did he come to your house that day?"

"No."

"Okay," Everly said. "But I have a question for Hallie. Did you pay your boyfriend to kill your father's new wife? Or," he turned back to Melanie, "did you pay him to kill the woman who stole your husband?"

Chapter Forty-Five

"I don't do a lot of criminal law, as you know m'dear." Mosley said to Grace as she moved around the office, turning off her computer and straightening up. "But I'd say it's a poor game when you save one client from an arson charge by letting two others implicate themselves in half-dozen other felonies."

"The real crime is that Sawyer blackmailed Melanie, but she might have been too dumb to realize it." Grace stopped and sat on the corner of the conference table. "It's a monumental mess, isn't it?"

"Let's review our accomplishments," Mosley hooked his thumbs under his belt and rocked back on his heels.

Grace smiled at his familiar posturing.

In his 'address to the jury' voice, Mosley summarized the hole their clients had dug for themselves. "Melanie says she paid Sawyer for Heath's debt, but Hallie insists she owed Sawyer the money for the drugs he lost in the fire she may have accidentally started." He paused for a breath. "Meanwhile, the police believe mother and daughter paid the young man off so he wouldn't tell his uncle — the real film producer — that it was Hallie's hashish and cocaine that were destroyed in the fire." Another pause before he added, "A lie, of course."

"Of course," Grace said. "Don't forget Everly also likes the theory that either, or both, mother and daughter paid Sawyer to kill the last Mrs. Overton."

Mosley held up a heavily veined hand and began to count. "Drug possession, trafficking, conspiracy to commit murder, murder for hire, murder in the second degree. Did I miss anything?"

Grace sighed. "Who knows? I wouldn't bet a nickel that Melanie and Hallie told us everything. At least right now there's no evidence to charge either of them with anything."

"That won't last long," Mosley said. "I don't think Sergeant Everly misses much, and Mac certainly doesn't, so we'd better work on our contingency plans."

"Tomorrow, okay?" She didn't know where Super Mosley had come from, but she was ready to send him back.

"Certainly, m'dear. Everly will be working, but I hear Mac may have other things on his mind."

"Please don't start, Cyrus. I'm going home." She got up and headed for the back door.

"No, no." Mosley followed her, still talking. "Wait, please. I want to say that, unlike Marjorie, I think it's grand."

She stopped so fast, he nearly ran into her. "Do you really?" she asked him, shocked.

He gave her a huge smile. "Why not? As usual, you went about it backward, but yes, if you're both happy, it's wonderful."

"Even with this complication?" She briefly touched her abdomen.

Mosley's smiled dimmed a bit.

She was too tired to finesse the announcement. "It's David's baby," she said and watched his face fall, then harden when she told him the rest. "Mac doesn't know, yet."

Actually, she thought Mac had guessed, but they hadn't discussed it. In fact, they didn't discuss anything at all in the brief time between the first kiss and resuming their work roles.

"Well, as I said, you went about it backward." Mosley managed another smile. "But I'm glad you came to your senses and made the right choice."

When she hugged him, he added, "Tell him soon, Grace."

~

"Are you happy now?" Marjorie demanded. "You've made a spectacle of yourself."

"Let me see," McNamara said, then smiled. "Yes, I believe I am. Quite happy, thanks. But I think you're exaggerating."

When he arrived home, Marjorie had been waiting for him, bursting with the news she gotten from the choir director at St. John's who had been passing by McNamara's office window at the very moment he was kissing Grace. There'd been no point in denying the gossip that Marjorie said was all over town.

"How long has this been going on?" Marjorie demanded. "And right under my nose, too. When were you going to tell me?"

"Not long, and I thought I'd enjoy myself for a while, first." He didn't want to argue. He wanted to keep the one bright spot of his day to himself.

For once, Marjorie was speechless. She sank down on a wrought iron patio chair and stared, unseeing, at the bed of roses her sister had planted two decades before. Ambushing her brother-in-law wasn't going the way she'd planned.

McNamara's happiness ebbed a bit in the face of Marjorie's distress. He dragged a chair up next to her and waited until she looked at him.

"Come on, Margie," he said. "You can't be rattled by a little gossip."

"Little? Want to see my messages? Do you have any idea what people are saying?"

McNamara shrugged. "If Mallard Bay statistics hold, it thrilled half of them, the others are outraged, and someone is worried about the scandal if I continue to coach junior football. Am I right?"

She shook her head.

He'd never seen her so angry. "Tell me the rest," he said. "It will be all right, just tell me."

She grabbed his arm, whether to anchor him or herself, he didn't know.

"What's going around now is nothing compared to what they'll be saying soon. Grace is pregnant, Lee. She's pregnant and that DC lawyer left her."

Grace wanted to call Mac as she walked home.

She wanted to hear his voice, but it was much too early in whatever it was between them for that kind of behavior. And there was the fact that he and Everly had sandbagged her clients.

An incoming text chimed on her phone. David was waiting at her house.

He was sitting on the front steps in full view of the neighborhood, and she knew it would add to the gossip.

"No key, remember?" he said before she could ask him what he was doing there.

"Not a good time," she said. But he still followed her inside and up the stairs to her apartment.

"Well, I've driven all this way, you can at least listen to me, can't you?"

"I've been listening to people all day. My ears are worn out. Please go home." She didn't think he'd leave, but she wasn't going to make him comfortable if he stayed.

"May I have something to drink?"

"No," she said. She finished unloading her briefcase and poured a Coke for herself.

He sat on her favorite chair, elbows propped on his knees, cordovan Gucci loafers firmly planted far enough apart to make him look dug-in, unmovable. She recognized his arbitration posture. He wanted to make a deal with her, but from a position of power.

"I need to apologize to you," he said.

Step One — his peace offering. For David, an apology was the ultimate gift, and he would want something in return.

"It seems my vasectomy may not have been as successful as I was led to believe. While it is definitely a long shot, apparently, under the right conditions, I'm capable of fathering a child."

The silence grew between them, with David waiting for a reaction, and Grace waiting to have one. She knew the conversation should wait until after she'd had time to settle all the issues in her own mind, but here they were. She realized with a shock that they would always be like this. The baby had cemented their relationship in a way that could never be completely broken.

"Do you understand?" Never patient, David fairly radiated nervous energy. "I'm saying I'm sorry. I know the child is mine, and I'm sorry I doubted you."

"Did you get tested?" she asked. Curiosity broke through her apathy and offered a bit of hope.

"Yes. That's what I'm trying to tell you. A couple of swimmers showed up, and all it takes is one."

His lopsided smile, the one that used to break all her barriers, only made her heart ache. "So, with scientific proof that I might not be lying, you've decided you can believe me."

"Oh, come on. You can't blame me for wanting to be sure. You've been jerking me around about the wedding for ages. I've done everything I can think of to make you happy, and you keep pushing me away. When you told me about the baby, I was sure there was someone else. It was the only thing that made any sense."

"I get it," she said. "I understand." And she did. He was only being David, and she'd never given him any reason to change the less than lovely aspects of his personality. Which, now that she thought about, was most of his personality. This led her back to his latest scheme. "Why did you lie about the house in Queenstown?" she demanded. "You've already bought it. Did you think I'd be happy about it?"

"Who wouldn't be?" he asked in a shocked tone. "How'd you find out, anyway? It was supposed to be a surprise."

"Oh, it was."

He shook his head. "Look, we're having a baby. We'll make it work. I'll change, you'll change. The world will change."

The day had seen relationships begin and end, and she didn't want to hurt anyone else. Not even David. She tried to be gentle when she told him it was over.

In a move that shocked her, he put his head in his hands. His next words were muffled, but she heard them clearly enough. "Please, Grace."

She tried to choose her words carefully, but they fell out on their own accord. "There's someone else. It's very new, and we've never, well, there's zero chance that this isn't your baby. But if you like, I'll have a paternity test done later on."

His eyes were enormous. "If I *like*! Someone else? What the hell, Grace? I was right?" He was on his feet and looming over her.

All she felt was pity. She thought if she reached out and tapped him, he'd fall back. She didn't love him, but she couldn't shut him out. It was his baby, too. She pointed to the love seat and said, "Sit down, David. We have to talk. I've seen a doctor."

She had to repeat everything twice before he absorbed all of it. Then, for a little while, they were just parents with a child in crisis. David reacted the same way he always did with bad news, questioning her every word, determined to find something she'd overlooked that would alter the situation.

"We'll get another doctor." He pulled out his phone and began punching numbers.

She put her hand over the screen. "We will not. I'll handle my own medical care, but I'm looking for another doctor for a second opinion."

It seemed to take everything he had to speak calmly. "Bed rest until you see the new doctor. Promise me."

"No. I won't do anything crazy, but you have to understand that I've led a very active life. If there's a miscarriage — "

"Quit saying that."

"What?"

"You're carrying my child! Not some collection of inconvenient cells for you and your new lover, but my child. The only one I may ever have. You can't take any chances, no matter how small."

She gritted her teeth, determined to ignore his arrogance. He was hurt, and a wounded David would never retreat. Picking up her own phone, she thumbed through her emails until she found Dr. Goulden's. She tapped the screen a few more times and said, "Check your email."

Seconds later, he was turning his own phone in circles and muttering, "What the hell is this?"

"A picture of our child." She righted the phone for him and pointed to a spot in the center of the screen. "That's the baby." She pinched the screen and shrunk the view. "This is my abdomen." The gray spot was now a pinhead.

He sat for a long time staring at the picture.

"You have to face some facts. I am thirty-eight. Our child has already beaten the odds of surviving a poor placement in my uterus. But there are other problems. You can read the report that's attached, but the baby is small, and according to Dr. Goulden, the pregnancy could end soon. Even if I don't miscarry, there may still be serious problems. Birth defects."

When he said nothing, she knew he finally understood.

"I'm going to bed. I don't want to hurt you anymore, but I can't take care of you. If you don't want to drive to DC, then stay in the first bedroom at the top of the stairs on the second floor."

He reached for her hand.

"I'm sorry," she said and pulled away.

Chapter Forty-Six

She was sleeping so soundly the cell phone's ring became part of her dream. When her sleep-numb fingers managed to push the answer arrow, she got an earful from Avril. The old woman's voice shook so badly it took several moments for Grace to understand her.

Hallie had run away, and she'd left a note for Avril.

"Read it again. *Slowly*," Grace said, and then listened. It was a very short note. "When did she leave it?"

"Something woke me around eleven-thirty," Avril said. "It took forever to settle Louise and go back to sleep. Then she barked and got me awake again about two. I didn't get up right away. If she hadn't been pacing around, I wouldn't have found the note until morning. She must have heard Hallie drop it through the mail slot in the front door, but I procrastinated long enough to give the child a good head start."

"You couldn't have known, Avril. What do you think she means, 'I can't unsee it or fix it'?" Grace asked.

"I don't know. I called Melanie, but she didn't answer. Then I panicked and called Lee. I couldn't think of anything else to do, except go next door and drag that poor excuse for a mother out of bed and shake her. I met Lee over there, and I thought Melanie would faint when she read the note, but she rallied. Half the kids were up by that point, and she asked me to leave. She didn't want Lee there either; said she didn't want anybody. When we left, she was sending the kids back to bed and telling them nothing was wrong."

"You've done everything you can."

"That's why I'm having a drink," Avril sighed. "I haven't had bourbon in the middle of the night in a decade, but there's nothing for me to do. Lee's at the station with Aidan, and they're trying to figure out where she's gone. I wanted to be there, too, but I think Lee's still peeved that I gave Hallie a heads up that the house was being searched. As soon as I told him what I knew, he sent me home."

Grace tried to think of something reassuring to say. "You've just been looking out for Hallie. For all of them. I'm sure he understands. Call me if you hear anything, and I'll do the same. It'll be light in another couple of hours; we'll see what we can do then to help out."

She hoped Avril believed her, but she had no intention of taking her own advice.

She'd dressed while talking to Avril. Now she grabbed crackers and water for her tote and left the apartment. At the top of the stairs, she stopped and listened. Niki had taken Leo to Aidan's for the night, but snoring from the nearest bedroom told her David had stayed over. She kept to the edges of the steps and winced with every creak as she hurried down to the first-floor kitchen and out the back door. If David woke up, she didn't want to explain why she was off to see Mac.

The Chief's call woke Niki, who made her unhappiness clear as Banks dressed to leave. He didn't tell her the call was about Hallie, or give her any details. He just held up his phone as his only defense. Niki said he could leave, but she wouldn't be there when he got back. He kissed her gently, then left the beautiful girl he'd once loved more than anything, knowing they were finished.

Five minutes later, he was at the station. Just being here made him feel like he was helping. He and McNamara went over all they knew about Hallie Overton, looking for a lead to her whereabouts. McNamara's focus was on apprehending a suspect, but Banks only wanted to find Hallie. His gut was telling him she wasn't running, she was in danger. A half-hour later, he had an ally when Grace arrived.

"Why didn't you call me?" were the first words out of her mouth, and Banks was glad they weren't directed at him.

"Why would I?" the Chief asked, looking confused.

"Avril called and told me everything. Didn't you think I needed to know?"

Banks felt like he was watching his parents argue. "We need to find Hallie," he interrupted, leaving 'you can fight and make up on your own time' unsaid.

For once, they both paid attention to him.

"She took the family's green Ford Transit," the Chief said. "I've reported the tag number to the State Police. Hopefully, they'll spot her before she gets too far."

"What if she's already where she wants to

be?" Banks picked up a copy of the note and began to read.

Everyone makes mistakes, but I can't unsee it or fix it. I know why Dad left and I need to go with him. I'm so sorry.

"She's talking about suicide," he said. "We have to do something."

"We're in a large, rural area," McNamara said. "Her mother said other than taking the children to the local parks and outings to Ocean City, Hallie hasn't been anywhere since they got here. We've checked the parks, and the OC police are on alert. If you have other ideas, I'm happy to try them."

"Maybe I can get something out of Melanie," Grace said.

"Really?" McNamara said, surprised. "She told me she'd fired you."

"So that's why you didn't call? Oh, for God's sake. Not to my face, she didn't, and she'll change her mind by tomorrow, but I see your point." She thought for a moment and perked up. "Whitney hasn't fired me. Can you get me through to her at the DOC?"

Three a.m. calls to inmates weren't usually well received by the Department of Corrections, but the nature of the emergency was compelling. Unfortunately, other than upsetting Whitney, they didn't accomplish much. Whitney confirmed to McNamara that Grace was her attorney and Hallie's, for all the good it did.

"Let me help," Whitney cried. "There has to be something I can do." Her voice blasted over the speakerphone. Banks scribbled on a piece of paper and held it up for Grace and Mac to see.

Grace nodded and said, "Whitney, where would Hallie go to be alone, if she didn't want to be found?"

Banks had written, 'where would she go to kill herself.' He balled the paper up and threw it in the trash. The meaning was clear in the anguish in Grace's voice.

Whitney didn't hesitate. "Near water. The beach." But she was short on new information. They weren't any closer to finding Hallie.

McNamara said, "There's nothing to be done here. Dispatch will forward any calls coming in. I'm going to recheck every accessible waterfront here in town and then spread out. Aidan, you go up to Kent Narrows and check for the van in all the parking lots near the water. She's probably been shopping up there."

"It's too public," Banks protested.

McNamara said, "Not at this hour. And it's easy to get to. That would be a draw for her. We'll have to rely on the MSP and the local departments to cover the highways. Check in with me by cell, but call dispatch first if you see anything."

"I'll go with you, Mac," Grace said.

But that wasn't how it worked out. If Banks had any doubts about the rumors of a new romance, they were gone after the Chief argued with Grace to go home, won, and still got a smile from her. They split up in the parking lot, Banks headed north to Route 50, and McNamara toward the harbor front.

Chapter Forty-Seven

Grace sat in the BMW until both patrol cars were out of sight. When she pulled out of the parking lot, she turned left, going out of town. She'd thought of one place Hallie might go, but it was such a long shot she hadn't brought it up. If Hallie remembered the uncomplicated route Felicia had taken when they followed Grace from Mallard Bay, she might go to the house David had bought on the Wye River. It would be hard to find a more private, accessible waterfront than the uninhabited property.

She'd only gone a mile when her phone rang.

"Where are you?" Melanie demanded.

"Out looking for your daughter."

"I need you. How soon can you get here?"

"Melanie, you told the Chief you fired me. Did you think I wouldn't find out?"

"You don't know everything. Please, come now, or it will be too late. The police will find Hallie, but we need you here. Something else has happened. Come to the back door."

Grace couldn't begin to guess what situations rated emergency status in Melanie's eyes. Probably anything she had to handle on her own would qualify. She said, "I have a stop to make first. I'll be there soon."

"No, now. Please…" The connection ended but was followed by an incoming text. *Phone battery dying. Get here ASAP.*

Grace looked for a place to turn around. When she'd pulled off the road, she brought up her contacts. Aidan would near the exit that would take him to the property. To her surprise and relief, he readily agreed to the detour.

"I'll be at Melanie's," she said as they wrapped up. "She's un-fired me apparently and now has a new disaster."

"Worse than a missing teenager?"

"I'm about to find out."

"Lucky you," Banks said. "I'll call as soon as I've checked it out."

"There's a long dock. I don't know if it has safety lights, but it should be light soon. It's not visible from the driveway, but that's where I'd check."

"I won't do a drive by, Grace. I'll walk the shoreline *and* the dock."

She knew she'd made him mad, and she didn't care. He might be more careful just to spite her.

She slowed as she reentered the village and ignored an incoming call from David. One problem at a time, she told herself.

She sat in her car and looked at the front of the Overton house. One van was missing, but otherwise, nothing appeared out of place for five in the morning. She took the walkway to the back door, as instructed. Through the window, she saw the cluttered den side of the great room. The television was on, but the room was empty.

"It's about damn time."

Grace whirled around to find Melanie standing behind her.

"Sssh!" Melanie whispered and pulled her off the step and into the deep shadows of a big fir tree. "Do you have your phone?"

Grace looked around. They might be alone, or there might be a dozen people tucked into the dark edges of the yard. "Yes," she whispered back. "Why?"

"The police still have mine, and the cheap one I bought to replace it fizzled out. It won't even text anymore."

"You called me because you want to use my phone?" Grace tried to get a better look at Melanie's face. "Let's go inside and talk."

"And wake them all up again? No." Melanie held out her hand, wiggling her fingers. "I want to call Whitney; I'll tell them it's an emergency."

"You won't get through until morning, if then. She's in jail, not a hotel." Grace fished the phone from her pocket, anyway. "Do you have the number for the DOC?"

"Of course," Melanie snatched the phone, then held it up to Grace's face to unlock it.

Seconds later, the ring tone rolling on, unanswered. So much for Melanie having the correct number, Grace thought. "How about if I call Chief McNamara and ask if there's news?"

"No. Abe and Zeke can handle the little kids when they wake up. I need to be with my sister while they search for Hallie. Will you take me?"

Grace thought she'd never heard a worse idea, but Melanie was shaking, so she said, "Sure, but after I call the Chief."

"Can't you do that while we're driving? Please, please take me to Whitney. I feel like I'm dying. That's why I called you. I waited out here so I wouldn't wake anyone up again. The kids have been up and down all night. I'll be forever grateful if you'll drive me."

No tears, no whining. Just desperation in Melanie's voice.

"All right," Grace said and reached for the phone, but Melanie slipped it into the pocket of her jacket.

"I'll keep trying to reach Whitney as we drive. Let's go."

There went her call to Mac and any hope of reinforcements. The situation was getting screwier by the minute, and Grace knew she needed help. She started moving back toward the kitchen door and the porch light and braced herself for an onslaught of tears. "This isn't a good idea. I'm worried about you," she said.

Then she saw the gun.

"Worry about yourself," Melanie's voice was steady, and her eyes were dry. "Now, let's go."

Banks didn't come to a stop at the dead end of County Road 249 and hit an uneven joint at the driveway entrance. His head slammed into the roof of the patrol car with a jolt that made him see stars. Grace hadn't said who owned the place, but he thought about suing them as he navigated the twisting lane. He was going to need some kind of income after next week, and worker's comp was sounding good. After nine years in uniform, this was the last case he'd work as a police officer, and he was beginning to think he'd made a mistake.

He was soon out of the woods and in front of the dark house. Grace had been right about the lights — there weren't any. But a half moon was low in the sky, and the pinkish tint of the sky said daybreak wasn't far off. He got out of the car and turned on his mag light.

The house was huge and appeared to be empty. He did one circuit and then a second, shining light into the windows. Nothing. It was when he swung the light toward the river that he caught the van in its beam. She'd driven it to the water's edge.

"Hallie!" he yelled as he ran, his voice echoing out across the water. "It's Aidan. Answer me!"

The van was empty and locked. He yanked at all the handles, trying to make sense of it, then saw the keys in the front seat. She'd made sure she couldn't leave.

He was still staring at the keys when he heard a splash.

"Hallie!"

The pier was new and sturdy, but its planks still vibrated under his pounding feet. The closer he came to the end, the more frantic he became. When there was no place left to run, he saw her — a dark form drifting a dozen feet out.

He was too late.

Later, he was amazed that he'd had the presence of mind to drop his duty belt before he jumped. He certainly didn't stop to consider that he couldn't swim. He hit the river bottom, and the deep silt anchored his feet just as the water closed over his head. Arms flailing, he struggled to pull himself free, but couldn't get his shoes off.

Willing himself to stop struggling, he swept his arms out as far as he could reach, hoping to snag her. If she wasn't too far gone, she could hang onto him until help came.

The briny water in his nose and ears hurt, and a burning sensation spread down into his chest. Panic took over and would have consumed him, if not for the pain. Something became tangled in his hair, pulling his head backward at an impossible angle. He opened his mouth to scream into the river, but his face broke through the surface, and there was air. Then an arm was under his neck, forcing his head up, and a shrill voice screamed, *kick! kick! kick!*

His final burst of adrenaline propelled him into the riprap at the shoreline, breaking two fingers and scraping the right side of his body raw. A small price to pay for being alive.

Even when they were out of the water, shivering on the rocks, he kept his grip on Hallie. It was only much later that he realized it was she who hadn't let go of him. In the dark water, in the minutes before dawn, the broken girl and the lost man had saved each other.

Chapter Forty-Eight

The van's steering took some getting used to. The alignment was out of whack, and there was a grinding noise coming from somewhere under the front bumper. Grace had clipped the passenger side of her BMW as she backed out of the driveway, and as they sped out of Mallard Bay, she prayed the damage to the van wouldn't result in a blowout.

It was hot, and despite Melanie's repeated juggling with the controls, the air conditioning refused to work. The odor of dirty diapers was overwhelming until Melanie lowered her window. Grace tried to focus on these details and not on how fast she was driving down a winding country road with a pistol pointed at her ribcage.

When she could breathe without gagging,

Grace said, "This is a bumpy road. Point that gun at my legs if you have to, but get it away from my belly."

A second or two later, the gun moved. "Don't try anything," Melanie said.

"What are you doing?" Grace fought to hold the van's wheel steady, but her hands were sweaty and shaking. "I know you don't want to hurt my baby or me."

"You think you know me?" Melanie's laugh was harsh. "You don't. Just like everyone else, you assume because I'm not strong, I must be weak. Well, I'm taking care of things tonight. That's what I'm doing."

Grace said, "I saw Hallie's note."

"Shut up." The gun appeared again and pressed against her arm. "I can explain everything when I have to." Melanie shifted to look over her shoulder, but there was nothing to see behind them. Grace knew because she checked the rear-view mirror every few seconds. They were nearing Route 50.

"Which way when I get to the red light?"

The question seemed to perplex Melanie, but as they approached the intersection, she said, "Go toward the bridge."

Grace dutifully made a left and said, "Not to Whitney, then?"

"Of course not. Speed up."

The van rocked as Grace edged the speedometer past seventy, and when the gun barrel poked her, to eighty-five. "What are you — " Another jab of the gun stopped her. Grace gave up on talking and concentrated on keeping the van as steady as she could. Surely at some point they'd attract police attention.

"Slow down," Melanie ordered, then added, "Way down."

They were approaching the Outlet Mall near the Route 50/301 split and were crawling at twenty-five when Melanie said, "We can both get out of this just fine if you remember your part. Screw it up, and it's all over. Got it?"

Grace nodded, not trusting her voice.

"You were with me, and you witnessed the attack. I had to defend myself. Understand?"

"What attack? What — "

"Understand?"

The gun ground into Grace's arm. "Yes! I understand," she yelped and hoped Melanie thought it was from pain, not the surprise of seeing flashing red and blue lights in the distance.

"Good, girl," Melanie said. "Good, good.... Turn. *Here!*" She grabbed the steering wheel and yanked it to the right.

Only by standing on the brakes and wrenching the wheel from Melanie did Grace manage to guide the van across two lanes and into a small parking area at the edge of the mall. The engine sputtered and died, and the smell in the car was worse.

"I give up. I can't do this!" Melanie cried. "Here, here!" She dropped the gun in Grace's lap and put her face in her hands.

Grace didn't need a second chance. She opened the door and threw the gun as far as she could, then jumped and ran, stopping only to wave her arms furiously at the patrol car pulling into the parking lot. Two state troopers were getting out when Melanie screamed, *"Gun! She has a gun!"*

The next few moments were a blur of rough hands and the pinch of plastic restraints on her wrists. Freezing where she stood wasn't a problem. Grace wasn't sure she could move if she had to. The troopers' guns looked much bigger than the one she'd thrown away.

She tried to explain, but even to her own ears, she sounded crazy. "Please believe me," she yelled at the officer holding her arm. "It's her gun. Be careful!"

But Melanie was sobbing and pointing to the rear of the van.

"Look in the back," Melanie cried. "Look what she did!"

And that's when they found Sawyer Renne,

rolled in a blanket and looking peaceful despite his wild ride and a bullet hole right in the middle of his forehead.

~

It was touch and go for a few hours, but Grace couldn't fault the young troopers who arrested her while treating Melanie with kid gloves. After all, Melanie was crying hysterically that she'd been kidnapped after witnessing a murder. Grace, on the other hand, had been driving a van with a dead man in the back. Eventually, though, things sorted themselves out. The gunpowder residue on Melanie's hands made a stronger case than Grace's fingerprints on an otherwise spotless gun. Handcuffs came off, handcuffs went on, apologies were made, and rights were read. In the end, everyone was satisfied except the first Mrs. Overton.

When McNamara arrived at the State Police Barracks to pick Grace up, Melanie asked about Hallie for the first time. Upon hearing that her daughter was safe, she immediately demanded an attorney and a private room 'suitable for a celebrity.' Grace suggested to Mac that they leave before her former client saw the holding cell.

The wailing started just as they reached the front door.

~

"Thank you for coming to get me," Grace said when they were in the Explorer.

McNamara only nodded. The silence stretched as they left Easton. He kept his eyes on the road, while Grace watched soybean and corn fields fly by.

"Are you ever going to be where I think you are?" he asked suddenly, making her jump.

"Probably not."

"You have to trust me if this is going to work, Grace."

"What do you mean? I trust you," she protested.

He didn't respond, which made her feel worse because she knew what he'd meant. She'd asked Aidan to search David's property because she was uncomfortable asking Mac. But he'd had it on his own list to check and had found Banks and Hallie within minutes after they'd pulled themselves from the water.

And then there was the secret she was keeping. She had no idea how to tell him about the baby.

"I'm sorry," she said. It was a down payment on the apology she owed him, but at the moment it was all she had.

Chapter Forty-Nine

MELANIE

I am *not* crying. I don't do that anymore. What's the point? They don't care about tears in here. Besides, all you want to know is why I did it. Like it's a big surprise a person would want to frame their own attorney. Think about it. She turned on me, didn't she? People make promises, and when they don't deliver, I'm the one who gets hurt.

I've never been strong, and people underestimate me because of it. Miss I-Know-Everything attorney thought she had us all figured out. She doesn't even have a family; how can she understand? Wait until she has her baby, she'll change her tune, see if she doesn't.

But back to me. Whitney says you're a kind soul, but she likes Grace too, and look where it got us. I want you to know I'm only talking to you because of what you did for us. You saved Hallie, and I owe you.

Keep your tissues, I'm not crying.

For the last time and for the record, here's what they sent you in here to get. Get ready, because when my lawyer shows up, he'll throw you out.

Shall we do Felicia first?

I got up to go to the bathroom and saw the door to Hallie's room was open. Felicia had locked herself in there earlier, and now the door was open. I hoped she'd left and went in to check. Hallie was standing by the foot of the bed, and it gave me such a shock to see her, I almost screamed. She was holding a pillow and didn't answer when I spoke to her.

Felicia didn't react, either. She was lying there in bed, and I knew what had happened. All I could think was I'd pushed my little girl too far. Just like I'd pushed her father too far. All of this was jumbled, you understand, but one thought was clear. I could save Hallie.

I took the pillow away from her and led her downstairs to bed and tucked her in. I told her she was a good girl, and everything would be all right.

Of course, Faith woke up. The child has an antenna for trouble. Anything goes wrong, and there she is, wanting to know what's happening. Hope's her shadow; so, I had to get both of them back to bed. Our babies are good sleepers. It's when they get older that they're a trial. That's why the older kids were bunking in the basement rec room. You make sure to tell the the State's Attorney. Premeditated murder! Tell her to live with eleven children and see where she puts the ones who make the most noise at night.

I'm wandering, but this is my confession. Deal with it.

Where was I?

Hallie, yes. I sat with her for a long time, thinking about what to do and giving Faith and Hope enough time to go to sleep. Hallie never said a word, even when I got up to leave her.

It was easy to go upstairs, pick up the pillow, and put it over Felicia's face. I thought she was dead, and I was only going to mess up the evidence. When she struggled, it scared me so badly, I pushed harder. It was a reflex, don't you see? I was frightened because this dead woman was fighting me. Anyone would have done what I did. Besides, it was Felicia's fault for taking those sleeping pills. If she'd awakened when Hallie was in the room, there'd just been another argument. None of the rest of it would have happened. She ruined everything from the day she walked into our lives.

The important thing to understand is Hallie didn't touch her.

Whitney lied, as usual, and not very well either. It was her idea. She only has two children to my seven, and she insisted on confessing. Who was I to argue with her? She's always looked out for me because I'm weaker. She asked you to visit me because she thinks you're kind and you'll understand how I'm suffering. I have nightmares about Felicia every time I go to sleep. It's a side-effect of my temporary insanity. The nightmares.

So. I've explained Felicia. Now, Sawyer. You all ought to thank me. One less dealer on the street.

I've preached and preached to my children that marijuana today isn't what we used to get, and sure enough, Sawyer was lacing it with cocaine, and who knows what else? If Hallie hadn't started the fire, he'd still be selling it. My daughter and I deserve medals.

I didn't know what he was doing until Hallie told me the day after the fire. Believe me or not, it's true. I made sure he never came near my children again, but he wouldn't leave me alone. He wanted money to replace his *products*. That's what he called the drugs, 'products'. He said he'd name Hallie and Heath as the dealers and say he'd covered for them. That kind of lie would ruin us, so I paid him what he asked. But I'd never been blackmailed, and I gave in too easily. He immediately demanded more money, this time for his lost profit. After Hallie gave her statement to the police, I knew Sawyer would be arrested, and he'd talk.

What can I say? I was out of my mind with shock and worry. Temporary insanity doesn't make you ineffective, you know. Well, not me anyway.

I called Sawyer as soon as we got home from the interview with the police. I said I had his money. He was at home in Baltimore and was his usual cocky self. That's how I knew the police hadn't caught up with him yet. I said he had to come and get the money before I changed my mind and used it for Whitney's bail. He followed instructions and drove to Kent Island and waited for me to call. I wanted him close enough to get here quickly, but I didn't want him hanging around where you could spot him. I was going to give him the money and tell him the police were on to him and he needed to run.

It was later than usual before the kids were asleep, and it was after eleven when I called him. I told him to park a few blocks away and come meet me outside, behind what's left of the garage.

Heath gave me a pistol before he left. He'd bought it from Sawyer — don't you love the irony? I only had it with me for protection, but Sawyer got so angry, he lunged at me. Now, see how cooperative I am? I only did what I had to. It was self-defense.

I can't explain why no one called 911. The shot certainly sounded loud to me, but there was only one. I waited a long time, but no one came. I guess in the middle of the night, a backfire is always the first thought.

You know the rest. I'm small, but I've been lifting kids almost as big as I am for the past fifteen years. It builds up some muscle — enough to haul him into the van. Don't bother asking me again if Hallie helped. I told you she didn't. And even if she had, she'd do anything for me, so it wouldn't be her fault. Leave her alone. She nearly drowned trying to get away from all of us. She's paid enough.

What's left? The nasty red-headed detective came to see me this morning. She tried to make friends and get me to talk by telling me what really happened to Heath. As if I didn't already know. So, you can prove it now. Good for you, but I knew all along who killed him. When he came to tell me he'd married Felicia and we might lose the show, I told him to do whatever it took to make things right, and my sweet, stupid man took me literally. He went back to the witch and told her I'd always be number one, and she had to stick to the original game plan, or he'd divorce her.

I'm sure you can understand why I could be out of my mind with worry when he disappeared and Felicia showed up like nothing had happened. Now, everything can be explained, and none of it is my fault. I'll be free before you know it.

Whitney and I are taking the kids to Disney World for a month when I'm out of here. Won't that be fun? We're going to ask if we can take Felicia's kids, too. It only seems fair. We wouldn't be collecting Heath's life insurance if their mother hadn't missed one set of fingerprints when she wiped down the railing on the hotel balcony. It's the little things that trip you up. Remember that while you're deciding what to do next with your life, Aidan, and choose wisely.

I know I will.

Chapter Fifty
AUGUST

"You will not go to court for that nitwit Whitney Overton, and that's final," David said as he paced around the kitchen. "You're reducing your schedule, and that's final, too. You only have four months left, and you're staying off your feet. I'll move in if I have to, Grace. Don't think I won't."

"Sorry big guy," Niki said. "We're booked. If you want a reservation for October, I can help you."

Grace ignored both of them and continued to plow through the chicken barbecue platter from Three Pigs. She'd already worked out a half-day schedule with Mosley, but stomping around like a jackass was keeping David entertained while she ate. She'd tell him about cutting back on work when she finished lunch.

"I also brought Smith Island cake," Avril said. "For *some* of you." She gave David her best stink-eye.

Dessert, Grace decided. She'd tell him after dessert.

"I'm surprised you have time to spend over here with everything you're doing for the Overtons," David said, smoothly transitioning from attorney-at-war to grade-school sniping with Avril.

"That family still needs help," Avril said. She was in the kitchen rocking chair, holding Leo in the crook of her arm like the plump, freckled baby he was. An unwary observer might have thought she looked grandmotherly until she kept talking. "You'd be surprised how many narrow-minded people judge that family without regard for the facts. Narrow-minded, *ignorant* people."

"Now Avril," Niki chimed in. "Just because they let Whitney go doesn't mean she and Hallie are totally innocent."

"She's right," David said, then looked confused when he realized he'd agreed with Niki.

"And," Niki continued, "it isn't good for the Inn at Delaney House to have attempted murderers in the neighborhood."

"There's no such thing as an attempted murderer," David said with a snort, ending their brief alliance. "And, I'm telling you, that's a pretentious, stupid name for an inn."

"Really? Believe me, David, no one cares what you think."

David's face went an unhealthy shade of red. He knew Niki wasn't talking about the inn's name.

"Children," Grace said as she cleaned sauce from her fingers. "Play nice or go home, please."

Niki smirked at David. "She means you. I live here."

"That can change," Grace replied. "We're not listening to anymore, understand?" She patted her rounded abdomen to reinforce who was included in the 'we.' Emotional blackmail was an unexpected bonus of pregnancy. Every day she vowed to only use her super power for good, and every day she failed, but she meant well.

"That's right," Avril said as if she weren't a part of the argument. "Besides, Hallie received probation. And court-ordered counseling, which that poor child desperately needs."

Leo grunted and shifted around for a better cuddle. Louise, who'd slept through everything else, woke and sat up to survey the situation. And to get ear scratches.

"Well, that was an easy fix for everyone,

wasn't it?" David snapped. After an apologetic glance at Grace, he turned his attention to checking emails on his phone.

Avril sputtered on about arrogant blowhards, while Grace and Niki ate cake.

It had been three months since Melanie had killed Sawyer Renne, and Hallie had saved Aidan from drowning. The Overtons still lived next door to Avril, and most conversations in the village wound around to them at some point.

"I'm representing Whitney," Grace said when she could see David was getting antsy again, "but since all the charges against her were dropped, it's only mopping up and handling a few odds and ends for Melanie's attorney. I'm doing most of that from home because you and Cyrus seem to agree about my work schedule. Besides, he has Jake now, and the two of them drive me crazy at the office."

She got up to clear away her dishes and cut another small piece of cake.

In typical David fashion, he wouldn't let it go. "You shouldn't be stressing out over things like this. I told you I'd take Whitney as a client."

"I'm not stressing over anything, and Whitney can't stand you, so drop it."

Niki and Avril, recognizing the changing timbre of Grace's voice, wisely kept silent.

"And stop winding everyone up about the

Overtons," Grace added. "Melanie will be sentenced soon, and the family will settle near her, which is unlikely to be anywhere on the Eastern Shore."

"Sorry," David muttered.

Grace smiled and said, "We're fine but tired of noise. Sweet Pea wants to enjoy her dessert in peace, so if you could dial it down a few notches, she'd be grateful."

"It's a boy," David said. "And you should be in bed, and give up sugar, but what the hell, I'm not going to win any arguments around here."

Grace stretched and yawned. "Actually, I feel like taking a nap. Why don't you count that as a win?"

Niki neatly distracted David by saying she'd heard Heath Overton had been sighted in Ocean City and in the Outer Banks. "There's a new story every time I turn around. What do you think about the rumors that he really isn't dead? Wouldn't that be something?"

"Why do you do that?" David asked. "I'm trying not to make Grace mad, and there you go throwing out asinine questions I can't pass up. Why would you repeat such a thing?"

Niki shrugged. "It could be true. Why not? The body was all mangled, and it's possible the DNA test was wrong. If it wasn't him in the dumpster, he got out free. That's something

Aidan says. Said. Whatever. Anyway, don't tell me it doesn't intrigue you a little. Maybe Heath just drove away in that Land Rover they never found and left the turmoil for everyone else to handle."

It was too much for David. "The Land Rover was dumped somewhere and probably chopped up for parts after his loving wife drove it to Atlanta. Before Grace's clients smothered her, that is. Why am I arguing with you? Any reasonable person believes an official autopsy." After another pointed look from Grace, he stood up. "All right, I'm off." He walked over, picked up her empty cake plate and kissed the top of her head. "Walk me out to the car?"

They ignored Niki's overly cheery 'Buh-Bye,' and Avril's mumbled parting shot, which would have required a fresh argument if David had acted like he'd heard it.

"So, you've gotten a contract on our house," he said when they reached his car.

Grace nodded. She'd given him the details in an email and didn't intend to discuss it. The issue of the house near Queenstown had been settled weeks ago.

"Let me know when you're ready to go to settlement," he said. "I have the baby's trust fund set up."

It was an acceptable solution to the awkward

problem of a house neither of them wanted. And because it seemed easy and straightforward, she knew trouble was coming, but for now, it worked.

A black pickup slowed to a stop in front of the house. If David noticed, he didn't show it as he gave her a quick hug, then fired up the Porsche and backed out of the driveway. If Mc-Namara heard the Porsche's gears grind when it took the corner, he didn't show it as he joined Grace on the porch.

"Everything okay?" he asked, and got his answer when she came into his arms.

"Everything is perfect," she said.

And for a while, it was.

Bad Intent had a rocky start, due in no small part to my own hubris. Sometimes my optimistic approach to life borders on the delusional. I have several special people to thank for pushing me to the finish line. You all deserve medals.

Ron Thomas — a marvelous chef and alpha reader with the patience of a saint. He is the best husband on the planet, and when I tell him so, he just says, 'what?'. That and 'I can't hear you,' keep him sane.

Helen Chappell — Editor and friend to Grace and me. Helen's amazing career as a prolific author, editor, and teacher make her a wonderful gift to all of us lucky enough to work with her.

Clara Ellingson, Cindy Haddaway, Olivia Hosken, Tarah Kleinert, and Roxanne Tury are eagle-eyed alpha readers who generously gave their time and energy to help me wrap up the final draft. I'm so lucky to have you all, and I am so grateful for the many hours you spent on my behalf. 'Thank you' just isn't enough for you wonderful people. Chocolate comes closer, don't you think?

The book that became *Bad Intent* began with the vague idea of a story about unconventional families — those that work, and those that don't, and those that might, if only. It was a fun book to write, and all along the way, I was reminded how blessed I am.

Ron, Patrick, Kate, James, and Jack — you have all my love. I'm grateful for each of you every day.

Easton, Maryland
March 2020